Praise for

The Last Marco Polo

"Ever so rarely a new writer comes along with a riveting love story that is progressively surprising providing readers with a rich experience of love blossoming between a young American and a beautiful Chinese girl during the turbulent and decadent period of Shanghai in the 1930s. So vivid is the writing, readers witness the horrifying events of one of the darkest times in Chinese history and see how human capacities for love, compassion, and hatred play out from a chance encounter to a life-altering experience. Such is the drama in Chen J. Ho's fluid and sweeping first novel, The Last Marco Polo."

--- Neville DeAngelou

The Last Marco Polo

Love was found, then lost

A
Novel

Chen J. Ho

The Last Marco Polo is a work of historical fiction. Names, characters, places, and events are the products of the author's imagination or are used fictitiously. Any resemblance to any actual events, locales, or persons, living or dead, is entirely coincidental.

ISBN 978-1-54396-867-5 eBook 978-1-54396-868-2

Book design by Chen J. Ho

My mother once told me:

> "When the Japanese attacked Shanghai, I ran out of the city like crazy…then a bomb exploded nearby and I fell into a pile of bodies. If I had died on that day, you wouldn't be here today."

Upon belated reflections of her good fortune, and mine,
I dedicate this book to her.

CONTENTS

CONTENTS

CHAPTER 1

A Thousand-Mile Journey...

The late morning sun shone through the window blinds, streaking his face in a pool of bright light. Jack Wells slowly struggled out of bed, trying to remember what time he went to sleep last night. A bunch of his friends had come over for his farewell party, Big Band music played late into the night, and drinks flowed into the wee hours of the morning.

Stumbling past two suitcases huddled in the shadow by his bedroom door, Jack staggered through the narrow hallway where the faded black-and-white photographs of his youth hung on the walls—beaming faces in the playground, dramatic gestures on the school stage, and proud poses in his graduation gown. He shuffled into a sun-drenched living room, grabbed his Camels off the bookshelf, and plopped down on the windowsill. From where he was sitting on the eighth floor, Jack could see a lone dog walker rambling in Riverside Park below and his two German Shepherds frolicking in the brown autumn leaves. Beyond the naked branches, he could see the George Washington Bridge in the distance. While still in high school, Jack had watched the two bridge towers slowly rise from the Hudson River like twin Egyptian obelisks, and the bridge workers dangle over the cables like little ants. He didn't realize then that when completed, it would become the longest suspension bridge in the world, another colossal symbol of America—the tallest building, the biggest dam, the deepest canal.

Slowly, he turned his gaze toward a church tower perched high upon a hill just south of the bridge. Over the black rooftops, he could see the Gothic stones of Riverside Church glistening under the clouds. On many a Sunday when he was young, he and his mother attended his father's services in the cavernous cathedral, and afterwards the whole family would have a leisurely picnic in the park overlooking the wide expanse of the glistening Hudson River. Jack recalled what his father had once said to him: "Son, you're very lucky to be born in this democratic Christian nation and to be living in a waterfront apartment on my clergyman's salary."

Jack had a charmed childhood, but that seemed so long ago. He had not been back to the church since his parents went to China on a missionary assignment. He wanted to visit them but didn't have enough money to make a trip to such a faraway place. Then, everything changed. In a few more hours, he would leave all this behind and embark on a year-long journey to China, an exotic world he had only read about in *Life* magazine or watched in the newsreels.

Jack graduated from Columbia University, about the time when his parents left for China in the spring of 1935. With an introduction letter from one of his father's well-connected friends, he had landed a job at the First National City Bank. Jack counted himself lucky. The lingering aftershocks of the 1929 stock market crash continued to ripple throughout the nation's economy, and some of his fraternity brothers were still out there pounding the pavement. His handsome face, six-foot frame and knack with numbers didn't go unnoticed, and soon he was promoted to Assistant Vice-President at their international banking division, where he worked with some of the big American corporations doing business overseas. And it was there that he first heard that the Hongkong and Shanghai Bank was looking to hire an American loan officer at their Shanghai headquarters. He jumped at the chance because, he figured, besides getting some real international banking experience, he could see his parents, all paid for by the bank. They picked him over the more experienced candidates; Jack didn't realize then that his father, Reverend Dr. Jonathan Wells, had already made a little name for himself over in Shanghai.

The Seth Thomas clock on the mantelpiece gently chimed the time. The hour hand reminded him that he was running late for his Sunday brunch with Joann Walker, a junior at the nearby all-girl Barnard College. Jack took another drag on his Camel before rushed back into the bathroom. He quickly finished his morning routine and donned a sharply-pressed double-breasted gray suit. At the front door, he smiled at himself in the hallway mirror as he squared off his black Stetson with a snappy sweep of his hand.

"Good morning, Mr. Wells," a short man greeted him as he crankily pulled open the folding elevator gate.

"Good morning, Max. How goes it?"

"Can't complain." Max placed his craggy fingers on a well-worn brass handle as the cab screeched down the floors. "How are your parents doing in China? They doing good?"

"Yes, they are doing fine. Thanks for asking."

"God bless them. I knew your mom and dad since you were this tall." He put his other palm closer to the cab floor. Max had been the elevator man ever since the building was first opened more than twenty years ago, the same year the Allied Powers declared victory over Germany. At the time, it was one of the most elegant apartment buildings ever built along the fashionable Riverside Drive on the Upper West Side of Manhattan—its facade sheathed in chiseled limestone, and lobby adorned with hand-painted Venetian murals. Jack's grandparents were among its first residents, and they left the place to his mother after they passed away.

"Of course, I remember. I still have the little wooden airplane you gave me for Christmas, though I've lost the propellers." Jack could hear the machine groaning as the Otis elevator jerked to a stop.

"I can fix that."

"Thanks. I'm too old to play with model planes." Jack just smiled.

"Have a blessed day! Please give my regards to your parents. I'm glad someone is spreading the Good Word over there."

"Sure thing, I'll tell them."

A chilly morning breeze blew across his face as he stepped out of the revolving brass door. Jack hurriedly pulled up his collar as he strutted up toward Broadway. Just before turning the corner, he stopped in front of Wong's Chinese Hand Laundry, tucked away forlornly at the bottom of an old brownstone; behind the rusty window bars, stacks of brown paper bundles of starched white shirts waited patiently to be claimed by their owners. Walking past a bank of garbage cans, he gingerly pushed open a broken screen door. A familiar little bell jingled.

"Mr. Jack, long time no see." A middle-aged Chinese woman greeted him with a practiced effervescent smile.

"Hi, Mrs. Wong. I need a rush job on these shirts."

"Tomorrow okay?"

"How about this afternoon?"

"Too soon! No time." She shook her head.

"Mrs. Wong, I really need them. I am going to visit your country later today."

"You go see father?"

"Yes, I go see father."

"Me go back too…someday."

Not far behind her, Jack could see her husband, a hunched figure behind a tattered cloth curtain. "That man used to go to Columbia," his mother had once told him. "His father was a high-ranking Mandarin official before the Chinese Revolution in 1911. After the collapse of the Chiang dynasty, his father could no longer afford his expensive education in America. He had to drop out; his manservant ran away, and his woman-servant became his wife by default."

"What is a default?" Jack was too young to understand.

"That means she didn't have much choice. She was sold to his family. No money and no degree, he would lose face if he went back empty-handed from the Beautiful Country; I think that is what Mrs. Wong calls America in Chinese," his mother told him.

Stuck together in purgatory, they opened up a Chinese laundry. The tiny basement store would become their sanctuary and their prison. Rain or shine, just a few steps down from the sidewalk, they would be busy washing, ironing, and folding until the sun faded from their backyard window. They kept much to themselves, as if they were just visiting, ready to go back one day to that China they once knew, but no longer existed.

"Four o'clock okay, Mrs. Wong?"Jack watched her write out a claim ticket.

"Yes, Mr. Jack," she agreed reluctantly.

"Can you put a little less starch on my shirts?" Jack said before leaving the store.

"Yes, Mr. Jack."

Jack dashed out toward Broadway, hurrying past Guido's Farm Market at the corner. "Hi, Guido, how's it going?"

"Good morning, Mr. Wells. Care for some fresh roses?" a short man yelled out in his heavy Sicilian accent. Guido was another fixture in Jack's neighborhood on the Upper West Side of Manhattan. He liked to brag about the freshness of the produce he brought in from his New Jersey farm every morning, and he liked to give free flowers to the Barnard College girls as they walked past his store.

"Maybe later. I'm gonna have lunch with my girl at the Plaza. I'm running a little late."

"How about just one rose, my compliment to such a *beautifur* girl." Guido plucked out a long stem.

"Sure, thanks. See you later."

Jack flew down the 116th Street IRT subway station. He dropped a token into the brass slot, pushed through the wooden turnstile. He had just missed it; he could see the small light on the back of the train slowly fading into the dark tunnel as pieces of newspaper danced between the shining rails.

"Shit!" Jack let out a heavy sigh. *The next train will be a while. Might as well get some sleep.* He slumped down on a wooden bench, stretched out his legs, and closed his eyes.

In the eerily quiet subway station, Jack suddenly heard his mother's soothing voice and felt her matronly gloved hand caressing his face. "Dear, can you take care of yourself while we are gone?"

"Mother, you've already bought me a month's worth of food."

"Jack, if you ever need some help, just call your Aunt Millets. She can cook up something and leave it in the fridge for you."

"Mother, it's okay; I am going to start working soon. I can take care of myself."

"I know, dear, but I still worry about you." She doted on her strapping son.

"Mother, why do you guys have to go so far? Some of our folks here need help, too."

"Do you know how many people are starving in China each year? At least our people are not starving." Jack heard his father say.

"Why can't they send someone younger? Isn't there some kind of civil war going on over there?"

"Son, China has been at war with itself ever since its last dynasty collapsed twenty-five years ago." Jack saw his father turn to tip a snappily dressed Negro porter. "But we are not going to China-China, so to speak. We are going to Shanghai; it is very safe there."

"Jack, dear, your father and I are very excited about his new assignment. We have read so much about China in *Time* magazine, and now we have a chance to see it for ourselves. Do you know that Madame Chiang is a Christian?"

"Who is she?"

"You don't know? She is the wife of China's President Chiang Kai-shek. He is also a Christian. We are going there to help them Christianize the whole country. You see, Jack, there is still hope for China."

"But how much can you two do over there anyway? China is so large and backward."

"That is all the more reason we Americans should do our best to help China. Just remember, Son, it is our Christian duty to help the less fortunate."

Reverend Dr. Jonathan Wells always had a keen interest in helping the poor. After graduating from Yale Divinity School in 1902, he was ordained at the Madison Avenue Baptist Church. A few years later, he became the Minister of Social Justice at Riverside Church. When one of his old friends at the International Missionary Consul told him that they were looking for a new pastor at the New Hope Church in Shanghai, he jumped at it. The idea of four-hundred million heathen Chinese thirsty for the teachings of Christ was just too compelling to ignore. This was his calling.

"Bye-bye. Jack, take care of yourself. Don't forget to write and send some pictures of your new girlfriends…you've had so many, and I begin to lose track of them."

"Yes, Mother.

"Goodbye, Son!" Reverend Wells brushed back his thinning salt-and-pepper hair.

"Goodbye, Dad and Mother! Godspeed!" Jack watched their train slowly rumble into the dark Park Avenue tunnel. Then everything became eerily silent again.

CHAPTER 2

Sunday Brunch at the Plaza

The downtown IRT subway suddenly roared into the station with a loud swoosh. Jack lurched up on his feet before the train screeched to a complete stop. He dashed in, plopped down on the padded straw bench seat, and stared out the window as the tunnel lights rushed past his reflection, hardly noticing all the straphangers gathered around him. When his train reached Columbus Circle station, there was only standing room. Picking his way through the crowd, Jack run out of the station into an empty Sunday morning street. As he scurried along Central Park South toward Fifth Avenue, he could hear the trotting hoofs of the horse-drawn carriages in the park. *I should take her for a buggy ride before I leave,* Jack thought.

"Good morning. Welcome to the Plaza!" A cheerful doorman in a red uniform held open a shiny brass door.

"Good morning. Palm Court?" Jack ran up the carpeted steps.

"Straight ahead, sir."

"Thanks."

"Sorry, honey, I'm a little late. This rose is for you." Jack saw Joann was already waiting for him on the other side of the lobby.

"Oh, thank you, darling." She ran toward him in her high heels.

"Honey, you look vivacious today."

"Thank you. I want to make sure that you will not soon forget about me." Joann tucked her hand into Jack's arm as they strolled briskly into the Palm Court.

"Not in a million years. Honey, it is nice outside. Let's take a walk in the park after brunch. Maybe we can even take a buggy ride."

"I'd love that."

"Welcome to Palm Court!" Two smiling waiters greeted them with stiff smiles, their gloved hands firmly planted on the backs of the white cloth-covered chairs. Under the softly lit Tiffany glass ceiling, the white tablecloths glowed, and the polished silverware glittered.

"So how did it go last night?" Joann carelessly dangled one leg over the other, showing off her brightly polished red toenails.

"We had a blast, but I wish you could have been there."

"Darling, I wish I could have been there too. You know how much I love to dance, but I couldn't miss my parents' thirtieth wedding anniversary."

"I am glad that at least we can have brunch together before I go."

"Darling, I wish your new job were in Paris or London. Why Shanghai, of all places?" Joann puckered her lips.

"Honey, do you know that I have never been outside the country other than the time when my father took me over to the Canadian side of Niagara Falls?"

"Really?" Joann eyed him as she took the menu from the waiter's hand.

"I know; I am not as well traveled as you are."

"My parents took me to Paris and Rome a few times. I love Paris. Their food is so…good."

"Well, Shanghai is not Paris; that's for sure."

"You can say that again. Darling, I wish I could go with you."

"I wish you could go with me too, honey. I will be back before you know it." Jack patted her hand reassuringly.

"But-but one year is a long time!" She curled up her red lips into a sad but adorable pout. Joann Walker was looking forward to becoming Mrs. Joann Wells after she graduates next year.

Jack didn't have the heart to tell her that he might have to stay another year if the bank wanted to extend his contract.

"How are your parents doing over there, anyway?"

"I think they are doing pretty well. My father said they already have over one-hundred Chinese parishioners."

"That's all?" Joann arched her pencil-thin eyebrows.

"Honey, I know that's not many. Converting Chinese into Christians is not easy. They have a different culture from us, you know."

"Whatever," Joann replied blithely. "Your dad always has this thing for the underdogs. I think you are a little bit like him."

"If you say so. What would you like? I don't know about you, but I'm starving, famished." Jack peered over his folded menu.

"I am not very hungry," she replied indifferently, laying down her menu.

"You want to order?" Jack saw a waiter approaching.

"Just some toast and a glass of orange juice." Joann tilted up her haughty jaw at the waiter.

"I'm going have the Eggs Benedict, honey-cured ham with hash browns, a glass of orange juice, and coffee, of course."

"Would that be all?" The waiter refilled their crystal water tumblers.

"Yes, for now." Jack handed back the menu.

"Enjoy it. It may be a long time before you have brunch at this place again."

"I know."

"Darling, why can't you go after Christmas? I will be very lonely without you here during the holidays."

"I've already asked, but the bank wants me to go now."

"No offense, darling, you are kind of young to be that important. Besides, what do you know about China anyway?" Joann took out her cigarette, cupping her hand next to Jack's lighter.

"I know. The only Chinaman I know is my neighborhood laundryman." Jack lit up his Camel.

"Darling." She paused, "What about us?"

"What do you mean? You are still going to be my girl. Nothing is gonna change."

"I know, but—"

"But what? We have been dating for how long? Five…six months?" Jack drummed his fingers on the table uneasily.

"Seven months and ten days, but who's counting? A girl can't wait forever, you know. I just don't want to be an old maid." She curled up lips.

"You will never be an old maid." Jack stared adoringly at her beautiful face framed by golden blond perms. "Darling, are you going to wait for me?"

"Of course, I will wait for you. It would be nice to have a little house on Long Island with a white picket fence and two little kids running in the yard," Joann crooned sweetly.

"That would be nice. I like the sound of that."

"I guess I just have to wait one more year," she sighed.

"Honey, maybe you can come to visit me during the summer. We could take a side trip to Japan."

"I'd love that. Maybe we can pay Akira a visit in Tokyo," she said, brightening up a bit.

"Akira, oh, yeah, sure, why not? I won't mind if you want to visit your ex-boyfriend," Jack said teasingly.

"Don't be silly. You know I have never dated a Jap before," Joann protested, tilting up her proud little nose.

"I am only joking with you. It's okay if you want to look him up."

"I got a postcard from him last week. He is engaged to a girl whose father is a general in the Japanese Imperial Army."

"Good for him. Have they set a date yet?"

"He said maybe sometime this summer. I would love to see a Japanese wedding with all their colorful kimonos and tea ceremony stuff."

"Honey, why don't you write to him and see if he would invite us?"

"I am sure he would be glad to have some Americans at his wedding. Gosh, I can't wait!" Joann shrilled.

Joann had to spend two hours a week tutoring English to foreign students to complete her school credits at the Barnard College. Akira Tanaka, a Japanese graduate medical student at Columbia, was her first pupil. But after only a few sessions, Joann began to notice that whenever she accidentally touched his hand, her Japanese student would blush and stutter. One afternoon, Jack showed up in the classroom, Akira saw them kissing, and his blushing soon stopped. Last month, Akira was suddenly called back to Japan. They took him out for a farewell dinner at a local joint on Broadway. He gave Joann a porcelain vase as a parting present, and she gave him a peck on the cheek. Jack remembered that night very well.

Sitting in the back of a taxi, Jack and Joann patiently waited for their turn behind a long line of yellow taxis, hardly noticing all the hurried footsteps in and out of the Grand Central Terminal—an imposing Beaux-Arts train station straddled on Park Avenue along 42nd Street in Midtown Manhattan.

"This is the same place where I saw my parents off to China. Now it is my turn." Jack looked up at the green vaulted ceiling hovering high above the cavernous Grand Concourse and then added somberly, "The difference is that they went over there to save souls and I am going there to make a buck."

"Darling, cheer up, at least you get to see them…I wish I could go with you."

"Me too."

"All aboard!" the conductor shouted, double-checking his pocket watch and waving his arm high. "The six o'clock *20th Century Limited* going to Chicago is on my left, and the commuter train going to Greenwich is on my right. All aboard!"

"Have a safe trip, darling. I love you."

"I love you too." Jack reluctantly let go of her hands.

CHAPTER 3
Pearl of the Orient

A long line of Pullman cars slowly emerged from the tunnel, rocking and rolling along the elevated Park Avenue train tracks, passing the tenement buildings in the Bronx and rushing through the tree-lined suburbs of Westchester County. Speeding along the Hudson River, the *20th Century Limited* came to its first stop at the Croton-Harmon Station. Outside his window, Jack watched railroad workers in their striped overalls rushing about to switch out the electric engine with a black steam locomotive waiting on a nearby rail spur, huffing and puffing like a young stallion. Twenty minutes later, with a blast of the shrieking whistle and billowing white mists, the *20th Century Limited* was on the move again, galloping west as empty wheat fields rush by with a whimper and nameless towns zipped past in a flash. The incessant rhythmic clanking underneath his feet soon lulled Jack into a deep sleep. Three days and another engine change later, his train finally rolled into San Francisco Bay, where the RMS *Empress of Japan,* one of the Canadian Railroad's Trans-Pacific luxury cruise ships, was already waiting by the dock, fully supplied and ready to sail.

After checking out his little cabin, Jack rushed back up onto the deck lest he might miss the last glimpse of the Golden Gate Bridge as the rocky shoreline slowly sink into the inky sea. Hours quickly rolled into days, and days came and went. Jack's life on the ship settled into a pleasant routine. He got up early each morning to work out in their indoor gymnasium. In the afternoon, he would do a few laps in their outdoor swimming pool and read a book on a lounge chair. There were very few young people on the boat, so he took his meals at a large table shared by several retired couples from New Jersey. After dinner, he would go up to the promenade deck and watch the *Empress of Japan* rushing west toward the bright azure skies. After the evening sun fell over the horizon and twinkling stars began to shine over the vast emptiness of the Pacific Ocean, he would return to the lounge to have another highball and smoke. Sitting at the bar, he watched a bunch of old folks shuffle around on the dance floor—elderly men, in their ill-fitted old suits, groping their partners with their aging bodies, and elderly women, in their white flapper dresses and laced pump shoes, gesturing inelegantly with their flappy arms. But beneath their wrinkled skins and plump waistlines, Jack could see their once-handsome faces and beautiful figures. As he watched them dance, Jack wondered: *When I grow old, will I be lucky enough to be just like them?*

Back in his cabin, he took out the stationery from the drawer and wrote:

Dear Darling,

This is my second week on this big beautiful ship. Everything was very exciting at first, but now I begin to find it pretty boring without you by my side.

In the beginning, the idea that I could swim in the middle of the Pacific Ocean was quite exhilarating, but it quickly became routine. I spent my days walking around the ship, exercising in their gym, and reading a book. In the evening, after dinner, I would have a drink in the lounge and watch some old folks dance.

There are many retired American couples on this ship, spending a small fortune from their life's savings traveling to exotic ports of call. As I watched them on the dance floor, I came to believe that they have lived their lives well. After surviving the bumps and bruises of life and the wears and tears of time, they are still together, and the flickers of their loves still burn strong—they have found their soul mates. When we grow old, I wish we could travel around the world just like them.

In another week, I will be arriving in Shanghai. And I can't wait. I will write to you again. Sleep tight, darling.

Love,
Jack

* * * * * * * *

"Good afternoon, Ladies and Gentlemen, this is your Captain McDonald speaking. The Empress of Japan will be arriving in Shanghai at 16:00 hours, 4:00 p.m. local time. I hope you all had a marvelous time sailing on this magnificent ship. But all good things must come to an end, I am afraid.

Today, we will dock next to the Customs House; all passengers shall disembark from the third deck on the starboard side of the ship. I hope you all have packed and put out your luggage outside of your cabin early this morning. Our petty officers will be available to assist you with any questions about transportation and lodgings in Shanghai.

It has certainly been my pleasure to be your captain, and I hope you will have a pleasant stay in the Pearl of the Orient and a safe journey to wherever your final destination may be. Welcome to Shanghai!"

Jack could feel palpitating excitement erupting all around him as his fellow passengers rushed through their meals, exchanged hasty goodbyes, and dashed out to the deck to take their first glimpse at the coastlines of the Asiatic Continent stretching out in front of them—the Middle Kingdom beckoned. Confidently, the *Empress of Japan* glided over the blue waters of the East China Sea and then plunged into the mouth of the Yangtze River. Tall reeds on the shores bowed in its shadows, and sampans bobbed up and down in its wake. Behind the early evening mists, they could see the gray smoke wafting from ramshackle farmhouses, bent human figures with straw hats toiling away in the rice paddies, and a lone water buffalo, with a boy riding on its back, moving sluggishly in the open field. China unfolded in front of them like an ancient Chinese scroll painting—a thousand-year-old image frozen in time.

Sailing self-assuredly up the Yangtze River, the giant steel hulk then made a sharp turn. The bubbling chatters suddenly began to die down as rice paddies, and floating sampans began to disappear, replaced by rusted metal warehouses, gray factory buildings, and bright billboards, littered along the banks of the dreary Whangpoo River.

This can't be the Pearl of the Orient everybody raves about. It looks more like Bayonne, New Jersey. What is the big deal? Jack thought as he looked on glumly at a blond Chesterfield billboard girl smiling seductively on top of a wooden scaffold and a Negro face with a set of white teeth beaming above a glowing neon sign: "Brighter Teeth with Blackman's Tooth Paste."

Just as the disappointed passengers started to drift away from the deck, the ship made another sharp turn. The Shanghai they came to see suddenly burst open in front of them. The British Union Jack, the American Stars & Stripes, and the Japanese Rising Sun all snapped loudly on top of big cruise boats and gray battleships. The square sails of a Chinese junk fluttered carelessly in the wind as it cut across the shimmering water. And the world-famous port of call of tall stone building and soaring Tudor Towers sparkled in the orange evening sky like a European city that had been magically transplanted upon this Oriental shore.

"Oh, honey, look over there! Look at that Chinese junk!" Jack heard an American woman holler.

"It looks just like the picture I saw in *Look* magazine!" another thrilled passenger exclaimed.

"You see over there, honey, that's the Cathay Hotel. That is where we will be staying."

"Now, this is the Paris of the East I have heard so much about!" remarked an older gentleman.

Along the teeming riverbanks, Jack could see swirls of activity as steel cranes of rusty cargo ships swung like giant octopuses, unloading bundles of imported goods from their bellies, and swarms of Chinese coolies in torn cotton jackets and rolled-up pants strained their leg muscles as they slowly pedaled away their heavily loaded tricycles. The RMS *Empress of Japan* joined in the excitement, exchanging a few playful toots with other luxury liners before letting out a final sonorous bellow announcing its triumphant arrival. As the ship inched closer to the quay, Jack watched dock workers trying to tie down this behemoth to the iron bollards with thick ropes, and red-turbaned Sikh policemen desperately shoved back a sea of blue suits and black fedoras swarming toward the Customs House. Waiting patiently to disembark, Jack slowly moved his gaze toward the bottom of the gangplank where a ruddy-faced man in a gray tailored coat was waiting, one hand holding an umbrella and the other in his pocket.

"Hello there! You must be Mr. Jack Wells!" He suddenly looked up with a supercilious glare.

"Yes, I am, and then, you must be Mr. Todd Spencer." Jack waved.

"Yes, indeed, I am. Welcome to Shanghai!" the proud figure replied with a richly resonant voice.

"I appreciate your coming out to meet me." Jack quickened his steps to shake the man's thick hand.

"It is my pleasure. I trust you had a pleasant journey."

"Yes, I did."

"Splendid, young man. This is not New York or London, but I hope you will find life in Shanghai agreeable," he said melodiously.

"I hope so. People tell me that Shanghai is a very cosmopolitan city, not like the rest of China at all."

"You are quite right. Shanghai is not—"

"Son!" A booming voice suddenly came from the direction of the Customs House.

"Dad!"

Todd Spencer quickly swung around and saw a tall man in a dark suit and a plump woman in a light-blue knee-high dress rushing toward them.

"How have you been, Son? Come and give your old man a big hug."

"Dear, I am so happy that you are finally here. Let me get a good look at you. Did you lose some weight?"

"Hi, Mother!" Jack hugged her.

"We missed you so much." Tears rolled down her powdered cheeks.

"I missed you too, Mother."

"Did you have a good trip?"

"Yes, pretty good."

"Why, it's our favorite Shanghai preacher. Good evening, Reverend Wells, and my lady." Todd Spencer ambled over, tipping his gray fedora.

"Yes, of course…"

"Oh, Mr. Spencer, I would like you to meet my parents." Jack quickly resumed his business composure.

"No need for the introduction, Jack. Your father and I—"

"Of course, Mr. Spencer, how are you? I believe we met at the Park Place Hotel a few months back."

"Yes, indeed, at the National Charity Ball. It has been a while. I hope everything is copacetic?"

"Yes, everything is just splendid."

"And how is our gentle lady?" He took Mrs. Wells' gloved hand as he ceremoniously bowed over it.

"I am doing well; thank you." Elizabeth Wells curtsied imperceptibly. "How is Mrs. Spencer? I trust she is in excellent health."

"Yes, she is quite well. Thank you."

"Mr. Spencer, it is very kind of you to pick up our son. I hope it is not too much trouble."

"No trouble at all, the pleasure is all mine. We don't want Jack to wander off to the wrong side of town, do we?" Spencer replied cheerfully.

"Son, where is your luggage?"

"I think the porters took it. I need to pick it up inside the Customs House."

"Jack, no need. I have already arranged to have your bags delivered to the Cathay Hotel."

"Oh, good. Thank you, Mr. Spencer."

"Jack, you are not going to stay with us?" His mother sounded a bit disappointed.

"Mother, I-I thought I told you guys that I would be staying at the Cathay Hotel."

"Dear, you did, but I just thought that was going to be later on in the week."

"Beth, dear, we've got plenty of time to see our son."

"Sorry, Dad, I thought you all knew," Jack fretted.

"Jack, I can change your reservation for a later date if you prefer."

"No, no, Mr. Spencer, please don't go through the trouble for me." His mother waved her hand emphatically. "Jack probably needs a couple of good nights' sleep anyway. Besides, Jack is a banker now, and a banker should be staying in a fancy hotel."

"Are you sure, Mother?"

"Yes, I'm quite sure, dear. You can come to see us after you get all rested up."

"Now, that's settled. Reverend, if you all don't have any prior engagements, would you like to join me for some libation at the hotel?" Spencer asked.

"A glass of white wine sounds excellent. This occasion certainly calls for a little celebration," Reverend Wells replied enthusiastically.

"Yeah, I could use a cold beer," Jack quickly agreed.

"Delighted. There it is. I shall see you all at the Horse and Hounds." Todd Spencer swung his umbrella toward a tall Art Deco structure perched along the arc of the harbor. "22 Nanking Road, you can't miss it."

"Yes, I know where it is. We will see you there then, Mr. Spencer."

"Reverend and my lady." Spencer tapped lightly on his umbrella and took a small bow.

"Son, shall we? Our car is just outside."

"Dad, you lead the way."

CHAPTER 4

Drinks at the Cathay Hotel

The streets outside the Chinese customs house were packed with foreign motorcars, rickshaws, and bicycles; a cacophony of honking horns, clanking bells, and sing-song voices assaulted Jack's ears. "Wow! This place is busier than Times Square on New Year's Eve!"

"Son, you have seen nothing yet. During the summer, you can't even walk around here."

"Dad, this is exactly how I had imagined Shanghai would be! It even smells Oriental!" Jack saw a European couple gingerly negotiating around the steaming food carts as they disdainfully declined the offerings of stewed duck's feet.

"Jack, did you grow taller?"

"I don't think so, Mother; maybe it is just that everybody seems to be shorter around here."

"How is Joann? Did you bring any new pictures of her?"

"Just the same pictures I sent you last time."

"Our car is over there." His father gestured toward a bronze Chinese man in an English shooting cap standing by a black Ford.

"Da Tu, can you drive us to the Cathay Hotel?"

"Yes, boss."

"Tell me more about what is going on between you two."

"Nothing much to tell." Jack followed her into the car.

"...have you two made any plans?"

"What plans?"

"You know."

"No, not yet. She might come to visit me this summer." Jack's eyes fixated at the window.

"Oh, that's great! I would love to meet her."

"Son, see that big gray building over there?" His father pointed out the windshield. "That is the Astor House Hotel. Your mother and I stayed there when we first arrived in Shanghai."

"Jack, we celebrated our 30th wedding anniversary in there, too."

"And that is Broadway Mansions."

"Jack, it is the tallest building in Shanghai. You can see the whole city from up there."

"It looks just like one of the apartment buildings on Riverside Drive." Jack craned his neck to get a closer look.

"Now that you mention it, it does, doesn't it?"

"Son, that street to the right is called Broadway East."

"They have a street named Broadway too?" Jack mused.

"Yes, they do. Many streets in Shanghai are named after our streets."

"Very interesting."

"Son, now we are crossing the Garden Bridge. The street in front of us is the world-famous Bund."

"So, this is the world-famous Bund. I heard people talking about it on the ship." Jack leaned forward and saw a red-turbaned Sikh policeman on top of a circular platform in the middle of a wide street, waving his arms this way and that as a flood of motorcars, trucks, and rickshaws rushed past him.

"Jack, you see that big building down there? That is your hotel."

"Is that the one with an emerald-green pyramid on top?"

"Yes."

"It looks very nice."

"Jack, I've heard that their rooms are all furnished with silk carpets and matching silk curtains. You can even draw your bath from a nearby well."

"Mother, have you guys ever stayed there?"

"No, it is a little too fancy for us...it caters mainly to foreign tourists and rich Shanghailanders."

"What are the Shanghailanders?"

"Your mother meant the expatriate Westerners. Son, Shanghai has over three million people but there are only 70,000 of us foreigners, and most of them live right here in the International Settlement Area."

"So where are you guys?"

"Our place is in Hongkew on the other side of the Soochow Creek that we have just crossed. Technically it is still considered a part of the International Settlement, though few Westerners live there if they can help it."

"Why is that?"

"Son, you can think of the international part of Shanghai as Manhattan Island surrounded by poorer neighborhoods like the

Bronx or Queens. The majority of foreign banks and international companies are located right here, and so are all the fancy restaurants, nightclubs, and apartments."

"Jack, this part of Shanghai is not like the rest of the city. It is very Western, and the other parts…not so much."

"Welcome to the Cathay Hotel!" Two white-gloved Chinese doormen greeted them in the punctilious manner of a British butler as they held open a pair of tall bronze doors.

Jack followed his parents into the boisterous hotel lobby where he saw some of his fellow passengers were already milling around in front of a green-marble reception counter and waiting for the Chinese bellhops in pillbox caps to load up their suitcases and ship trunks.

"Good evening," a man in a double-breasted suit greeted them graciously.

"Good evening. We are here to meet Mr. Todd Spencer."

"Yes, sir. He is waiting for you over there." He pointed toward the man sitting in a high-back red leather chair.

"Hello again." Todd Spencer quickly stood up and walked over. "Reverend, this is Freddy Silverman. He manages this establishment."

"How do you do?" The hotel manager nodded politely.

"Freddy, this is Reverend Wells. I am sure you have heard of him."

"Reverend Wells, my apology. Are you and Mrs. Wells going to stay with us tonight?"

"Oh, no, our son is."

"Freddy, I believe we have made a reservation under the name of Mr. Jack Wells."

"Yes, of course. I believe we have just delivered Mr. Wells' luggage to his room."

"A room with a harbor view?"

"Yes, of course, one of our best. Mr. Spencer, are you and your guests going to dine with us tonight?"

"Freddy, we are going to have some cocktails at the Horse and Hounds."

"Excellent. If you need anything else, please let me know." He enunciated his words in an Oxford accent.

"Of course. Shall we, Reverend and my lady?" In the affected manner of a host, Todd Spencer led them along a vaulted hallway aligned with black marble pilasters and glowing angular Art Nouveau sconces.

"Good evening, Mr. Spencer." The maître d' was already waiting by the door.

"May I take your coat and hat, sir?" A Chinese girl in a Western dress bowed.

"By all means." Spencer nonchalantly handed her his umbrella and coat. "We would like to have a private booth."

"Certainly, Mr. Spencer. This way, please." The maître d' led them into a corner alcove surrounded by fox-and-pheasant paintings on the green velvet walls.

"Mr. Spencer, we haven't seen you and Mrs. Spencer for some time. I hope everything is well."

"Yes." Spencer slid into the green-leather booth.

"What will be your pleasure today?"

"Mrs. Wells, how about a glass of their lovely Cabernet Sauvignon?"

"I don't know. Why don't you pick one for me?"

"The lady would like to have a glass of Cabernet Sauvignon 1932."

"Excellent choice." He nodded.

"And for you, Reverend?"

"Make it the same for me. A glass of Cabernet Sauvignon sounds fine."

"What about you, sir?"

"The usual—Bombay Gin with a dash of tonic water. Jack, what would you like to drink?" Spencer lounged back into the booth, arm dangling over the backseat.

"How about a beer?"

"Jack, after such a long trip, you look like you may need something stiffer." Todd flashed a tempting smile.

"Okay, then, I'll have a scotch-and-soda."

"Certainly, Johnny Walker or White Horse?"

"I will try Johnny Walker."

"Oh, my, my, when did you start drinking hard liquor?"

"Mother, I only drink a little," Jack replied sheepishly as he glanced around the bar room. "Sir, is this place always so busy?"

"Yes, especially at Christmas. Everybody is having a party. Tonight, in our Grand Ballroom, there is going to be a gala for one-hundred people, and next week, we are expecting some of your Hollywood entourages to stay with us."

"Here in Shanghai?"

"Yes, sir. Many of your famous Americans have stayed with us. Just recently, we had Douglas Fairbanks, Will Rogers, and Miss Marlene Dietrich as our guests. The Cathay Hotel is *the* place to stay if one wants to be seen."

"Dimitri, where did you learn to speak English so well?"

"Moscow University."

"Yes, it is one of the finest universities in the world," Reverend Wells added.

"It was; until the Bolsheviks managed to ruin it." Spencer snickered. "What a bloody shame."

"Yes, indeed, what a bloody shame," the maître d' replied somberly.

"Thank you, Dimitri. That will be all."

"Thank you, Mr. Spencer. Please let me know if you need anything else." He quickly retreated.

"Mr. Spencer, they all seem to know you very well. Do you come here often?"

"Mrs. Wells, please call me Todd."

"Okay, then please call me Beth."

"Alright, Beth…when I was younger, my wife and I went out a great deal during the week, from club to club, from garden parties to dinner parties; we tried to attend every ballroom dance and charity ball on weekends, and sometimes even during the weekdays. On many nights, we would wind up here for a nightcap. We had lovely times," he ruminated.

"Mr. Spencer…Todd, how long have you been living in Shanghai?"

"Since 1912…I can hardly believe it has been more than a quarter of a century," Spencer said nostalgically.

"That was the year the Titanic sank," Jack marveled.

"Jack, that was same the year you were born."

"If I recall, that was also the year when that Sun Yat-sen fellow overthrew the last Chinese dynasty and established China's first republic."

"Mr. Spencer, then you have witnessed one of the most momentous periods in Chinese history. You are truly an Old China Hand."

"You flatter me, Reverend. I don't know China as well as I should. I would venture to say you probably know more about the country than I do."

"Why do you say that? I have been here not even for two years."

"Reverend, my world revolves around my bank, the Trinity Cathedral Church, the Shanghai Country Club, and my humble abode. I don't associate much with the locals, other than my Number One Boy, of course."

"Our lives revolve around the church. We don't get around a lot either. Todd, do you and the Mrs. go out to eat a lot? You must know many good restaurants in Shanghai."

"Not really. We have tried a couple of French and Hungarian restaurants, and once we even tried a Chinese restaurant. What the devil is that name?" He paused. "Oh, yes, yes, Sun Ya. People told me it was the best Chinese restaurant in the city, but frankly, once was enough for me. Nothing is better than a juicy leg of roasted mutton or crisply grilled quails washed down with a pint of Guinness, and afterward, some rice pudding and a glass of sherry for dessert." Spencer lit his pipe.

"We don't go out to eat much either. Thank goodness, I have someone to help me do the cooking."

"That is one good thing about living here in Shanghai. You can get a lot of good and inexpensive domestic help."

"Todd, what do you and the Mrs. do in your leisure time?"

“There isn’t a lot to do here in Shanghai…I play a round of cricket or shoot a few holes of golf on weekends. My wife prefers gardening and takes her tea with her friends at the Shanghai Country Club on Lady’s Day.”

“It sounds like you and Mrs. Spencer lead a pretty comfortable life.”

“Yes, we are quite comfortable, but still, it is not Home. Shanghai is not London…so, Beth, what do you and the Reverend do in your leisure time, may I ask?”

“Other than praying?” Jack’s father said self-mockingly.

“Other than that,” Spencer deadpanned.

“I tried to learn how to speak Chinese.”

“But why?”

“I figured if I could speak their language, I would be better at my job.”

“That is quite admirable, Reverend. Fortunately, I don’t have that need. All my fellow Brits conduct our lives in our mother tongue.”

“I studied French in college. Chinese is much too hard to learn,” Mrs. Wells agreed.

“Don’t feel too bad, Beth, even some of us who were born here could only manage a few gobbled-up Chinese words. It is a bloody shame that we have to speak that mangled pidgin English so they can understand what we want. All that gibberish is such an affront to my ears.”

“We are very lucky to have a nice Chinese girl to do the translations for us.”

"My Number One House Boy does that for me." He picked up his gin from the bamboo coaster. "Jack, welcome to Shanghai. Cheerio!"

"Cheers!" Jack took a greedy swallow of his highball.

"Reverend, we are quite happy that your son can join us here in Shanghai."

"Thank you for your confidence in our son. Mr. Spencer, may I ask you a question?"

"By all means, Reverend."

"I am sure there are a few talented English chaps already living here in Shanghai, so why did your bank go through such expense to bring Jack all the way from New York?"

"Ah, an excellent question, Reverend." He took another sip of his gin. "You see, my good man, ever since our bank was founded in 1864 in this very city, we have only employed young lads from good families and good schools, such as Eton and Oxford. We value trust above everything else; money is much too important a matter to leave to anyone else."

"So where does our Jack fit into the scheme of things?"

"Good breeding, smart presence, excellent schooling, and quick with numbers are some of the qualities we see in your son. Beth, now I can see the connection."

"Thank you. Jack, you hear that?" His mother could hardly contain her pride.

"Frankly, Beth, there is another reason."

"Which is?"

"Beth, times have changed. For much of the nineteenth century, our trading houses, such as our East India Trading Company, pretty much dominated most of the foreign trade in Asia, but now it is your American companies playing that role. We need to adapt to a new economic landscape, and we need someone like Jack to help us deal with your American companies."

"Son, this sounds like a very good career opportunity for you." His father beamed.

"Yes, indeed. Jack, I think you will find your new position at our bank both exciting and rewarding."

"Mr. Spencer, I look forward to the challenge."

"Care for another?" Spencer savored the last drops in his glass.

"Dad, care for another glass of wine?"

"Son, I think we have taken up enough of Mr. Spencer's time. Maybe another time." Reverend Wells stared lingeringly at his empty glass.

"Jack, your father is right. We should be running along."

"No, no, you all should stay. Catch up a bit. Mrs. has a little supper waiting for me." Spencer patted his mouth with a white napkin.

"Mr. Spencer, when should I report to work?"

"Jack, you'll need a few days to get acclimated with the city. Spend some time with your lovely parents. It is Christmas." He rose from his chair. "Ah, Reverend, speaking of Christmas, our bank is hosting our annual cocktail party at the British Consulate tomorrow night. If you all don't have any prior engagement, would you be so kind as to drop by and share some of the holiday spirits with us?"

"No, we don't have anything special planned, do we, dear?"

"Thank you, Mr. Spencer. We'll look forward to it."

"Excellent, then I will see you all at 6:00 p.m. Of course, you know where it is."

"Yes, we do."

"Delighted! Good night." Spencer strutted out.

"Have a good evening, Mr. Spencer." The maître d' bowed ingratiatingly at the door just as a crowd of holiday revelers in white dinner jackets and long Chantilly dresses streamed in, talking and laughing as they took up all the empty seats along the mahogany bar.

"This is a nice place." Jack stared at the good-looking crowd.

"Jack, you should get some rest. Your father and I will see you tomorrow."

"Are you guys leaving already?"

"Aren't you tired after all that traveling?"

"No, Mother. I am not tired at all. It is only 8:00 a.m. in New York." Jack looked at his wristwatch. "You guys hungry?"

"We probably could use a light supper, but I heard things are very expensive here." His mother looked at her husband.

"Don't worry, Mother. I am a banker now. Remember?" Jack glanced around. "Hey, Dimitri, where can we grab something to eat?"

"We have many restaurants in the hotel. What kind of food do you prefer?"

"What do you recommend?"

"Well, we have the Tower Restaurant on the roof where you can get a very good view of the harbor. The Dragon and Phoenix Restaurant is just upstairs if you like Chinese food. If you prefer something casual, there is a little French bistro cafe just outside."

"What kind of food do they serve over there?"

"A little bit of this and a little bit of that. I've heard their Cordon Bleu is excellent."

"That sounds good. I haven't had that for a long time," Jack's father said enthusiastically.

"Do they serve hot dogs?"

"I am afraid not, but they serve excellent steaks. Australian beef, not American."

"That sounds even better. Mother, what do you think?"

"Jack, beef is very, very expensive here in China. Are you sure?"

"Of course, Mother. My treat. Let's go."

"Dear, this will be the first time we're having a meal together as a family in two years." She smiled happily, walking between her two men.

CHAPTER 5
The British Consulate

After seeing his parents leave the hotel, Jack finally got a chance to check out his room. He couldn't believe how nice it was—a black leather sofa in the corner, a large mahogany bed in the alcove, and a basket of fresh flowers on a square glass-and-chrome coffee table. After hanging up his coat behind a mahogany closet door, he quickly checked out the marble bathroom, unpacked his clothes, brushed his teeth, and took a quick shower under its gold faucet. Jack finally settled into his bed. He lay wide awake as his ears fixated on the incessant humming outside his hotel room. Though it was past midnight, Shanghai still buzzed like a beehive. After a while, he got up, walked to the window, and lit another cigarette. As he looked down into the street below, he was surprised to see streams of motorcars, rickshaws, and bicycles jostling along the Bund as if it was still afternoon. He could hear street vendors hawking on the sidewalks and smell the petrol and garlic wafting in the air. Over in the harbor, he could see large cargo ships moving about and small tugboats chugging upstream; every square inch of this Oriental port throbbed with life. But on the other side of the harbor, everything suddenly blurred; a dark sea of gray-tiled wooden houses crisscrossed by dimly lit narrow alleyways. *That must be the wrong side of town*, recalling what his boss had said. Jack took another puff on his smoke before slowly closed the casement window. He didn't know when he fell asleep, but when he woke, his mother was already calling him from the hotel lobby.

"Jack, did you sleep well?"

"Like a log."

Cueing behind a long line of two-toned Cadillacs, yellow Studebaker coupes, and silver Rolls-Royces, their black Ford slowly drove past an imposing wrought-iron gate guarded by two white-turbaned Sikhs. At the end of the gravel driveway, bordered by meticulously trimmed hedges and velvety Bermuda grass, Jack saw a large English Renaissance building; elegant and stately. A crowd of white dinner jackets, black tails, and sparkling evening gowns had already gathered at its front steps, and uniformed Chinese waiters rushed about under its brightly lit veranda.

"Oh my, my, everybody is so dressed up. I thought this was just going to be a little cocktail party."

"Mother, you know the Brits, they're very big on proper attire." In his dark gray Brooks Brothers business suit, Jack too began to feel a little out of place as he looked around the fancy guests, drinking and laughing as trays of hors-d'oeuvres and champagne floated around on the parquet oak floor.

"I think these are the same groups of people we saw at the other parties," Jack's father said, looking disdainfully at some Frenchmen and their dazzlingly dressed ladies bantering in their lyric tongue. In another corner, a group of Germans in their dark military uniforms were talking and laughing loudly as they clinked their champagne glasses.

"Yes, they do look somewhat familiar. If I had known this was going to be formal, I would have dressed up a little more." Jack's mother fretted in her green crepe de chine dress.

"What is wrong with what you are wearing? You don't want to look ostentatious like them."

"It is so plain compared to what those women are wearing."

When Elizabeth Pattison was attending the Nightingale School, an all-girls private school on the Upper East Side of Manhattan, she went to many fancy parties on Park Avenue and beach outings in Southampton. She missed those riotous dances in her white flapper dresses and clam-bake gatherings on the beach in her one-piece swimming suit. She met Jonathan Wells at a church function when he was an earnest young minister in training. They fell in love. No regrets, but she sometimes wished she had enjoyed one more year of freedom before becoming a preacher's wife.

"Too bad Joann couldn't be here," his mother said. "I am sure she would love this kind of thing, dressing up and dancing the night away. Jack, after you two get married, take her to parties and have some fun. Don't be a big bore like your father."

"I hear you, Mother."

"Beth, my dear, you find this sort of thing fun? A couple of these parties a year would be enough for me," said the erudite preacher, holding his hands behind his back and looking ill at ease.

"Oh, Jonathan, lighten up. Have some fun; don't be so serious."

"My dear, I am being paid to be serious. That is my job."

"That's well and good, but don't be such an old fuddy-duddy. Where is that ebullient young man I once knew? Parties are what people live for in this city. What else is there to do in Shanghai anyway?" She forcefully pulled on his arm.

"Okay, dear, I will try to look like I'm enjoying it!"

As they slowly made their way onto the parquet floor, he suddenly whispered, "Son, do you see that man over there?"

"Yes, Dad. Who is he?"

"That's the British Consul, A. H. George." His father discreetly pointed with his index finger toward an impeccably attired Englishman standing under the archway as if he was surveying his country estate.

"He looks like he owns this place."

"Figuratively speaking, he does…and that's the Japanese Consul-General Horiuchi and his wife." His father moved his gaze toward a short Japanese man in a black top hat followed by a kimono-clad lady shuffling obediently behind him. As they approached the archway, the British Consul-General immediately broke out with a broad smile and his peremptory glare softened. In that peculiar British decorum, with one hand behind his back, he took a step forward to shake the Japanese man's hand, stiffly gracious and condescendingly imperial.

"Son, do you know why he is so nice toward him but not so much to others?"

"They must be good friends. I don't know." Jack shrugged.

"No, they are not friends. In this part of the world, the Brits are very careful not to offend the Japanese."

"Why? I thought the British were still in charge here."

"For now, they are, but I don't know for how long. The Brits don't want to see the Japanese challenge them here in Shanghai because they no longer have all the resources to protect this far-flung outpost of their empire."

"Is that why I see him doing some serious ass-kissing over there?"

"If you want to put it in such a succinct way." His father chuckled. "Fascinating to watch, isn't it? Son, if I hadn't gone into religion, politics would be my career choice."

"Neither profession makes any money."

"Your mother always pokes fun at me about that. As I have always said, Beth, my dear, we are blessed because we're neither deprived of money nor burdened by it."

"Dear, I've got news for you; here in Shanghai, money *is* everything! People eat and sleep with it. Those with money want to flaunt it, and those who don't have it are dying to get it, literally and figuratively."

"Excuse me, madam." A Chinese waiter suddenly appeared from behind, holding a tray of bubbly champagne and a sizable can of black Beluga caviar.

"Oh, my, my, isn't that nice? If you don't mind, I would like to have an itty-bitty of that caviar." Beth gleefully watched the man dab a little spoonful of the shining black eggs onto a cracker. As she waited, she saw a man in a white dinner jacket slowly work his way toward them.

"Jack, isn't that your boss? He is heading our way."

"Yes, I think that's him."

"Merry Christmas, Reverend and my lady!" Todd ambled over. "I hope you all are having a jolly good time."

"Merry Christmas, Todd. Lovely party. The hors-d'oeuvres are just excellent and caviar simply scrumptious."

"Crosse and Blackwell on Avenue Edward VII. Beth, you ought to give it a try. They carry all sorts of delectable accoutrements."

"Of course, I shall make a note of that." She nodded as if she were going to shop there.

"Reverend, I am so glad you all can join us tonight."

"Mr. Spencer, this is the eve of the birth of our Lord, Jesus Christ. We Christians all around the world rejoice in His coming."

"Yes, indeed, I am glad that we can all gather here so far away from our homelands to celebrate His birth."

"Mr. Spencer, in due time, I hope not just here in Shanghai, but the whole of China will be celebrating this important day.

"I hope you are right, Reverend...I hope you are right."

"Mr. Spencer, you don't sound too positive."

"Reverend, don't get me wrong. I am glad that you Yanks are still so enamored with the idea of Christianizing the Chinamen, but do you really think those heathen Chinese understand the true meaning of being a Christian?"

"Mr. Spencer, they might not understand every word in the Lord's Prayer, but I do think they all can feel His love."

"Reverend, I am sure you have heard the term 'rice Christians'?"

"Yes, I have. I have met a few of them who came to our church just for the food, but then again, praying on an empty stomach is a hard thing to do. Poverty in China, if you will, is like a disease; it is curable, just give it some time. And we can help them. As the Bible says: 'Blessed is he who considers the poor.'"

"My dear Reverend, poverty is just one of the many problems China is facing today. It has many more insidious diseases that are harder to cure."

"Such as?"

"After centuries of slow decays, China is plagued not just with abject poverty but rampant corruption. In fact, the whole country is in such dire shape; I wouldn't be a bit surprised that it would fall apart like a rotten pagoda with a gust of a strong wind. Frankly, I think China is beyond redemption."

"I am afraid I have to disagree with you there, Mr. Spencer," the Reverend replied sternly. "China has over three-thousand years of continuous civilization, and many of their Confucian moral codes are very similar to our Christian values. Granted they have lost their way for the past century, but I do not have any doubt that once they accept our Lord Jesus Christ as their Savior, China will bounce back again. It is our hope that China will not just become a Christian nation but a democratic one, too. A new China, if you will."

"I say, you Yanks' evangelical zeal is quite inspirational…if not a bit delusional. Converting one Chinaman is hard enough—but the whole of China?"

"Yes, the whole of China! That is the reason we are here."

"My dear Reverend, even if your wish does come true, I am afraid that it may take quite a while…certainly not in my lifetime, or yours."

"Why not?"

"Beth, our Protestant churchmen have been trying to convert these heathen Chinese ever since the early 1600s. After two hundred years, they have little to show for their efforts."

"Mr. Spencer, have some faith; Rome was not built in a day."

"My dear Reverend, for the past two centuries, we British had been trying to teach the Chinese our Christian ways of doing things, but they stubbornly clung to their old customs, wallowing in the quagmires of feudalism and Confucianism. The Chinese would never change. In my humble opinion, Reverend, West will always be West, East will always be East, and the two shall never meet."

"Mr. Spencer, you are too pessimistic. Do you know that Dr. Sun Yat-sen, the father of the new Republic of China, believed in our Western democracy? And he was a Christian."

"Todd, do you also know that Generalissimo Chiang Kai-shek and his lovely wife, Soong Mei-ling, are also Christians?" Beth quickly added. "They were just named 'Man and Wife of the Year' by *Time* magazine; their church wedding even made the front page of the *New York Times*. We do not have any doubt that China is on its way to becoming a Christian nation in a not too distant future."

"Beth, I was at their wedding. When her sister, Soong Ai-ling, got married to the head of the Bank of China, Mr. Kung, I was at their church wedding, too. But frankly, I think the whole thing was just an elaborate charade to make them look Westernized for the news cameras."

"Why do you say that?" Beth asked incredulously.

"Beth, they might put on white wedding dresses and black tails, attend our universities and take on Anglicized first names, but deep down, it is very difficult for us Westerners to understand their inscrutable Oriental minds."

"Todd, do you know that Madam Chiang graduated from Wellesley College? She understands our American values, and she speaks excellent English."

"And she also knows how to play up to the Americans' fantasies of Christianizing China," Spencer countered.

"Todd, I am really surprised that you would say that," Beth said agitatedly.

"Mr. Spencer, perhaps you are a bit too cynical," the Reverend chided.

"Reverend, with all the foreign aid you Yanks have given to China, do you know how rich the Soong families and their in-laws have become?"

"No, I don't suppose I do."

"They practically own the Bank of China."

"I thought the Chinese government owns it."

"They are the government! My dear Reverend, you don't suppose all the Yanks' financial aid and military equipment sent to Chiang Kai-shek went to convert the Chinese or fight the Communists? Do you?"

"They should...what are you implying?"

"A lot of your American aid has found its way into their personal bank accounts."

"Eh...are you sure?"

"Quite! I am a banker. I should know this sort of thing."

"Todd, I don't know much about their family finances, but I do know that the Soong sisters are good Christians. They attend church regularly."

"Beth, there is a saying in China about these three famous Soong sisters: One loves money, one loves power, and one loves China, but does anyone know which one of them loves God?" Spencer then paused. "And on that note, I should be running along. After all, this is Christmas Eve; we shouldn't be discussing such a frightfully boring subject. You all do have a jolly good time. Merry Christmas, Reverend and my lady." Spencer took a slight bow.

"Mr. Spencer, Merry Christmas!" Jack watched him stride into another crowd. "I will see you on Monday."

"Yes, of course. Bright and early."

"A pretty opinionated fellow, isn't he?" the Reverend said glumly.

"A little bit, but all you men are pretty opinionated."

"Dear, maybe we should call it a night."

"Dad, are you sure you guys don't want to stay longer?"

"Jack, why don't you stay? We old folks can't stay up that late."

"I don't want to stay here all by myself. Mother, how about we all take a walk in the harbor? I heard it is a very popular night spot."

"Jack, your dad and I used to go there a lot, but we haven't been there for a while."

"Let's go then!"

"I will tell Da Tu to pick us up at the Cathay Hotel."

CHAPTER 6

Strolling along the Bund

As they waited patiently by the curb for the light to change, Jack heard a skinny Chinese man trotting close to the sidewalk in a pair of worn-out straw sandals call out: "*Lau Ban, Big Boss*, want a rick-shaw ride?"

"*Beu Yo, Beu Yo!*" His father waved his hands.

"What did you say to him?" Jack asked.

"I told him that we don't want any ride."

"*Lau Ban!* Only fifteen cents!" the man persisted, trotting closer.

"Come on, Jack. Let's cross."

"Okay, Dad." Jack followed him into the crowded Bund as two young Chinese girls in body-hugging chi pao and high heels strutted toward them.

"They are showgirls. I can tell," his mother sneered under her breath.

"There are just too many nightclubs and brothels in the city." His father shook his head.

All along the crowded river promenade, foreign tourists stopped here and there to admire the busy harbor and take pictures of the enchanting skyline, and over the moonlit waters, tall cruise ships, rusty cargo boats, and Chinese wooden junks sailed past each other as if they were engaged in some sort of unrehearsed dance, each moving to its own rhythm.

"Son, what do you think of Shanghai so far?"

"I like it."

"Son, do you see over there? That's Lloyd Triestino's *Conte Verde*...and that one is the Japanese ship, *Chichibu Maru*...and the big cruise ship over there is the *Empress of Japan*. Son, after I retire, I will take your mother on a world cruise on that ship."

"I think you and Mother would enjoy it. I saw lots of retired people on that ship."

"But that will have to wait a while...Son, do you see over there? That is Warship Row." His father pointed to a group of gray battleships moored further downstream. "That is *Izumo*, the flagship of the Japanese Asiatic Fleet, and over there, that is one of our ships, U.S.S. *Panay*, a bit small, but it gives us missionaries the needed protection inland."

"Dad, I've never realized that Shanghai had so many foreign warships...fascinating."

"Turn around and look at that skyline! Over there, that is the Bank of China, and the one next to it is the Chinese Customs Building." His father waved his arm like a tour guide.

"You mean that tall building with a big clock on top?"

"Yes, they call it Big Ching because it looks and sounds like Big Ben in London. They did a pretty good job copying it." He chuckled.

"Son, you see that building with a big round dome on top? That's the Hongkong and Shanghai Bank."

"It looks just like one of those buildings on Wall…" Jack suddenly felt a hand tugging at his coat, and he looked down and saw a small Chinese boy staring up at him imploringly. "No mama, no papa, no food!"

"Where did he come from?"

"He must have come out from there. Behind that small concrete building, that is where the International Settlement ends and the Old Chinese City, Nantao, begins." His father pointed toward a pile of old wooden jetties further upstream.

"He has only one leg." Jack saw the boy was leaning on a makeshift bamboo crutch. Instinctively, Jack reached into his pocket, but before he had a chance to place the quarters into his little hand, a small mob of young boys in rags quickly encircled them, besieging them with loud cries. "*Lao Ban! Lao Ban*! No mama, no papa, no food!"

"You just get so numbed by all these poor little kids." His mother opened her purse, shaking her head helplessly.

Before she had a chance to hand over her few coppers, the boys started to scatter helter-skelter. Jack turned around and saw a tall, red-turbaned Sikh policeman running toward them, waving a big wooden stick and yelling, "Hey, you Chinks! Get out of here! How many times do I have to tell you not to come to our side to bother our foreign guests!"

"Sir, we are okay. They didn't bother us at all." Jack's father tried to stop him.

"I'm so sorry, sir! I have warned these kids time and time again not to come over to our side. They're like a bunch of rats, totally incorrigible. They're scaring away our foreign tourists. I am sorry, sir!" the Sikh policeman said apologetically.

"It is quite all right. We are not tourists," Beth quickly added.

"Ma'am. I'm just doing my job. Where are their parents anyway? Good evening." He made a slight bow and continued with his patrol.

"Jack, let's not overdo it tonight. I think you should get another good night of sleep to catch up with the time difference."

"Son, your hotel is back there."

"Jack, we will see you tomorrow at the church."

"Okay, I will see you tomorrow. Good night." Jack watched them enter their black Ford already waiting by the curb.

Now all alone, he slowly panned his eyes down the lively riverfront, full of new sounds and exotic smells. *I can't believe I am here in China. Well, not exactly China,* Jack thought. Back in his hotel room, he took out the hotel's stationery from the mahogany desk and wrote:

Darling,

After three uneventful weeks at sea, I have finally arrived here in Shanghai. I'm staying at the Cathay Hotel. Like I've told you, it is just as fancy as the Plaza.

My room came furnished with mahogany furniture, silk curtains, and monogrammed Irish linen bed sheets. And they even have a telephone and a Zenith radio in the room! (It is playing Benny Goodman as I am writing to you.) I think you would love their walk-in closet, marble bath, and soft towels. I heard they even pipe in their water from a nearby well.

Yesterday, my boss (his name is Todd Spencer) picked me up at the dock. Mother and Dad were there too. We had a drink with him at the hotel, and he invited us to the bank's Christmas

Eve cocktail party at the British Consulate. You should have been there; all the guests were dressed to the nines, and they even had a string quartet playing Haydn in the background. I have never imagined that Shanghai would be like this!

After the party, we took a walk along the Whangpoo riverfront next to the world-famous Bund. The city skyline looks exactly like the pictures in Life magazine, but you need to be here to experience the sight, sounds, and smells. Tomorrow night, I am going over to my father's church to have Christmas dinner. I can't wait to see their place.

Darling, I wish you were here. Till then, sleep tight.

Love,
Jack

CHAPTER 7

The New Hope Church

When he awoke, a symphony of sounds outside his window was already in full swing. Lying in bed, Jack slowly moved his eyes around the room, admiring the floral designs of the ceiling moldings and the silk coverings on the walls. Suddenly, the telephone on the nightstand sprang alive. For a moment, he wasn't sure who would be calling him here in China. He grabbed the black receiver. "Hello?"

"Jack, did I wake you?"

"Mother?" Jack mumbled.

"Did you forget? You are supposed to come to see us at the church today."

"No, I didn't forget…What time is it?"

"It is almost one. Do you need more time?"

"No, I'm awake."

"I will send Da Tu to pick you up around two. Is that okay?"

"Sure, I'll be ready. Do I need to bring anything?"

"Just your toothbrush. You are staying overnight, right?"

"Yes, of course."

A little after two, Jack strode across the rose-marble hotel lobby. His Chinese chauffeur was waiting outside.

"Good afternoon, boss." Da Tu quickly took off his shooting cap and threw away his smoke on the sidewalk.

"I hope you didn't wait long, Da Tu. Did I say it right?"

"Right, right, boss." He held open the door.

"Just call me Jack." Jack slipped into the backseat of the black Ford.

"Okay." Da Tu lurched the car into the traffic.

"Da Tu, is Nanking Road always this busy?"

"Yes, many shops."

"I can see that." Jack saw throngs of shoppers darting into one store, rushing out from another.

"Boss, that is Wing On, very big store…that is La Kai, very good silk." Impatiently, he honked at the rickshaw trotting in front of him.

"Hmm…interesting." Jack wasn't listening. His eyes were on a pretty Chinese woman hanging on the arm of a much older man in an embroidered Chinese silk gown. They looked rather incongruous together, one modern and one ancient, but she didn't seem to care. All bundled up, her face glowed warmly as her fluffy fur coat shivered against the blustering winds blown in from the East China Sea.

"Da Tu, do you like to shop here?"

"Me no buy here, too high price."

"How far are we from my father's church?"

"No far, other side." Da Tu pointed out the windshield at a rusted bridge straight ahead. As they rode closer, Jack saw the name

"Thibet Road Bridge" affixed on the top of the steel girder and small sampans anchored by the algae-covered embankments below.

"What is this river called?"

"Soochow Creek."

But this can't be the same creek I had crossed a couple of days ago at the Bund. He looked down at the rakish water, and he could see Chinese women, with babies wrapped around their backs, doing their laundry by the edges of their fishing boats, oblivious to the rumbling traffic overhead.

As their black Ford slowly rolled across the bridge, the bustling Thibet Road suddenly became drab. No more foreign motorcars cruising in the street, or blond mannequins standing in the windows; all Jack could see were dreary wooden houses with clotheslines hanging over the balconies, electrical wires dangling in the air, dirty bicycles strewn on the broken sidewalks, and bamboo tables and chairs cluttered in front of small noodle shops

"Da Tu, where are we?"

"Chapei."

"I thought my father's church was in Hongkew."

"Yes, yes, left side. Chapei, right side, Hongkew."

"I see." Jack leaned back from the window with a sinking feeling. *This doesn't look too promising.*

"Boss, that is Shin Won Tang," Da Tu called out a few minutes later.

"I beg your pardon?"

"Your father's church. We called it Shin Won Tang in Chinese."

"Oh, I see it." Jack slowly sat up. At the end of a narrow side street on the right side of Thibet Road, he saw a modest gray-brick building with a white cross on top and a rosary window below. *This couldn't be the New Hope Church they often raved about.* Before Da Tu had a chance to open the door, Jack was already standing outside of the car and staring up at the three gold Chinese characters high on the wall. "How do you say it again in Chinese?"

"Shin Won Tang. Come, come, father inside." Da Tu eagerly pushed open a weather-beaten wooden door.

Squinting his eyes, Jack surveyed the dimly lit church filled with rows of old wooden benches on a bare concrete floor and red paper with cursive Chinese characters adorned the walls—a world away from the soaring Riverside Church his father had left behind.

"Son!" A back door suddenly flung open, letting in a shot of bright light.

"Hi, Dad!"

"What do you think?"

"Dad, it's...very nice." Jack managed to hide his disappointment.

"Da Tu, I won't be needing you anymore today. Thank you."

"Thanks for driving me."

"Okay, boss."

"Son, we've got enough room here for more than two-hundred people for our Sunday services."

"I see." Jack stared vacantly at a small wooden cross hung over a cloth-covered altar, and an old upright piano sat by the side.

"And there is also a garden behind the church." Sensing his son's disappointment, Reverend Wells tried to direct his attention away from the empty altar. "Let me show you."

"You have a garden?"

“Wait till you see it.” His father placed his hand on Jack’s elbow, pulling him toward the back door.

“Dad, it is so different from everything around here!” Jack cried out. “I never would’ve expected to see a Chinese garden hidden behind these narrow alleyways.”

“What do you think?”

“It is very nice! Even the air smells different here!” Jack took in a deep breath. “How did this place become a part of your church?”

“This garden and several of the houses around here used to belong to a very rich man called Mr. Lu. When he passed away, he left the whole place to Pastor Henderson. Mind you, in those days we had very few Christian converts in China, let alone such a devoted one. Son, let me show you this tree.” His father pointed at a dwarf tree in a large, blue, glazed ceramic pot. “This little Chinese Elm is over fifty years old. I wouldn’t be surprised if Mr. Lu might have planted this one himself.”

“It looks like a miniaturized tree.” Jack leaned over for a closer inspection.

“The Chinese have been cultivating these miniature trees for thousands of years. They call them *penjing*.”

“Is this like the Japanese bonsai?”

“Similar. The Chinese shape the tree by pruning it and then letting it grow naturally; the Japanese use wires to form the tree into the shape they desire.”

“I didn’t know that.”

“Son, do you see those rocks? They were dug up from the bottom of the Taizhou Lake in Soochow,” the Reverend said offhandedly as if his son knew where Taizhou Lake was.

“What is so special about them?”

"I was told that these stones have a certain ethereal quality about them. You see those holes?"

"Yes, what about them?" Jack stared perplexingly at the strangely shaped rocks.

"Just like Michelangelo's sculptures, they are not just stones. These solids and voids represent the interplay of the yin-and-yang forces found in nature—female and male; weak and strong; soft and hard. Chinese find these rocks poetic because, through these solids and voids, they see a certain harmony."

"They do have that strange look to them." Jack turned his attention to a school of fish swimming in and out beneath the white and pink lotus flowers floating around the rocks. "I like those fish. They are so colorful."

"They are called 'koi.' They're very popular in China."

"This Chinese garden looks so serene and peaceful. Dad, now I see why you like this place."

"Yes, I do like it a lot. With what is going on around the world these days, this place is like a cloister, a peaceful place to contemplate and reflect, a little piece of paradise on earth, if you will. Son, let me show you where we are staying."

"Sure." Jack followed him through a moon-shaped opening. At the end of the cobbled path, nestled between swaying bamboo groves, he saw a wooden building with curvy roof overhangs and red-lacquered screen windows.

"This little pavilion used to be Mr. Lu's private study, and now it is our residence."

"It, it looks so...so Chinese." Jack could not help but wonder how different it was from their spacious waterfront apartment in New York.

"Yes, it is authentically Chinese. They don't build these kinds of buildings anymore," his father said enthusiastically.

"Oh dear, when did you come in?" His mother strode in, wiping her hands on her apron. "Very different from the States, isn't it?"

"Hi, Mother. Dad was just showing me around."

"Sit down, sit down. Do you want anything to drink?"

"I would like to have a beer if you have one."

"We do. Jack, we've got you set up here in the study. I hope you don't mind." She eyed an elaborately carved wooden bench with embroidered silk cushions.

"Son, this place is not going to be like your fancy Cathay Hotel."

"I know that, Dad. If you guys can rough it, so can I."

"Son, when was the last time you used an outhouse?" His father winked at his mother.

"When I was a boy scout camping out on Bear Mountain. Why do you ask?"

"Well, you might have to rough it tonight. Our bathroom comes only with cold running water, and you have to do your things outside or in a little potty," Jack's father said teasingly.

"Jack dear, many places in Shanghai—especially outside of the International area—don't have indoor plumbing as we do in the States. A lot of us have to learn how to use a chamber pot." His mother noticed his discomfort.

"I-I think I can deal with that…at least for one night," Jack stammered.

"Jack, let me go get your beer."

"Thanks." Jack followed his mother into the kitchen. "Mother, what are you cooking? It smells good."

"Beef stroganoff, your favorite." She handed him a beer. "It will be ready in a few more minutes."

"Can't wait. I am starving."

Jack sat between his parents at a small square table facing the garden, and just as he was about to take a sip of his beer, Jack saw his parents lowering their heads to pray. "Thank you, Lord, for giving us this opportunity to be together on this special day."

It had been a long while since he had said his prayers. Jack put down his beer to join them, but he could only manage to say a few words before his father suddenly declared, "Amen. Let's eat!"

"Let me serve you some rice." Jack's mother offered.

"Mmm, everything smells so good! I don't think Aunt Millets' beef stroganoff was ever as good as yours."

"Thank you, dear. How much rice would you like?"

"Mother and Father, I want to make a toast to both of you." Jack raised his beer. "I am so happy that I can share this Christmas holiday with you, just like we have always done before. I am so very proud of what you two are doing here in China for the Chinese people. I wish your congregation at the New Hope Church will continue to grow, and God willing, He will continue to bless you both with good health."

"Jack, one of the hardest things your father and I had to endure was not being able to spend Christmas with you. I thank our Lord for giving us this opportunity to celebrate this special day together here in China. Oh, I want to cry." His mother put down her wine glass.

"There, there." The Reverend gently patted her hand.

"Mom, I love you. Dad, I love you. I missed you guys." Jack reached out for their hands.

"I'm okay, dear." She regained her composure. "These two years have been tough. We've had our shares of ups and downs, but overall, it has been a very rewarding experience, doing God's work in China." She took up her wine glass and dried her eyes.

"Son, your mother and I are very fortunate to have had Pastor Henderson lay down the groundwork before he passed away. He built up the whole congregation practically from nothing. Compared to him, what we have done here was relatively easy stuff. We still have much to do."

"Jack, do you know that he almost got killed during the Boxer Rebellion?" his mother asked softly. "But he stayed the course. God bless his soul."

"Praise the Lord!" They tinkled their glasses.

It was well past midnight. Jack lay awake on the Chinese settee with his feet hanging over the armrest. The room looked ancient, redolent with Chinese relics, and the ceiling rafters were dusty, covered with cracked red lacquer. Jack could hear the intermittent crickets chirping in the garden, the gentle strumming of a lute through the screen windows, and high-pitched falsetto singing at a nearby balcony. *When are these people going to sleep?* Jack twisted and turned; his body began to feel sore.

An hour went by, then another, and finally, he gave up. Jack lit another Camel. As he was puffing on his smoke, a loud sing-song cry came over from the other side of the white stucco wall. It was the cry of the night soil man making his rounds in the alleyways. Jack took a look at his watch; just one more hour to go before dawn. *I better get some sleep*, Jack mumbled.

"Good morning, Jack. Are you awake? It is almost nine o'clock."

"Mother?" Jack answered groggily.

"It is almost nine o'clock. We are waiting for you to have breakfast."

"Okay, I will be right there." Jack cleared his eyes with the back of his hand.

"Mrs. Lin made tea and some scrambled eggs for you. I'm still working on teaching her how to use the coffee percolator. I am dying for a good cup of coffee."

"Chinese don't drink coffee; they drink tea." His father strode into the room. "Good morning, Son. Slept well?"

"Not really. How do you guys get used to all those noises at night?"

"Son, there are at least four times the number of people packed together in these narrow alleyways than in our typical streets back in the States. Life goes on at all hours of the day and night. It takes a little getting used to, but after a couple of weeks, you won't hear a thing." His father sat down on a wicker chair facing the garden.

"Hard to believe, isn't it? We are fortunate to have this place all to ourselves." His mother poured his tea, and suddenly she called out, "Good morning, Lily!"

Jack turned around and saw a pretty Chinese girl carrying a basket of flowers on her arm walking toward them.

"Lily, please come over here. Let me introduce you to our son." His mother put down the teapot and motioned her to come closer.

"Good morning, Mrs. Wells and Reverend."

"Hi, I am Jack." He stood up, held out his hand.

"How do you do, sir." She nodded politely.

"How…do you do?" Jack asked eagerly.

"Jack just came from New York a couple of days ago. He is going to be working here in Shanghai."

"Mr. Wells. I hope you like Shanghai," she said softly, casting down her big almond eyes.

"I think I will," replied Jack, still standing.

"Reverend, Da Tu and I have made up one-hundred-thirty Christmas gift bags. We made a few more just in case. Last year we were a little short."

"That is good news! Lily, let's hope we'll give out two-hundred bags next Christmas." Reverend Wells beamed. "Lily, here is my Sunday sermon. Please look it over. We've got half an hour."

"I will take a look at it right away. Mr. Wells, it is nice meeting you." She picked up her flower basket.

"Same here, it is nice meeting you too." Jack put out his hand, but she had already walked away.

"A lovely girl, isn't she? I don't know what we would do without her. She is a godsend."

"Where did you find her?"

"Oh, it's a long story." His father took a sip of his green tea. "A few years ago, Pastor Henderson found her wandering in the streets of Chapei."

"That is the Chinese section on the other side of us," his mother quickly interjected. "She was homeless because she ran away from an arranged marriage she hated. He then took her to a place called the Door of Hope. That is where we foreigners take in the runaway Chinese girls who have been sold by their families."

"They still can sell people in China?"

"Chinese don't call this kind of thing selling; they call it arranged marriage or apprenticeship," his mother said. "Anyway, after spent a year there and learned enough English, she went to work for Pastor Henderson as his assistant and translator. We are very lucky that she stayed on after he passed away. She is now helping me with the church chores and your father with his Sunday sermons."

"She sings the hymns like an angel," his father quickly added. "Lily is a smart girl. We should help her go on with more schooling. China certainly needs more educated Christian women like her."

"I am going to talk to the headmistress at the McTyeire School for Girls next week. I want to see if I can get her in on a scholarship."

"That is an excellent idea, my dear. I will go with you." Reverend Wells quickly drank up his tea and jauntily rose from his wicker chair. "I think I am ready for my Sunday sermon."

Following his mother into the dimly lit New Hope Church, Jack quietly closed the door behind him. He squinted his eyes at the shriveled figures packed tightly on the backless pews. From their hunched shoulders and gray hair, he could tell most of them were women, and full of years. Towering over them, Jack saw his father standing behind a white cloth-covered altar, with that Chinese girl by his side. She had changed into a shapely white blouse, black satin trousers, and matching cloth shoes. Her shiny black hair was braided into a long pigtail and her oval face, unadorned with makeup, glowed under the light. She looked up at his father, eagerly waiting.

"My brethren and sisters," Reverend Wells boomed in an unnaturally loud voice. "Jesus Christ is the Son of God and our Lord. He died for our sins." He paused. Lily nodded and then turned to the congregation. In a soothing voice that sounded more mature than her age, she intoned softly: "*Wo dei tung boa jei mei men, Yesu si Shangdi dei erh zie, da wie wo men de zui siwang.*"

"He, He alone, can lead his true believers into the kingdom of Our heavenly Father…Psalm 23: The Lord is my Shepherd. He leads me in the paths of righteousness…."

Jack looked on as his father piously waved his dog-eared Bible; he roared, he whispered, and he then waited for her to translate. His sermon spoken in Chinese danced off her tongue like a melodic tune; her sing-song voice rose and fell as he nodded approvingly. "*Ta, zhiyou Ta, koyi lingdao wo men zhun tiantang….*"

Even though Jack didn't understand anything she was saying, her words did not sound strange to his ears, for he seemed to have heard those words spoken before.

As the sermon droned on, Jack saw his mother quietly take her seat at the old upright, arms raised; she waited for the scrapings and hacking coughs to subside. With a slight nod, she started to play, and the Chinese girl began to sing:

Amazing Grace! How sweet the sound
That saved a wretch like me!
I once was lost, but now am found;
Was blind, but now I see…

Following her lead, everyone started to sing. Swaying gently on their small bound feet and with yearnings on their faces, the old parishioners looked up hopefully at a small transfixed figure of a gaunt man hanging on the back wall. He didn't look Chinese; he did not even look the least bit like the fat Buddha. With his arms stretched out on a wooden cross, head mournfully drooping and eyes peacefully closed, they were told that this emaciated Jewish man hanging on a cross is the Son of God and that he died for their original sin—an idea as foreign as the words rolling off this tall preacher's tongue. But the promise that He, He alone, could save them from their abject poverty and lead them into paradise, was all they came to hear.

Now I can see why they called this place the New Hope Church, Jack thought, and he too began to sing.

"Hallelujah! Praise the Lord!" Jack heard his father thunder, waving his Bible in exultation.

"Shei-shei ni men…thank you all for coming." He saw the Chinese girl take a small bow.

"Dad, that was a very beautiful service." Jack quickly rushed over.

"Thank you, Son. You should come every Sunday then."

"Mother, you played beautifully, as always."

"Thank you. Jack, let me introduce you to some of our parishioners. Mrs. Chan, this is our son."

"Ai Yo! Mrs. Wells, your son so tall. You very lucky." Mrs. Chan touched Jack's arm with her trembling hand.

"Yes, I am very blessed." His mother beamed proudly.

Soon others began to surround him; their adulations made Jack squeamish as he haplessly stood in the center of this unwanted attention, smothered by all the veiny hands.

"Old Heaven has condemned me to a bitter fate. I only have a girl, and even she couldn't give me a grandson," another old lady grumbled in Chinese.

"Ai Ya! Mrs. Wu, what are you saying? Your daughter is only twenty-five. She has plenty of time to give you a grandson."

"Wu Tai-Tai, lady Wu, you must burn more paper money to please Guanyin so that she will grant your wish."

"Mrs. Yang, don't talk such superstitious things. Our Reverend don't like us talking that way in the church."

"Why not? Guanyin is our goddess of mercy."

"Yang Tai-Tai, remember, we are all Christians now," another said in an admonishing tone. "Reverend told us there is only one true God. Our gods are not real. They are just a bunch of clay figurines."

"Chang Tai-Tai, don't worry; he don't speak Chinese."

Amid all the jabbering, Jack suddenly heard that Chinese girl call out, "Mrs. Wells, can you come here for a minute?"

"Jack, come, I need to help Lily with the Christmas goodies.... Yes, what is it, Lily?"

Thankfully, the old ladies soon started to move away from him when they saw the little Christmas bags were being handed out by the church door.

"Mrs. Lin wants another Christmas bag, and I told her one bag per family."

"Lily, I know her husband is a rickshaw puller, and you know rice is probably the only thing they can afford to eat the whole day. Putting a little more rice and some meat in their stomachs is the least thing we can do." She put another bag into her eager hand.

"*Shie-shie.* God bless you. Your kindness will be repaid in your next life."

The prayer room soon began to thin out as the last bags of rice and sausages were handed out. Jack's father and mother waved by the church door, "Merry Christmas!"

"Reverend, if you don't need me anymore, I will be back tomorrow."

"Lily, thank you. The sermon went well as usual."

"Thank you, Reverend. It is your sermon. I am just repeating your words."

"No, no, not my words, God's words, and you spoke them so beautifully in Chinese. I wish one day I could speak Chinese as well as you do so I can convey the true meaning of the scripture directly to our parishioners. Lily, you must teach me."

"Reverend, I am honored. Then you must help me improve my English." She blushed.

"That's a deal."

"Reverend and Mrs. Wells, I will see you tomorrow. Goodbye, it is nice meeting you, Mr. Wells."

"Same here; hope to see you next Sunday."

"Jack, do you want to stay for lunch?"

"What, Mother?"

"I said do you want to stay for lunch?"

"Sure."

CHAPTER 8

First Day at the Bank

Jack was awakened early by the muted groans of the foghorn in the harbor; and by seven o'clock, he was already downstairs in the elegantly appointed dining room ordering poached eggs, fried bacon, and coffee. Curious about what was going on in this Chinese port city, he casually picked up a neatly folded *North-China Daily News* placed on top of the white tablecloth. Aside from the headlines about what Hitler was up to in Europe, there were local news and some announcements about the last night's meeting of the Shanghai Municipal Council. In the society column, he saw pictures of well-dressed English men and women at a fancy Christmas party and smiling faces of weekend golfers gathered in front of the Shanghai Country Club. Jack quickly folded the paper as he discreetly looked around the hushed dining room. Other than the white-uniformed Chinese waiters, everyone seemed to look alike—dapperly dressed Americans and European businessmen with little white handkerchiefs peeking out from their dark double-breasted suits. *They are all older than me.* Jack smiled, drank up the last drops of his English Breakfast tea, and casually dabbed his lips with a white napkin.

"Can I get you anything else, sir?"

"No, I am fine. Just put the bill on my room."

"Certainly, Mr. Wells."

"I hope everything was satisfactory, Mr. Wells." Another Chinese waiter rushed over, pulling out his chair.

"Yes, everything was excellent."

"Have a pleasant day, sir."

If only my friends could see me now. A faint smile curled up at the corners of his mouth.

The biting wind swept across his face on this cold Monday morning as Jack strode briskly along the crowded Bund, past the tall bronzed doors of the Charter Bank and the Big Ching of the Chinese Customs Building. Then, there it was. Flanked by two fierce-looking bronze lions and protected by an array of black wrought-iron bars, the Hongkong and Shanghai Bank building loomed ahead; it looked more like a fortress than a bank building. Standing underneath the tall archway, the two Sikh doormen immediately snapped into erect attention when they saw Jack approaching. "Good morning, sir! Welcome to Hongkong and Shanghai Bank!" they declared in unison, holding open a pair of giant bronze doors.

"Good morning." Jack nodded as he strode past the lobby murals into a cavernous banking hall. Below the high-vaulted barrel-ceilings and nestled between the soaring Corinthian columns, he saw rows of battle-gray metal desks placed neatly on a vast gray granite floor. Many young English men, all about his age, hunched by the green shaded lamps, already busy at work.

"Good morning, Mr. Spencer. I saw everyone is already working. Am I late?" Jack then saw his boss, impeccably dressed in a navy-blue Savile Row suit, ambling toward him.

"No, no, young man, you are quite punctual. Our staff starts at 8:00 a.m., and officers at 8:15. Let me show you your office." Spencer tilted up his head toward a glass-enclosed mezzanine hovering over the gray metal desks.

They are going to give me an office? Jack had not figured on that.

"Our retail banking functions are on the main floor, officers are on the second and third, senior management is on the fourth, and our private dining and meeting rooms are on the top floor. We don't go up there unless we're invited." Spencer casually dispensed some of the bank rules.

"Understood. We have a similar arrangement back in New York, too." Walking behind, Jack nodded and smiled at anyone who happened to look up from his desk.

"Here we are. This is your office." Spencer casually pushed open a heavy mahogany door.

"Is this my office?" Jack asked unsurely as he peeked into a spacious room with a clear view of the harbor.

"My good man, we certainly didn't intend to bring you all the way from New York to have you sit down there working on the bills of lading. Oh, I almost forgot—your secretary." He turned to a pretty woman standing behind a metal secretarial desk. "Miss Mary Lane, please come here for a minute."

"Yes, Mr. Spencer." She quickly stepped out from behind her Underwood typewriter.

"Miss Lane, this is Mr. Jack Wells. From now on, you will be his secretary."

"Certainly, Mr. Spencer." She curtsied.

"Hi, I am Jack." He held out his hand.

"How do you do, Mr. Wells. I look forward to working for you." She curtsied again.

"Thanks, Mary."

"Miss Lane, can you bring us two cups of tea?"

"Yes, Mr. Spencer, I will be right back."

"She is very pretty." Jack watched her walking away.

"Yes, I must admit. Bewitchingly exotic, isn't she? That is usually the first thing most men notice about her."

"Of course, how can you miss?" Jack tried to sound casual.

"But Jack, if you look more closely, you'll notice that she is not quite our sort of people."

"What do you mean, Mr. Spencer? She has such a lovely English accent."

"Jack, she is what we call a mixed-blood. You didn't notice her slanted eyes?"

"Now that you mention it."

"She is a Eurasian, an unfortunate by-product of a mixed union between a Chinese woman and an Englishman, one of the few rogue employees we ever had at the bank. A good English chap, actually—quite a pity." He paused. "Getting involved with a Chinese woman is a definite no-no for our employees—bank policy, you know."

"I see…So, what happened to him?"

"We had to terminate his employment for the appearance of propriety. The poor fellow never did recover from that. He was ostracized from our Shanghai society and could not find another suitable position to support himself or his Chinese wife. I managed to send him back home to his first wife and found him a position with another bank in London."

"He was already married?"

“I am afraid so, but he was a decent enough fellow to send a hundred pounds each year to support Mary and her mother.”

“Do you know her mother?”

“Not really. I just delivered the money to her outside the bank whenever he wired in the funds. But that all stopped when he passed away a couple of years ago and I never saw her again…and not long after that, Mary came to see me for a job, so I offered her a secretarial position. I simply could not see her working at nightclubs like so many other Eurasian girls. She turned out to be an excellent secretary, and I think you will find her quite satisfactory.”

“I’m sure she’ll do just fine.”

“Splendid.” He paused for a moment. “Oh, by the way, if you need to use the facility, please do use the lavatory designated for us foreigners only; the Chinese staffs have their own.”

“Yes, I understand. We have separate restrooms back in the States, too.”

“It certainly makes things more manageable. Jack, I shall leave you to get acclimated with your new office. Mary has already left some files on your desk. Look them over, and we will talk again at lunch. Shall we say 12:30?”

“Okay, that would work.”

“Carry on!”

Jack slowly walked behind the mahogany desk, sank into his leather chair, and ran his hands over the green felt desk pad. His office even had a black leather sofa with two matching side chairs in the corner and two paintings on the walls. *Not bad, not bad at all for a junior banker*. Jack smiled.

"Mr. Wells?" Mary gently knocked. "Where would you like to take your tea?"

"Uh, I don't know. Just put it anywhere. Mr. Spencer has just left. Mary, thank you, anyway."

"Mr. Wells, would you like to have a cup of coffee then?"

"No thank you. Mary, just call me Jack; we Americans are not that formal."

"Mr. Wells, I am not allowed to do that. Is there anything else I can do for you?"

"No, not now. Let me first get used to this place. I will call you if I need anything else."

"Okay, I will be right outside." She quietly retreated, closing the door behind her.

Jack picked up his teacup and took a loud sip as he turned his attention to the yellowed file folders with Standard Oil, Westinghouse, R. J. Reynolds Tobacco Company, and a few other familiar American company names marked on the edges. He picked up one file and started to flip through it and soon forgot the time when he heard a knock on the door.

"Shall we?"

"Sure, Mr. Spencer. Where are we going?" Jack quickly closed his files.

"The Shanghai Club. I thought you might like to try some of their roasted duck for lunch."

"Back in New York, we only have forty-five minutes for lunch. I would usually have a sandwich."

"Jack, here in Shanghai, we have more leisurely working hours. We give our officers two hours for lunch, or to do whatever one needs to attend to around the city, but we do have to work half a day on Saturday."

"We have to work on Saturday in New York, too." Jack straightened his tie.

CHAPTER 9

The Shanghai Club

At first glance, the Shanghai Club at Number 3 Bund did not look particularly remarkable; but once inside, this two-story English Renaissance structure exulted an unmistakable air of the exclusivity of the nineteenth-century colonial days. Surrounded by dark walnut panels, Englishmen in tailored suits gathered along the brightly polished brass rails, chatting, laughing, and waving their empty glasses at the uniformed Chinese barmen behind the well-worn mahogany counter.

"Good afternoon, Mr. Spencer." A white Russian maître d' greeted them at the door. "This way please."

"Mr. Spencer, he seems to know you pretty well."

"Jack, I have been a member of the Shanghai Club for a long time, and I always dine at the same table—a sort of tradition here."

"The usual? Bombay Gin with a dash of tonic?"

"Yes, of course."

"What about you, sir?"

"I would like to have a beer."

"Sir, do you prefer a Guinness?"

"Eh…you know what, I changed my mind. I would like to have a Bombay Gin too."

"With tonic water?"

"Sure."

"Excellent. I will be right back." The maître d' quickly disappeared.

Spencer leaned back in his chair and pointed toward the window. "Jack, that's the famous Hundred-Foot Long Bar; it goes all the way back into the other room."

"I have never seen a bar that long." Jack turned his head to look.

"We English like to gather around this watering hole after work…there is no place like it in Shanghai—or London, for that matter."

"I can see this is a pretty popular spot." Jack surveyed the crowded bar.

"You see those gentlemen over there?" Spencer politely nodded toward a small group of immaculately dressed men sitting by the large bay windows overlooking the harbor.

"Yes, what about them?"

"The gentleman sitting closest to the window is the managing partner of Jardine and Matheson, and the man sitting next to him is the head of Butterfield and Swire."

From where he was sitting, Jack could tell they were well-bred men of high social standing, lording over the Shanghai Club with that certain patrician air. "Is your boss over there?"

"Our senior managing partner is currently in London, but my boss is sitting over there." Spencer pointed toward another group of men standing a few feet away from the bay windows.

"Why is he not sitting with them?"

"He has to take his drinks with his peers," Spencer replied matter-of-factly.

Jack saw small groups of Englishmen gathered along the brass rails a few empty seats away from the clear view of the harbor. "How do they all know where they should sit?"

"Jack, ever since the Shanghai Club was first opened in the late 1800s, we had the same sort of tradition we had back Home: Men of high social standing always sit by the bay windows; the Knights, Dukes, and the lesser ranks in that order would take their seats a little away from them."

"Interesting. I don't think we Americans have that kind of tradition."

"Jack, I am quite sure that your Vanderbilts and Rockefellers wouldn't think..." Spencer suddenly stopped in mid-sentence and jumped up from his chair. "By George, I thought you were still in London. I did not expect to see you back in town for another week!"

Jack quickly turned around and saw a tall man with a headful of silver hair approaching their table.

"I came back a couple of days ago, and I was about to give you a ring." He looked in Jack's direction.

"Oh, yes, allow me to introduce my new assistant, Mr. Jack Wells."

"How do you do, sir?" Jack quickly stood up.

"Jack, this is Mr. Mathew Atkinson, a very dear old friend of mine."

"American? I presume."

"Yes, Mr. Atkinson."

"Matt, Jack is Reverend Wells' son."

"Oh, yes, yes, of course."

"Jack, Mr. Atkinson has been in Shanghai as long as I have. He knows practically everybody who is of any consequence. He is what we call an 'Old China Hand.'"

"I hope you are not referring to my age, old sport," he said jauntily. "Young man, you are very fortunate to be working for the strongest bank in Shanghai. Even some of our English lads could not get their foot into the door."

"Yes, I am very fortunate, Mr. Atkinson."

"Can I give you some advice, young man?"

"Certainly, Mr. Atkinson."

"Buy yourself a nice tailored white dinner jacket. Shanghai has many good Chinese tailors. I am sure you can have one made at a very decent price. Proper attire is a must if you want to be invited to some of our better parties in the city."

"Thank you, Mr. Atkinson. I shall remember that," Jack said deferentially.

"Young man, have you been to our country club yet?"

"No, I haven't. I just arrived a few days ago."

"Todd, let's set up a golf date at the club. I have an interesting business proposition to talk to you about. Do bring this young man along."

"Certainly, old sport."

"Cheerio!" Atkinson waved with the back of his hand as he strutted toward the bay window.

Spencer sunk back into his chair as he watched his old pal bantering jovially with the managing director of Jardine & Matheson.

"Jack, after all these years, I have yet to share a drink with him over there by the bay window."

"Mr. Spencer, I am sure that someday you will."

"Not anytime soon, I am afraid."

"Why not?"

"Jack, you're young; you don't appreciate how hard it is to change one's station of life that you were born into."

"I guess not, but just look at it this way, Mr. Spencer, after a few shots of this Bombay Gin, does it matter where you sit?"

"Jack, you may have a point there." Spencer took another big swallow of his gin, as raucous laughter erupted from the back of the Hundred-Foot Long Bar. "Let's change the subject."

"Okay." Jack put down his drink.

"Jack, our bank is currently having a small problem with this Robert Ferguson fellow at Standard Oil."

"I think I saw his name in the files."

"He runs the cash management department for their China operations. Recently he has made some noise about moving their accounts to Barclay Bank, or Yokohama Specie Bank, God forbid. Standard Oil has been one of our most important clients for many years, and we certainly don't want to lose them."

"Why does he want to do that?"

"This Ferguson fellow thinks that one of our employees has mishandled some of his company's funds. Nothing serious, just some small loss of interest involving his overnight deposits. It was all due to some misunderstandings."

"Okay, you want me to talk to him?"

"Yes, from one American to another. Perhaps, you can take him out to dinner, a cabaret show, or whatever...." Spencer swiveled his gin in his chubby hand.

"I will see what I can do," Jack said eagerly.

"Splendid! Jack, try the duck. Tell me what you think."

"It looks good." Jack eagerly picked up his knife and fork.

"Mr. Spencer, I've never thought I could have such a delicious lunch on my first day at the bank. Thank you." Jack followed his boss out of the Shanghai Club.

"Extraordinary, isn't it? Sometimes even I find it hard to believe that we could have such a civilized meal so far away from home."

"Mr. Spencer, I've read that Shanghai used to be just a little fishing village. The changes here have been nothing short of a miracle." Jack cast his eyes around the bustling harbor.

"Yes, indeed. It is quite remarkable, if I may say so. For almost one-hundred years, we Brits have steadily transformed this muddy riverbank into one of the most cosmopolitan cities in the world, and that is why people call it the Paris of the East." Spencer glanced up proudly at the gleaming skyline.

"Yes, you Brits have done a remarkable job. Just look at those buildings."

"Unfortunately, the Chinese don't appreciate what we have done for them," Spencer said scornfully. "No one has come up to me and said: 'Mr. Spencer, thank you very much for what you have done for us Chinese people!'"

"I guess the Chinese still consider the International Settlement as a part of China."

"Yes, but no...after they lost the Opium War in 1842, the Chinese, under the Treaty of Nanking, had agreed to cede this part of

Shanghai to us as a treaty port in perpetuity. So technically, it belongs to us. No matter. Just imagine, if we had left it to the Chinese, this place would probably still be the same as we first found it," he paused and then added exasperatedly, "For all we had done for them, why aren't the Chinese more grateful?"

"Lao Ban, want rickshaw ride, only twenty-five cents!" a rickshaw man trotting close by them suddenly called out.

"No, we don't need any ride today." Jack waved his hand.

"Lau Ban, rickshaw ride, cheap, only twenty cents!"

"No, no ride today, thank you," Jack repeated.

"Want girls?"

"Hey, look here! Are you deaf! Stop pestering us, you little vermin!" Spencer barked, flashing a contemptuous glare as he waved his forefinger. "Chinese! Sometimes we must be a little sterner with these people!"

"Mr. Spencer, it is okay. He is just trying to make a living." Jack didn't know what else to say as he watched the frightened rickshaw puller quickly trot away.

CHAPTER 10

Lunch at Little Jimmy's

Mary Lane quickly got up from her secretarial chair when she saw them walking out the mezzanine elevator. "I hope you gentlemen had a pleasant lunch."

"Excellent. The roasted duck is really good."

"Would you care for some tea?" Mary was poised in front of them wearing a pink blouse and a shorter pleated skirt.

"Mary, can you go get Mr. Robert Ferguson's files?"

"Mr. Spencer, they are already on Mr. Wells' desk."

"Mary, you look very nice today."

"Thank you, Mr. Wells." Mary curtsied.

"Mary, you do look a bit different…a new outfit?" Spencer took a casual glance at her.

"Yes, Mr. Spencer."

"Splendid! Carry on."

"Mr. Wells, do you need anything else?" Mary followed him into his office.

"Not for now. Mary, what is this Ferguson fellow like?"

"I don't know. I have never met him."

"Can you get him on the phone for me?"

"Certainly, Mr. Wells."

A moment later, Mary was back at the door. "Mr. Wells, he is on the phone."

"Mr. Ferguson?" Jack picked up the receiver.

"May I know who is calling?" a woman's voice answered.

"This is Mr. Jack Wells from the Hongkong and Shanghai Bank."

"Just a moment, please."

"This is Bobby," a man abruptly answered, as if he had snatched away the receiver from the woman.

"Good afternoon, Mr. Ferguson, this is Mr. Jack Wells. I am from the Hongkong and Shanghai Bank."

"Okay, what can I do you for?"

"I was assigned to handle your Standard Oil account. I'd like to introduce myself, or perhaps pay you a visit," Jack said courteously.

"You sound like an American. What happened to the other guy?" His irritable voice softened a bit.

"Mr. Winthrop? He went back to London."

"Good for him. He is a real jerk." He cursed.

"Uh..." Jack was a little taken back. "Perhaps I can come to your office...uh, or maybe we can meet for lunch or dinner?"

"No dinner, lunch is fine. You name the place and time," he replied gruffly.

"Mr. Ferguson, I am kind of new in Shanghai. You want to pick a place?"

"You like to have some down-home cook'n?"

"Sure, you know Shanghai better than I."

"I know this joint that serves the best bowl of Texas chili west of Hawaii."

"No kidding—in Shanghai?"

"No kidding. It's called Little Jimmy's, just a few blocks behind your bank. It is just a dive, nothing fancy."

"Okay, it sounds good. What time is good for you?"

"How about this Friday around twelve?"

"That will work. I can arrange a chauffeur to pick you up."

"Nah, I can walk. I will meet you over there."

"Great! I'll see you there." Jack then heard a click on the other end. *This Bobby Ferguson fellow sounded like a good ol' boy.* "Mary, can you give me the address of Little Jimmy's?"

As he walked close to the Little Jimmy's, Jack spotted a man in a dark suit that looked one size too small for his sturdily built body, and his powder-blue striped tie was too pretty for his weathered face. "Hi, Mr. Ferguson!"

"Hi, there! I see you've found it." Flashing an easy smile, Bobby Ferguson extended out his hand. "It ain't the Shanghai Club, but I hope you don't mind."

"No, not at all." Jack quickly stepped up.

"I think you'll like this place if you like chili."

"I've had chili a couple of times before." Jack followed him into a small space cluttered with red-and-white tables on a black-white linoleum floor.

"Let's grab a table over there…hey, Jimmy, how's it going?" Bobby Ferguson hollered, waving at a man standing by the kitchen door.

"Is that *the* little Jimmy?"

"Yeah, that's him."

"He is not too little. How did he wind up running a joint like this here in Shanghai?" Jack studied this improbable-looking American diner in the middle of a Chinese port city.

"He used to be a U.S. Marine stationed in the Far East. After he got out of the service, he decided to stay. I heard he has a Chinese girlfriend stashed somewhere."

"This place looks pretty authentic. You come here often?" Jack surveyed the movie-star posters on the walls.

"Whenever I am in the mood for a bowl of hot chili. Lots of American sailors come here at night." Bobby Ferguson slouched in his chair, pushed aside the plastic-covered menu, and then stuck a paper napkin into his collar. "They serve steaks too if you want one."

"I had some Australian beef a few nights ago—not too bad."

"It ain't Texas Long Horn, but close."

"Chili would be fine."

"Hey, Jimmy, give us two bowls of your spicy chili and two beers. Put it on one check."

"Let me pick up the check, please," Jack insisted.

"It's okay; I got a business account."

"Okay, my treat next time."

"If you want…I understand you come from New York."

"Yeah, this is my first week in Shanghai."

"I'm going on my tenth year," Bobby Ferguson said nonchalantly.

"Really? You like living here?"

"Well…not bad, just different."

"Mr. Ferguson, I see you are an Account Manager at Standard Oil." Jack picked up his business card by the side of the table.

"It pays the rent."

"Mr. Ferguson, I understand you're thinking about switching banks. Is there anything I can do to change your mind?"

Cut right to the chase. Bobby suppressed a smile. "Where did you work before?"

"First National City Bank in New York."

"Good, then you should know something about banking."

"I hope so."

"Your predecessor don't know shit about banking. I am glad that you took over his place."

"I have never met the guy, but they told me that he was transferred back to London because Shanghai was not his cup of tea."

"Really? Is that what they told you?" Bobby Ferguson snickered, arching his eyebrows. "You wanta know the real reason?"

"Okay, tell me."

"The real reason is," he said, leaning over the table, "he got caught with a Chinese teenage girl in an opium den one night. The Shanghai Municipal Police could have him up on narcotics charges and throw him in the slammer."

"They didn't tell me that. I thought the opium stuff was banned a long time ago."

"It was and still is, but you can still find lots of opium dens all over the city. Yeah, smoking opium is still a big business in China. Even some of us foreigners got hooked on that stuff."

"No kidding?"

"No kidding. Anyway, after the police handed him over to the bank, they quietly shipped him out of Shanghai before he became local news." Bobby Ferguson paused, cupping his beer in his hands. "I could see the headline: 'British Banker Busted in a Chinese Opium Den!'"

"I guess that would make the bank look pretty bad."

"No shit! Just imagine what that would do to the bank's sterling reputation. You know, the white man's image thing." He chuckled, almost laughing. "What an irony, one of their own got hooked on the same dope they have been peddling to the Chinese for one-hundred years. It serves them right." He slammed down his beer.

"Mr. Ferguson, it is a good thing that we Americans never had to deal with that stuff."

"We sure did." He leaned back in his chair. "Jack, do you know that next to the British East India Trading Company, we Americans were the second biggest dope dealers in China back in the 1800s."

"Mr. Ferguson, you're kidding me, right? I have never heard such a thing."

"That's a historical fact. During the 1860s, Warren Delano Roosevelt, our president's grandfather, was one of the biggest opium dealers in China. And he was not the only one either. Astor, Samuel Russell, Cushing, Forbes, and Low, just to mention a few. They had all gotten very rich off the Chinese on this dope trade."

"But why? I thought they were all Christians."

"Money, what else."

"I find that hard to believe. Mr. Ferguson, where did you get all that stuff?" Jack asked skeptically.

"You just don't hear people talk about it back in the States. Jack, do you know that much of the ground that Yale University stands on today was bought with the opium profits donated by Astor?"

"C'mon, Mr. Ferguson. You are bullshitting me, right?" Jack began to feel a little offended. "My dad graduated from Yale."

"Would I make up such a thing to make us Americans look bad?"

"I find the whole thing hard to believe."

"Anyway, I don't care if you believe me or not; it is a good thing that we don't sell that stuff anymore. The Chinese Green Gang now controls the dope trade. And lately, there have been a lot of turf wars going on in the streets. You've got to be careful where you go at night, even in this part of Shanghai. You don't want to get caught in their cross-fire."

"Thanks for telling me."

"Care for another?"

"Sure, why not. Mr. Ferguson, if you don't mind my asking…"

"Bobby, just call me Bobby."

"Okay, Bobby, are you from Texas?"

"Yeah, born and bred." Bobby smacked his lips.

"Where about in Texas, may I ask?"

"Midland," Bobby drawled with a more discernible accent.

"How the hell did you wind up in Shanghai?"

"My dad used to work for Standard Oil. When he was transferred to their headquarters in New York, I went with him. I spent a year in the city, and I even went to school there, but I had to quit after my old man suddenly died of a heart attack. Got a job as an oiler with the same company back in Midland and worked my way up to the Middle East as a supervisor, then Jakarta, and now Shanghai is my home."

"That's a long way away from home. Married?"

"Used to be. Wife split after just six months. She couldn't stand living here."

"Don't you ever want to go back to the States?"

"Sometimes, but I ain't got nobody back home. Mother remarried twice. I like it here pretty good."

"So, what do you do for fun?"

"Work, sleep and play a little golf at the Columbia Country Club on weekends. Sometimes I go to the Del Monte Club or Ciro's with friends, to watch a cabaret show and dance with some big-tittie White Russian women."

"It sounds like you are getting along pretty well here in Shanghai."

"Most of the time…everything is so much cheaper here compared to the States."

"That is what I have heard."

"And lives here are cheap too. Girls are a dime a dozen. Jack, do you know you can hire a Chinese girl as your live-in maid for less than $100 a month? She can do a lot of things for you; you know what I mean?" He winked.

"I don't know about that." Jack shifted uncomfortably in his chair.

"If you don't like Chinese girls, you can always have some of them white Russian or Eurasian girls, but the problem you have there is that they would do anything to trick you into marrying them." He threw back his drink.

"You know my secretary is a Eurasian?"

"Yep, that's what I've heard. Someone told me that she has got a really nice rack. She must have got that from her English father."

"Bobby, I would rather not talk about my secretary that way, if you don't mind," Jack fretted.

"Sorry, I don't mean her any disrespect."

"Have you ever met her?"

"No, never had the pleasure. She sounds mighty stuck-up over the phone with that snooty English accent."

"Bobby, once you get to know her, she is actually very nice. Not as unapproachable as you think."

"Maybe I have misread her."

"You have. Why don't you drop by my office? I can introduce you to her."

"Uh...I've always wondered what she looks like."

"You wouldn't be disappointed. I can assure you."

"Okay, but please don't tell her what I said before."

"Hey, don't worry about that."

"Thanks…Jack, I reckon you've not gotten around to see much of the city yet."

"No, not yet."

"If you like, I can show you around sometimes." Bobby drained his second beer.

"Sure, it sounds good."

CHAPTER 11

The Rickshaw Man

The elegantly prepared breakfasts in the morning and neatly folded linen bedsheets at night were something Jack could easily get used to, but they all came to an end too soon. After three weeks at the Cathay Hotel, Jack moved to a one-bedroom apartment in the French Concession area of Shanghai, just a few blocks from where he worked. To his surprise, living in this part of Shanghai—called "French Town"—was not too bad either.

Now, on his way to work in the morning, he could pick up a freshly baked croissant and a cup of strong Russian coffee at the downstairs bakery. After work, he would have a bowl of French onion soup at a local bistro. At night, he would often enjoy a glass of wine at some small sidewalk café, while listening to some out-of-work White Russian musicians play on their violins. With trams rumbling along in the tree-lined Avenue Joffre and foreign tourists walking by his table, Jack felt like he was living in Paris. He wrote to Joann about how much he liked living in this part of Shanghai, and she wrote back: "It may not be Paris, but it sounds like a very exciting place to visit."

“Good morning, Jack.” Spencer stood in front of his office, one hand leaning against the door.

“Good morning to you, sir!” Jack replied cheerfully, rising from his chair.

“Sit, sit! You are pretty chirpy today. Have you settled into your flat?”

“Yes, I have.”

“I hope you find your new accommodations satisfactory?”

“Yes, it is very nice. It is right on the Avenue Joffre. It came all furnished.”

“Jack, you have made an excellent choice. Many of our new employees have found living in the French part of the city quite agreeable, especially in an area called ‘the Little Moscow.’”

“Yes, it is very nice. It is a little like living in Paris.”

“Excellent! Now that you have settled in, are you ready to join Mr. Mathew Atkinson and me for a game of golf at the Shanghai Country Club?”

“Sure. What time?” Jack replied snappily.

“Shall we say this Saturday at one o’clock?” Spencer paused. “Jack, do you know what kind of business he is in?”

“Import and export?”

“No. Mr. Atkinson is one of the largest rickshaw-license owners in Shanghai. We call him the Rickshaw Man.”

“Really? How did an Englishman get involved in the rickshaw business?”

“I have asked myself that same question. Jack, you see, over twenty years ago, there were more rickshaws than motorcars running in the streets, and the Shanghai Municipal Council decided to regulate this unruly Chinese business by issuing license plates so they could collect some revenue on them. Mind you, most of us foreigners had little contact with the Chinese rickshaw pullers and still don't. So, when Mr. Atkinson bought five thousand of those little plates at five dollars apiece, we all thought he was mad, spending such a sizable sum on such a dreadful Chinese business. But as it turned out, that was his serendipitous moment."

"How so?"

"Jack, you see, the Municipal Council issued only a limited number of rickshaw license plates to us Shanghailanders, and no Chinese were allowed to purchase any of them."

"It is kind of like a monopoly."

"Exactly! But I failed to see it that way. I asked myself who in their right mind would want to deal with these dreadful Chinamen running around in their dirty straw sandals?" Spencer remarked rhetorically. "But Mathew Atkinson didn't have that in mind at all. He simply leased out all his license plates to the local Chinese contractors, who in turn would rent them out to the rickshaw pullers. He charged them one dollar a day for each of his license plates, which initially cost him only five dollars to buy. You do the math. Mr. Atkinson got bloody rich off these Chinese rickshaw pullers, and he had never owned a single rickshaw!"

"You should have bought some."

"I should have, but frankly, I just didn't have his vision." Spencer sighed. "Long ago, he had predicted that Shanghai would become a safe haven for many Chinese who wanted to live in a foreign-controlled territory as the rest of China gets mired deeper and deeper in civil wars. As years went by, the city's Chinese population began to swell by hundreds of thousands, and so did the demand for rickshaws. His prediction was prescient," Spencer said enviously as if he was wondering why he didn't see it coming. "Now he is thinking about selling all his rickshaw licenses."

"But why?"

"Good question. Mr. Atkinson thinks that in a not-so-distant future, as Chiang Kai-shek and the Chinese communists are busy killing each other, the Japanese will take over China, and I am afraid that we British might eventually have to cede our control of Shanghai to these little yellow men. If that happens, he thinks his rickshaw business would lose much of its monopolistic value."

"Really? You think he is right?"

"Jack, Mr. Atkinson has often been right in the past. I don't see any reason to doubt him now."

"Do you know what price he has in mind?"

"I'm sure he wants a pretty penny for it." Spencer re-crossed his legs. "I'm going to get in touch with some of our rich Chinese clients to get a feel for their level of interest."

"What do you want me to do, Mr. Spencer?"

"I need you to look over his numbers and come up with a good price that he is willing to sell at, and the amount of loan our bank can safely provide him."

"Okay, I can do that."

"Excellent! I've asked Mary to bring you his files." Spencer saw Mary already standing by the door. "Mary, do come in."

"Thank you, Mr. Spencer." Mary put down the files on the desk.

"Thank you, Mary."

"Do you want anything else? A cup of tea?" Mary wiggled a little on her heels.

"Yes, I could use a cup of tea."

"Mr. Wells, I will be right back."

Their chauffeured Bentley slowly rolled into the Shanghai Country Club. Mathew Atkinson was already waiting for them under the canopy of a large white English Tudor mansion.

"Good afternoon, gentlemen." He strutted toward them with the relaxed manner of an English country squire.

"How are you, Mr. Atkinson? It is nice meeting you again."

"I am glad you could come, young man." He graciously draped his arm over Jack's shoulders as he started toward a glass-enclosed patio.

"Good afternoon, Mr. Atkinson. Your table is ready," an elderly Chinese waiter greeted them. "What will be your pleasure today, sir?"

"My usual." Atkinson nonchalantly plopped into a white wicker chair as another Chinese waiter fussed over him with his white napkin.

"Mr. Spencer, what can I get for you?"

"Bombay gin with a touch of tonic water."

"Certainly, and what about you, sir?" the waiter turned to Jack.

"A scotch and soda, please." Jack tried to look relaxed as he casually glanced at the velvety expanse of Bermuda greens outside the patio. "Nice golf course."

"Jack, do you play?"

"A little, when I was in college, but I liked baseball better."

"Baseball…is that a bit like cricket?"

"A little bit. Have you ever heard of Joe DiMaggio or Babe Ruth?"

"The names sound familiar. I don't much follow any of your Yankee sports. Other than golf, making money is the only other sport I follow."

"Matt, speaking of making money, how many rickshaw plates do you now own?"

"Over seven thousand, give or take a few," he replied blithely. "Jack, do you know how many rickshaws are running in the streets of Shanghai as we speak?"

"About seventy thousand, and you own about ten percent of the market."

"I see you've done your homework, young man."

"Old sport, how can our bank be of service?"

"What do you think my business is worth?" He swiveled his single malt scotch in a slow circular motion.

"Well, it all depends on who the buyer is. At this moment, I think the Chinese are your most logical buyers."

"Yes, I agree. I presume you already have someone in mind?"

"Yes, I do. Mr. James Tung. He is one of the richest Chinese men in Shanghai. I know he had an interest in acquiring some rickshaw licenses even way back then. I am sure he still might be interested."

"My good man, I'm afraid the French Flying Stars might have already approached him."

"Matt, are you sure?"

"Quite."

"I am going to his Chinese New Year party next week. I can feel out his level of interest in doing a deal with them."

"Todd, I've heard this Chinese man is a real shrewd character. I don't want him to play my deal against theirs."

"Don't worry, old sport. I know how to handle the Chinese," Spencer replied with bravado.

"Excellent, old sport! After the deal goes through, I will see to it that some of my profit will go to our Trinity Church."

"Jack, besides being a very good businessman, Mr. Atkinson is also a very good Christian. During Christmas, he often gives five-hundred dollars to the Shanghai Rickshaw Men's Mission, so they too have something to cheer about."

"My good man, that is the least I can do. After all, these poor little fellows did all the pulling for me," he said chirpily.

Back in his apartment, Jack poured himself another scotch, sat down on the leather sofa, and wrote.

Darling,

Just came back from a golf game at the Shanghai Country Club. I played with one of the richest men in the city. He is known around here as "the Rickshaw Man" because he owns 10% of all the rickshaw licenses in Shanghai! He wants our bank to help him sell his business, and I would be helping my boss to come up with a good price and find him a buyer. Not too bad for a 25-year-old junior banker....

I've also met an interesting, good 'ole boy from Texas. He has been living here for a long time, and he is going to show me around. It is nice to know another American here in Shanghai. Anyway, everything is going swimmingly well. I wish you were here.

Love,
Jack

CHAPTER 12

Chinese New Year

Large black-and-gold Chinese characters painted on pieces of red paper seemed to appear in the streets of Shanghai overnight—on doors, inside shop windows, and around telephone poles; one could even see them on the backs of rickshaws, buses, and trams. Throughout the day, sounds of firecrackers echoed between buildings and the beating of drums rumbled in the alleyways. Colorful dragon troupes danced and twirled from store to store as smiling shopkeepers handed out little red envelopes with money stuffed inside, pleased that the evil spirits had been scared away by the dragons and that more good fortune would be smiling upon them in the coming new year.

Curious foreign tourists looked on with amusement as Shanghai's Chinese residents, in their best satin robes and silk chi pao, rushed about on the crowded sidewalks and stopped here and there to greet each other with folded palms and bending bodies: "*Kon Shi Fat Chai!*" Even the rickshaw pullers seemed to have forgotten their daily toils as they trotted bouncingly along the congested Nanking Road, hoping for better luck in the coming of the Chinese Lunar Year 4635, the Year of the Ox.

As their chauffeured Bentley slowly cruised along Bubbling Well Road, Jack stared out the window, fascinated by what was going on in the streets.

"Jack, the Chinese celebrate the New Year like the way we celebrate Christmas. It is quite an event every year."

"Mr. Spencer, do you know what all those Chinese characters mean?" Jack pointed to pieces of red paper on the back of a tram.

"I do, as a matter of fact," Spencer replied confidently. "The single characters on the square red papers mean 'Happiness' or 'Prosperity.' The four characters on the long strips of paper mean 'Congratulations on your new fortune' or 'Have a smooth sailing in your new business.' The one over there with gold characters on window means 'Happiness and Prosperity,' It is pronounced *Kon Shi Fat Chai!* Or so I was told."

"Mr. Spencer, you seem to know a lot about Chinese culture."

"Not really…Jack, have you ever been to a Chinese New Year banquet before?"

"No, never been to one."

"Every year, this Mr. Tung fellow invites hundreds of his friends and business associates to his mansion for an elaborate Chinese New Year feast complete with a full production of the Peking Opera; it goes on and on, well into the night."

"Can't wait to see it. Thanks for inviting me."

"Not at all. Mrs. Spencer is quite glad that you can go in her place. Our bank gets invited every year, and this year is my turn to go, again," he sighed. "How many times can a poor fellow bear to watch those tedious dragon dances, or have his ears assaulted by those loud gongs? Frankly, I find the whole thing terribly boring."

"So why are you going?"

"Business, my good man. Our banking relationship with his family goes back to the last century, and we have to keep up the appearance of cordiality."

"So how did this Mr. Tung become so rich?"

"His grandfather started their family business as a comprador at Jardine and Matheson back in the early 1800s."

"What is a comprador?"

"A sort of middleman between our trading houses and the local Chinese. During the early 1800s, his grandfather had set up a distribution network deep inside of China where few of us foreigners dared to go. As a business agent, he managed to milk 10% of profits from everything we sold to the Chinese, including opium."

"It sounds like his grandfather was a pretty good businessman."

"Yes, indeed. His father continued that legacy, and after he passed away, Mr. Tung took his family's business to another level. He branched out into textiles and shipping, and he even set up shoe factories in Hong Kong. Quite an enterprising man, just like his grandfather. He is now one of the richest men in China, and he owns one of the largest mansions here in Shanghai."

"Mr. Spencer, do you live around here?" Jack began to notice the stately stone parapets of English Tudor houses and barrel-tiled roof lines of Spanish villas hidden behind the white-washed stucco walls.

"Jack, not everybody can afford to take up residence in this part of town. I live further out in the Western Settlement."

"Where is that?"

"A bit further west from here…ah, that's the House of Tung." Spencer pointed as their car slowed down behind a long line of shiny Rolls-Royces, Broughams, and Mercedes.

"This is a pretty impressive place." Jack leaned forward to get a closer look as they inched past a pair of tall red doors flanked by two strange-looking stone animals. Moving slowly along a gravel driveway, they came to a stop in front of a large English-styled château. Before Jack had a chance to open his door, a retinue of white-uniformed Chinese servants had already swarmed around their car, holding open the car doors on each side.

"Welcome to Mr. Tung's residence. May I take your coat?"

"Kon Shi Fat Chai!" Jack heard that familiar refrain again. Chinese men, clad in shimmering embroidered gowns, greeted each other with beaming smiles and folded palms, and Chinese women, decked out in glittering chi pao, bowed as their green jade bracelets dangled on their wrists; smooth porcelain skin and young, not the kind of dark, weathered faces Jack often saw on the streets. Milling close by, he also noticed several burly Chinese men, in their plain black-cloth gowns, white linings rolled up over their sleeves, and gray fedora cocked over their oily hair.

"Those fellows are their bodyguards," Spencer whispered.

"Why such tight security? I thought this was a Chinese New Year Party."

"Jack, these rich Chinese are all deathly afraid someone might kidnap them, or their sons. They bring these menacing-looking fellows along wherever they go."

"Welcome to Mr. Tung's residence. Happy New Year! May I bring you gentlemen some libation?" A Chinese man in a blue Chinese robe approached them.

"We are here to see Mr. Tung."

"Sir, the Old Lord is in the Great Hall. I shall take you there."

"No need, I know where he is." Spencer brusquely strode past him.

"Mr. Spencer, you seem to know this place pretty well."

"I have been here a few times." He kept walking.

"This is a pretty big place." Jack strutted closely behind, recalling the Chinese garden at his father's New Hope Church, much smaller but very similar.

"Jack, this James Tung fellow is the only Chinese taipan I know of who can afford to have both a Western-style mansion and a traditional Chinese residence all in one place. He had spent a considerable amount of money and time on building up this place so he could live in the best of both worlds, one Oriental and one Western." Spencer paused and then added with a hint of envy, "He makes some of us Englishmen look like paupers. Ironic, isn't it?"

Standing under the curvy tiled-roof of a large, pavilion-like building, Jack saw a tall Chinese man dressed in a black silk Mandarin robe, surrounded by a group of anxious well-wishers. *That must be Mr. Tung, the master of the house.*

As they walked closer, the man suddenly looked in their direction, flashing a wide grin. "Ah, Mr. Spencer, long time no see!"

"Yes, long time no see." Spencer threw up his hands ceremoniously.

"How many moons ago did we last meet? You are looking well." He impetuously waved away all the well-wishers.

"Many moons ago." Spencer shook his hand with an imperceptible bow.

"Mr. Spencer, I am honored that you could come. I hope the Year of the Ox will be an auspicious year for all of us."

"I hope more fortunes will visit upon you in the coming New Year." Spencer knew a thing or two about how to greet the Chinese.

"Mr. Spencer, there is another good reason for us to celebrate this New Year."

"Which is?"

"Our great leader, Generalissimo Chiang Kai-shek and the Chinese Communist bandits, have just agreed to form a United Front to fight the Japanese. I hope once and for all China will get rid of those little pests off our back."

"Congratulations are in order then," Spencer replied perfunctorily. "We in the West also want to see the Japs out of China."

"China needs all the help we can get from the West, especially from the Americans."

"Speaking of help, Mr. Tung, this is my new assistant, Mr. Jack Wells." He motioned for Jack to come closer. "Jack, this is the Honorable Mr. James Tung."

"How do you do, sir?" Jack eagerly stepped forward to shake the old man's bony hand.

"American?" He narrowed his dark brown eyes.

"Yes, American."

"You, Harvard man?"

"No, Columbia."

"Jack, Mr. Tung's Number One Son has just graduated from Harvard. He is very proud of the fact that his son is now a member of the very prestigious Harvard Club of China."

"Congratulations, sir. Harvard is one of the best universities in America."

"Thank you," he replied proudly. "Young man, I understand that your president, Franklin Roosevelt, is also a Harvard man."

"Oh, I didn't know that."

"Do you know that many of our Chinese leaders are graduates from your American Ivy League schools?"

"No, sir."

"The head of Bank of China, Mr. T.V. Soong, is a Harvard man, and China's finance minister, H.H. Kung, graduated from Yale."

"My dad is a Yale graduate too," Jack quickly added.

"Mr. Tung, Reverend Jonathan Wells is Jack's father."

"Yes, I have heard of him." He slowly turned his attention to the leather attaché case Jack was carrying. "Why are you still carrying that thing, young man? It is Chinese New Year."

"Uh..." Jack hesitated.

"Mr. Tung, we have a very interesting business proposition to talk to you about," Spencer hastily interjected.

"Really?" His interest was piqued. "Perhaps we can talk in my study. I will call my son to join me if you gentlemen don't mind."

"Not at all."

"Then, shall we?" He gestured graciously.

"Honorable One, wish you a happy and prosperous New Year!" someone shouted.

"Mr. Tung, I wish many fortunes will visit upon you!"

"*Kon Shi Fat Chai* to you all!" The master of the house waved dismissively with the back of his hand.

With an ink portrait of an ancient Chinese man hanging on the wall and a bronze incense burner placed on a long altar table underneath his stern old eyes, Mr. Tung's study looked more like a family shrine than a study. In the center of the room, there was a large silk carpet with a golden dragon and a green phoenix embraced in an eternal dance of yin-and-yang. The only hint of his scholarly pursuits Jack saw were rows of paintbrushes and a hefty ink block placed on a large carved wooden table by the screen windows.

"Jack, that's where Mr. Tung practices his brushstrokes. Do you know that, besides being a successful businessman, he is an accomplished Chinese calligrapher? I have one of his scrolls hanging at my house."

"Mr. Spencer, you are too polite." James Tung clasped his hands together to show his modesty. "Just dabbling, just dabbling…please sit, please sit. Can I offer you gentlemen some refreshments, green tea, or something stronger?"

"Bombay Gin with a dash of tonic water."

"And you, my young American friend?" Mr. Tung turned to Jack.

"Uh…a scotch and soda, if you don't mind, sir."

"Excellent, I'll take my tea," he addressed to no one in particular.

"Father, do you want to see me?" A sharply dressed young man in a tailored Oxford suit strode into the room.

"Gentlemen, this is my Number One Son, Winston Tung."

"How do you do?" He nodded before retreated to his father's side.

"Young master, would you care for some libation?" the head servant asked in English.

"*Bu yao!* I don't want anything." The Number One Son waved his hand impetuously, just like his father.

"Si, Sau Ye! Yes, young lord!" The head servant bowed and quickly left the room.

"So, Mr. Spencer, what are we here to talk about?"

"Mr. Tung, not long ago, you expressed an interest in buying some rickshaw licenses, but then our Shanghai Municipal Council had a few restrictions."

"Yes, I did express some interest back then."

"Well, an opportunity has now been presented to me by one of our most valued clients. He is getting on in age and wants to dispose of his rickshaw investments in Shanghai and go back home to live like a country squire."

"One day I too want to go back to my hometown to retire, but for now, I have to wait for my Number One Son to learn the business. His head is full of only book knowledge." He paused, waiting for the servants to serve their drinks.

"I am sure he will be a quick learner under your tutelage, Mr. Tung."

"You are too kind. So how many rickshaw licenses does he want to sell?"

"About seven-thousand. Only a few men such as you will have the means to buy them all," Spencer said in a deferential voice usually reserved for his superiors.

"You are referring to Mr. Atkinson, aren't you, Mr. Spencer?"

"Yes." Spencer tried not to sound surprised. "Have you been approached by him?"

"No, Mr. Spencer, it is just an educated guess. It is no secret that he is one of the last foreigners in Shanghai still holding on to those rickshaw licenses." Mr. Tung gently stroked the cover over his teacup. "I certainly could understand why he wants to sell. Everyone is concerned about the unstable political situations here in Shanghai, not to mention all the problems in Europe."

"Mr. Tung, we are all concerned about the political instabilities around the world, but whenever there are uncertainties, there are opportunities."

"Mr. Spencer, political winds are like women; their moods are never stable, but one must not get caught in their wrath. While I do have some interest in looking at the deal, there are many risks."

"Mr. Tung, you are a very savvy businessman. Frankly, I must say you Chinese, like some of our European Jews, are quite smart in seizing the opportunities while others are frightened," Spencer replied without his usual haughty air.

"Mr. Spencer, I take that as a compliment," he replied dryly, sipping loudly on his green tea. "One man's recklessness is another man's courage. This is a very large transaction even for me."

"Mr. Tung, I understand your concerns, but this will be a chance for you to acquire a substantial chunk of rickshaw licenses in one fell swoop, and that would give you control over much of the rickshaw business in Shanghai."

"Does he have a price in mind?"

"Certainly north of twenty-five million pounds."

"It sounds like it is fully priced."

"Our bank can provide you with excellent finance. I am sure the French wouldn't be able to do that for you."

"Mr. Tung, we can structure the loan where you can recoup your investments in about five years," Jack eagerly added.

"That is, if the British are still in control of Shanghai by then, young man."

"Mr. Tung, we British have been in Shanghai for one-hundred years, and I am quite sure that we will be here for another hundred years." Spencer signaled to Jack to take out a large yellow envelope from his briefcase. "My assistant has done a thorough financial analysis of Mr. Atkinson's holdings along with our proposed financial structure. I'm quite sure you will find our proposal compelling."

"Mr. Spencer, I'm a simple businessman. I don't understand these fancy numbers, but I will let my son take a look at them."

"Are these numbers accurate?" His son stepped forward.

"Mr. Winston Tung, I can assure you that these financial statements accurately reflect Mr. Atkinson's business operations."

"I know much of his business is in cash. How can we verify his numbers?"

"Mr. Winston Tung, of all the people I have dealt with, Mr. Mathew Atkinson is one of the most scrupulous men I know. He never lies."

"People who claim they don't lie, are usually pretty good liars. I don't trust his numbers because there is no way to check them!"

"Shhh-h," Mr. Tung hissed with much annoyance, raising his index finger in front of his dried lips.

"Father, I'm just trying to—"

"*You don't need to talk too much in front of foreigners. You can tell me later*," his father muttered petulantly in Chinese. "Mr. Spencer, you must excuse my son's impetuous behavior. That is what happens when you send them to America. They are always anxious to express their opinions even though their heads are only half full; they talk too much and listen too little."

"Our English lads have similar problems after they go to America." Spencer nodded in agreement.

"Young man, I am sure you have done an honest job in presenting Mr. Atkinson's business. We will take a look at it. Give me a good price; I will take the problem off his hand."

"Mr. Tung, I am sure Mr. Atkinson does not consider his business a problem asset. It is a great piece of business, and many others would love to buy it."

"Mr. Spencer, I will give you an answer in a few days."

"Splendid! I will wait for your answer." Spencer abruptly stood up and took out his gold pocket watch. "Mr. Tung, I must be running along."

"That is a beautiful watch."

"Yes, indeed. This is an 18K gold minute repeater Patek Philippe handcrafted in 1892, a superbly crafted timepiece, a perfect blend of art and technology."

"Mr. Spencer, we Chinese still have much to learn from the West, and I hope that one day, China too will be able to make such a beautiful watch."

"Someday, I'm quite sure you people can…someday," Spencer replied nonchalantly.

"Mr. Spencer, you and I have known each other for many years, but we have yet to have a meal together. How about staying for dinner as my honored guest? This year I have hired two former imperial palace chefs to prepare some of the most delicious dishes eaten only by the Empress Dowager T'zu-hsi. It is going to be a rare treat, even for me." He slowly got up from his chair.

"Mr. Tung, I would love to, but unfortunately, Mrs. Spencer is a bit under the weather. I am afraid I can't stay. I say, Jack, you must stay to enjoy Mr. Tung's fancy feast."

"Sure, I will stay," Jack replied eagerly.

"Splendid! Goodbye, Mr. Tung. It is my pleasure to meet you again. Perhaps we can have dinner at another time."

"Yes, perhaps another time," James Tung replied tersely, his smiling face tightened as he watched Todd Spencer strutting out into the courtyard. Slowly, he turned to Jack and smiled. "Young man, have you ever had shark-fin soup before?"

CHAPTER 13

A Chance Encounter

Jack meandered into the garden, stopping here and there along the cobbled walkways, pretending to examine this potted dwarf tree or admire that group of rocks. *I am the only foreign face here.* Jack suddenly became self-conscious as he smiled at the curious passers-by. *I am just going to stay a little longer*; he quietly told himself as he wandered over a small stone bridge spanning over the koi pond. As he ambled through a moon-shaped door, he heard the noisy banging of drums and gongs. Behind a large crowd, he saw a group of actors, with painted faces and colorful costumes, singing and tumbling on a wooden stage emblazoned with colorful flags and banners. He walked closer; suddenly Jack spotted a head full of sandy hair amidst the gray hairs and black fedoras. Pretending to look for a seat, he inched toward him.

"Hey, what the hell are you doing here?" The man suddenly turned around as if he had sensed someone was staring at him.

"Hey, I was about to ask you the same thing!" Jack felt greatly relieved. "Bobby, since when have you become a connoisseur of Chinese opera?"

"Nah, I'm just killing time. I'm waiting for my lady friend. What about you? This would be the last place in Shanghai I would expect to run into you."

"My boss and I just had a meeting with Mr. Tung to discuss some business."

"Have you had a chance to try their food yet?"

"No, not yet. I understand that Mr. Tung has hired two former imperial-palace chefs for this event."

"Yeah, that was what I've heard. They probably are gonna cook up some weird stuff, like stir-fried snakes," Bobby said jokingly. "Hey, if you don't feel like sticking around, you want to grab a bite to eat somewhere else?"

"What about your girlfriend?"

"She is not really what I'd call a girlfriend; you know what I mean?" Bobby winked.

"I could use a bowl of Texas chili."

"Great! Let's go to Little Jimmy's."

The clanking of the thimbles began to get louder, the beatings of the drum faster, and the high-pitched falsetto voices more thrilled.

"It looks like the show is over." Bobby turned to the stage and then saw a young Chinese woman in a pink chi pao and high heels walking toward them.

"Hi, Bobby, I am ready."

"Hi, China doll, I'd like you to meet a good friend of mine, Mr. Jack Wells."

"How do you do, Mr. Jack Will."

"China doll, there is a change of plan. Jack and I have to go somewhere."

"This is Chinese New Year. You promised to take me out to a fancy restaurant!" She shook her body coyly.

"We can do it another time, okay?"

"Hey, Bobby, how about we take her along?" Jack looked at her apologetically.

"Jack, no sweat; she is okay with it."

"No okay, but what can I do?" She pursed her lips.

"I will come to see you at the club, okay?" he cajoled her.

"Come tonight, then. You come too, Mr. Will." She cast him a coquettish side glance.

"Okay, I will try. See you later, China doll." Bobby waved.

"What's her name?" Jack watched her walking away dejectedly.

"I don't know her Chinese name. I just call her Jasmine."

"What does she do?"

"She is a cabaret dancer at the Paramount Night Club; a nice place, just like the Copacabana in New York except it is a little bit more risqué. Have you ever been there?"

"No."

"Wanta go?"

"When?"

"How about after we eat?"

"Eh…sure, I have nothing better to do."

The glittering lights blinked on and off along the edges of a semi-circular building, and the three large Chinese characters glowed brightly high on the marquee.

"Jack, that's the Paramount Night Club. In Chinese, it means 'Gate of One-Hundred Pleasures.'"

"It looks a little sleazy." Jack looked up at the pink neon.

"It is classier than most other joints in Shanghai. They got some of the prettiest Chinese girls in there. You'll see."

Gathered in front of the club on the other side of the street, Jack could see a coterie of Chinese men in tailored suits and silk ties, and women in flowing Western dresses and slinky evening gowns. "Bobby, this is a pretty fancy crowd."

"Jack, they are Shanghai's smart set, la crème de la crème of China, young, Western-educated, and rich. At five dollars a pop and with a two-drink minimum, not too many Chinese could afford to come to this place."

"I can see that." Jack stared at a group of Chinese women; all decked out in shimmering gowns, sparkling diamond earrings, and white pearl necklaces. Their fingernails were painted bright red or dusted with gold.

"Pretty nice, eh?" Bobby saw him watching. "Some of them even speak better English than me. Is that crazy or what?"

"Interesting, but I don't see any American faces here except us."

"There is one over there." Bobby tilted his head. "Most of us usually don't come here unless we have a Chinese girlfriend."

"Is that why you come here?" Jack just smiled.

Walking slowly behind the well-dressed crowd, they entered into a semi-circular dance hall with maroon velvet drapes covering the walls, glowing chandeliers hanging from the ceilings, and tiers of white-clothed tables hovering above an empty dance floor. Sitting next to a stage, Jack saw a group of young Chinese women, all dressed in figure-hugging, colorful chi pao with slits running up to their thighs, casually chatting and giggling.

"After the show, if you want, you can ask one of them to dance."

"I thought we are here just to watch the show."

"We are. Jack, you can have a really good time here. It all depends on how much you want to spend. You know what I mean?"

"I got your drift." Jack slipped into the booth.

"Gentlemen, what would you like to drink?" A waiter rushed over.

"A gin sling."

"What kind of drink is that?"

"Some sort of local concoction. Wanta try it?"

"Sure."

"Make it two."

Soon the lights began to dim, a drum started to roll, and a young woman stepped out on the stage. "Ladies and gentlemen, Happy New Year! *Kon Shi Fat-chai!*"

"*Kon Shi Fat-chai!*" the audience responded enthusiastically.

"I hope 1937 will be a happy and prosperous New Year for all of you!" she cried out, first in Chinese and then in English. "To start our celebration of the Year of the Ox, we proudly present to you The Lotus Girls!"

The girls sitting at the bottom of the stage began to form a single line against a backdrop of the Shanghai skyline at night, complete with a yellow paper moon.

"For your pleasure, they will sing for you one of the most popular songs today: 'The Shanghai Night!'"

The audience clapped enthusiastically as the Lotus Girls began to sway their arms and wiggle their hips. A chorus of seductive voices started to sing:

Shanghai nights, Shanghai nights.
You are a city that never sleeps.
Glittering lights, traffic sounds,
dances, and songs.
One sees only her smiling face,
but not her wounded heart.
To live a nightlife just to survive,
Wines don't make people drunk,
people get themselves drunk.
A life spent without purpose,
a wasted youth.

"I have never seen to this kind of shows before." Jack strained his eyes at the shimmering hot pinks, grass greens, and sky blues.

"Jack, if you want to dance, I can get one of them girls for you after the show."

"Let's just watch the show." Jack took a big gulp on his gin sling as he watched people returning to their tables from the dance floor.

"That's her." Bobby saw one of the cabaret girls walking toward them. He had left word with the club manager where they would be sitting.

"Hey, Bobby, did you see me on the stage?" she asked chirpily.

"Sure, you were great!"

"Hello, Mr. Jack Will, I am glad you can come too."

"Hi, Jasmine." Jack rose from his seat to shake her hand.

"Hey, China doll, can you fix my buddy up with one of them girls? Only the classy ones, okay?"

"Mr. Will, I have just the right girl for you. Today is her first day, you very lucky man."

"It's okay. I don't know how to dance."

"Who says you have to dance? She can sit here to keep you company. I think you will like her. She talks good English. Okay, Mr. Will?"

"China doll, Mr. Wells, not Mr. Will."

"Whatever," she snapped her fingers at the waiter standing nearby. "Lau Tan, tell Lee Li-wha to come over."

"Right away, Miss."

"Mr. Will, I think you will like her."

"No, really. It is okay," Jack said uneasily.

"Jack, relax. Have another drink. Enjoy what Shanghai has to offer."

Just then, Jack saw another cabaret girl walking across the dance floor, all dolled up in a peach-colored chi pao, face powdered white, lips painted bright red, and hair tied up in a smooth bun. As she approached their table, a sudden chill raced down his spine, and she too became crestfallen. Abruptly, she turned to walk away.

"Where are you going, Lee Li-wha?" Jasmine yelled out in a restrained voice.

"Zheng Ting, what is the meaning of this?" the club manager rushed over.

"Lau Ban, nothing, she is just shy."

"Lee Li-wha, you come back here right now!" the club manager barked.

"Jack, do you know her?" Bobby asked suspiciously.

"Eh…yes, she works at my father's church," Jack replied haltingly. "Let's get out of here." Jack started sliding out of the booth.

"Sir, can I get you another girl?"

"No, I gotta go. Bobby, are you coming?"

"Hey, Chan, everything is cool. We are just leaving."

"Sir, she is new. This is her first night, a virgin. I am surprised that you gentlemen don't appreciate a piece of good merchandise." The club manager taunted them with a creepy smile.

"Mr. Well, please, this is her first day. Please be nice to her." She looked up pleadingly.

"Eh, Jasmine, I am sorry; I can't stay. I—"

"Ladies and gentlemen, now it is my privilege to present to you tonight a very special guest, the one and only, Miss Zhou Xuan!" A sudden shrill voice came from the stage. "By popular request, tonight she is going to sing for you 'When Will You Be Back Again?' Please welcome Miss Zhou Xuan!"

The crowd roared with applause as a petite woman accompanied by a man with a two-string instrument walked onto the stage.

"Mr. Will, she is one of the most famous singers in Shanghai today. We are very lucky to have her here tonight. Can we just listen to her, okay?" she coyly tugged at his arm.

"C'mon, Jack, let's wait for her to finish her song, and then we go," Bobby whispered.

"Jasmine, I can't…" Awkwardly, Jack just stood there not knowing what to do as the lady on the stage began to sing:

Good flowers don't blossom often and
Good sceneries don't last.
With sadness, I smile

With tears, I will remember
Tonight, we shall say goodbye
When will you be back again...?

"*Lee Li-wha, go sit next to this gentleman or else you are fired!*" Jack suddenly heard the screeching voice of the club manager and then saw Lily running across the crowded dance in tears.

"Lily, wait!" Jack reached out helplessly.

"Mr. Will, now you have hurt her feeling."

"Jasmine, I am sorry, but I didn't mean to…" Jack stammered.

"I don't understand. If you don't want to have fun, why you come here anyway?" Her voice hardened.

"Hey, Jasmine, my friend is just as embarrassed as she is. He didn't expect a church girl would be working in a place like this." Bobby came to his defense.

"I am sorry. It is just that…I am sorry…" Jack apologized profusely.

"Gotta go, China doll." Bobby got up from the booth.

"Gentlemen, the night is still young. We got many other girls. I can bring them over, and you can choose the one you like."

"No thanks, not tonight, Chan." Bobby dropped a five-dollar bill on the table. "China doll, I will take you out next week. Okay?"

"No okay. We don't matter to you Americans, but we got feeling too, you know!" Indignantly, Jasmine snatched up her purse and slid out of her seat.

Outside the club, Jack glanced aimlessly around the street as if he was looking for a taxi.

"Hey, buddy, I am sorry about what happened back in there. I hope she didn't ruin your night." Bobby flicked off his cigarette butt into the street.

"It is not her fault. Man, out of all the places; this is the last place I would expect to run into her." Jack shook his head in disbelief.

"Jack, I think she was just as surprised as you were. It happens." Bobby looked up at the pink neon.

"My mother is trying to get her a scholarship to the best girls' school in Shanghai…Man, if they ever find out what she does at night!"

"They won't know if you don't tell."

"Bobby, why does she have to do this kind of shit? I don't understand it!" Jack stomped his feet.

"Maybe she needs some extra cash." Bobby offered his take.

"But…but she is supposed to be a good Christian! Back in there, she looked so…."

"Jack, back in there, girls can make more money in one night than they can make in a week anywhere else."

"Bobby, you make it sound like she is…I…I just can't believe it!"

"Jack, at places like this you can get any girl you want, young and pretty," he said nonchalantly.

"Bobby, it hurts my ears just to hear you talk about her like that!"

"Talk like what?" Bobby stared at him critically. "Jack, if I didn't know any better, I would think you have a crush on that girl!"

"What gives you that idea?"

"Jack, it ain't my business, but I can tell you this much. Things are not always what they seem here in Shanghai. Some of these girls might look sweet and innocent, but they ain't. You can have fun with them but don't take them too seriously."

"I don't think Lily is like that!" Jack replied angrily.

"Look, I am not making any judgment on these girls. To tell you the truth, I kind of feel sorry for them. They are selling their bodies so their little brothers and sisters won't die of starvation. But then again, what can I do? It is what it is."

"But...but I just wish she didn't have to do that!" Jack couldn't fathom the hurt in his heart—her effervescent smiles flashing across his eyes and her angelic voice ringing in his ears.

"Jack, what happened back there is just a chance encounter. Hey, it happens," Bobby shrugged.

CHAPTER 14

Lily's Secret

That painted face and those dangling fake diamond earrings still swirled in his head when Jack walked into the New Hope Church, dreading that awkward moment if he sees her again.

"Jack, your father can't start his Sunday service. Lily is not here!" His mother cried out agitatedly.

"Good morning, Mother." Jack felt relieved. "Has anyone tried to look for her? She might still be sleeping."

"She is always on time, never missed a day. I have no earthly idea of what could have happened to her." His mother sounded frazzled.

"Does any one of them know?" Jack looked at the old ladies pattering around her; it was obvious that they didn't know either.

"Da Tu went to get the car. He is going to Chapei to find her. Can you go with him? Just in case she might be sick, or something."

"Eh…I hope nothing happened to her." Jack began to worry.

Soon Jack found himself on the other side of Thibet Road. As they traveled deeper into Chapei, the wide streets narrowed, and paved roads became unpaved. Beyond the crumbling roof overhangs and wet laundry lines, Jack could see billowing smoke spewing out from gray factory buildings and haggard men streaming in and out from the barbed-wire gates—a dreary nineteenth-century industrial landscape, Chinese style. As their black Ford slowly moved along the narrow alleyway, Da Tu suddenly stopped, rolled down the window, and hollered at an old man sucking on his brass water pipe. "Whey, you know where Lee Li-wha live?"

The old man unhurriedly got up from his four-legged stool and spat vigorously into a slimy water puddle before disappearing behind a wooden door.

"Boss, he don't know." Da Tu drove on. A few minutes later, he hollered at a Chinese woman busy kneading on a washboard. "Whey! You know where Lee Li-wha live?" She stood up, slapping her wet hands and pointing at a door across the alleyway.

"Shie shie. Thank you." Da Tu quickly got out of the car.

From the backseat, Jack watched the Chinese woman adjusting the baby strapped on her back before squatting down to her washing. Behind her, he saw a tiny room crammed with her stuff on a mud floor—a bamboo table, four wooden stools, two bunk beds, and stacks of oily brown boxes. A Chinese movie-star calendar on the back wall added the only bright colors to her cramped little home. *My hotel room is bigger than that*, Jack thought as he watched Da Tu pattering back. From his sappy walk, he could tell that he didn't find her.

"Boss, nobody saw her." He leaned into the car.

"Nobody knows where she could be?"

"No, they don't know nothing."

"Mother, we couldn't find her." Jack saw the disappointment on her face as soon as he walked into the door.

"Jack, what are we going to do?"

And then he saw his father stepping in from the garden. "Come, come, dear, I am sure there is a good reason why she is not here this morning."

"But who is going to do the translation for you, dear?"

"Let's wait a little longer. I am sure she will be here."

"What if she doesn't? I have just made an appointment for her to meet the headmistress of the McTyeire School later this afternoon. She is a very busy woman," she said agitatedly. "Jack, do you know the McTyeire School is one of the best schools for Chinese girls in Shanghai, if not the whole of China? Even Madame Chiang graduated from there."

"Yes, Mother, you have already told me."

"I think Miss Richardson might even consider giving her a scholarship. I hope she will show up soon."

"Mother, maybe she has something else to do." Jack had an urge to tell her about last night, but he knew it would stress her out even more.

"But what could it be? I just hate to see her miss an opportunity of a lifetime to get a good education!" she said exasperatedly.

"Mother, don't worry; she will be here." *She will miss the opportunity of a lifetime if she does not show up soon. I must go back to the Paramount Night Club to tell her.* Jack quietly decided.

"I'd like to talk to Lily. Is she here?" Jack asked through a small crack of a leather-padded door.

"Wha'? Nobody here," a man shouted from inside, refusing to open the door further.

"Sure, you do. I just saw her here last night," Jack insisted, pushing on the door.

"Nobody here. We no open. Come back later." He wedged his foot against the bottom of the door.

"Lily works here as one of your hostesses. I want to talk to her, please," Jack softened his voice.

"No Lee Lee, come back later if you want another girl."

"Goddamit! I don't want another girl! I just want to talk to her for a minute!" Jack shouted, ramming his shoulder against the door.

"Nobody here, we no open," the man repeated.

"Mr. Jack Will, you are back." A painted face suddenly peered through the crack.

"Hi, Jasmine! I want to talk to Lily. Is she here?"

"No, she not here no more. I thought you don't like her." She chewed on her noodles, wiping her lips with the back of her hand.

"Please, it is important that I talk to her."

She nodded to the man, and he let go of his foot.

"This guy said he does not know who Lily is. I know he is lying." Jack quickly stepped in.

"Her Chinese name is Lee Li-wha. She don't have a stage name. So why do you want to see her for? You change your mind?" she asked facetiously.

"She did not show up at the church this morning, and my parents are very worried about her."

"What's going on?" The club manager walked over. "Is she giving you a problem again, sir?"

"No problem, Chan, we're just talking."

"Lau Ban, this American wants to talk to Lee Li-wha."

"I just want to talk to her for a few minutes."

"But she not here no more. Zheng Ting, why don't you take this gentleman to the booth? He might be thirsty."

"I am not here for that."

"No waiting here. You block door, bad for business." The manager waved his hand grumpily.

"Mr. Will, boss don't like you stand by the door if you are not a customer." She pulled on his hand.

"Okay, I will stay just for a couple of minutes." Jack reluctantly followed her across the empty parquet dance floor. Even before he had a chance to sit down, a smiling waiter rushed over. "Lao Ban, what is your pleasure?"

"I told you guys I'm not here to drink." Jack glanced around the tiers of bare tables, naked under the harsh spotlights. *Whoa, this frickin' place looks even seedier than I first thought.*

"Two drinks minimum, house rule." The waiter smiled solicitously.

"Look here, Jasmine, I have told you I just want to talk to her." Jack laid into her. "Why do you people keep hustling me?"

"Hassle, what you mean, Mr. Will?"

"C'mon, is this whole thing an act?" He rolled his eyes. "And please don't keep calling me Mr. Will. My name is Jack Well…s! With an 'S'!"

"You don't need to shout, Mr. Well…s."

"Look, I am just here to tell Lily that she may have an opportunity of a lifetime to get into the McTyeire School for Girls. I'm sure you have heard of it. Your president's wife graduated from there."

"Okay, I'll tell her when I see her." Jasmine looked at him without any reaction.

"And that's it? Did you hear what I said? The McTyeire School is the best Chinese school for girls in Shanghai, if not in the whole of China!" he said loudly, not sure he was madder at her or at that pestering waiter.

"Mr. Well…s, everybody knows the school. It is for rich Chinese girls only. Lee Li-wha don't have that kind of money to go there anyway," she replied calmly.

"Jasmine, my mother is trying to get her in on a scholarship. She wants to help her to get a good education so she can become somebody!" Jack shot a harsh look at her expressionless face. *What an ingrate!* "How the hell did she get mixed up with a woman like you anyway?"

His words plunged into Jasmine like a sharp knife; her placidly calm façade suddenly collapsed. "I am…so sorry…you think Lily is a bad girl." She sounded wounded.

"No, I don't think she is a bad girl," Jack retorted. "Please just tell her what I've told you. I am out of here!" Jack got up, grabbing his Camels from the table.

"Leaving so soon?" The club manager rushed over.

"Get out of my face, Chan!" Jack glared at him angrily.

"Mr. Wells, would you please sit down, please? You don't know the whole story." She looked up at him imploringly.

"Okay, I am listening."

"Mr. Wells, can I have a cigarette?"

With some hesitation, Jack slipped back into the booth, handed her one, and held his lighter close to her mouth. Under the flickering lights, Jack could see the hard living etched on her young face. She took a big drag, held it, and slowly blew out her smoke. In an almost whispering voice, she pleaded. “Please don’t tell your parents, Mr. Wells, that will ruin her future. You must not blame her.”

“Look, I haven’t told my parents. They don’t know anything.”

“Thank you.” She smiled wanly. “It is all my fault. I shouldn’t have let her work here.”

“So, why did you?” Jack waited, cigarette dangling from his mouth.

“…Mr. Wells, I wasn’t always a dance hostess, you know.”

“No, I don’t!”

“I came to Shanghai five years ago to study acting. I’ve always dreamed of becoming a movie actress. I wanted to be the Vivien Leigh of China.” She paused, wiping her hand back and forth over the table edge. “But like many young Chinese girls, I didn’t make it, and so I became a dancer…not here but in a real dance studio. Last year, I tried to open up my own. I figured at least I can make a living from teaching dancing, but the Green Gang wanted too much protection money, so I had to close it down, and I ended up owing my friends a lot of money. So here I am. I am not proud of what I’ve become.” She sighed heavily, her cigarette burning between her fingers.

“Why can’t you do something else? Bobby said you are a smart girl.”

“It is not that easy. Mr. Wells, you don’t know, in Shanghai, youth and beauty are what we Chinese women can sell. For some of us who are not so fortunate to get married early or rich, men only want our hands and our bodies.” She said it in such an accepting way as if she was merely stating the facts of life, without protest or rancor, but her face grimaced with pain.

"Jasmine, you are still young. I am sure you will have no problem finding yourself a good husband." Jack ratcheted down his condescending voice.

"Mr. Wells, for us Chinese women, our fates are tied to the stations we are born into. Poor marry poor, and rich marry their own kind. I don't know what I did wrong in my last life to deserve this kind of punishment from the Old Man Heaven." She choked back her tears, but Jack could see her hurt quivering at the corners of her hardened mouth.

"So how did you two meet, anyway?" Jack asked after a long moment of silence.

"She and I happened to live in the same neighborhood in Chapei when we first met. After I learned that she came from a nearby village where I came from, we soon became very good friends. She tried to talk me into becoming a Christian, and I taught her how to dance." She paused and then said quietly, "Lee Li-wha is now my best friend. She is like a sister to me."

"Oh yeah, right." Jack rolled his eyes. *What kind of woman would do that to her own sister?* "And that is why she wound up here?" Jack said sarcastically.

"No. She needed money to pay off her father's debt," she replied plainly.

"But why? I thought her father died a while ago."

"He did, but his opium debts were not paid in full before he died."

"I didn't know her father was an opium addict," Jack mumbled; his mother had never told him about that.

"Mr. Wells, Lee Li-wha's father used to be a rich farmer. When she was only thirteen, she was betrothed to the Number One Son of a very rich family in town. Soon after that, her father got hooked on opium and borrowed heavily from them to support his habit. Two years later, he lost most of his land except a small piece of the family burial ground. When Lee Li-wha turned fifteen, her father couldn't even afford to feed her. So, he sent her there to work as their daughter-in-law in training, ten hours a day and seven days a week."

"It sounds more like indentured servitude than an arranged marriage."

"Eh?"

"I said it sounds like she was more a slave than a future daughter-in-law."

"Yes. She hated the whole thing. A year later, she ran away, and her father had to send her younger brother there to work as their houseboy. A few months later, he too ran away. Her father tried to pay down his debt, but couldn't. He died heartbroken. Now the House of Zhou wanted the little piece of burial land still in her family's name."

"But it is not her fault."

"You don't understand, Mr. Wells. Her mother and father were buried on that land, and she and her brother have their plots there, too." Jasmine paused. "The idea that they will plow over her parents' graves and let her parents' souls wander in the underworld for eternity was just too much for her to bear."

"How much money are we talking about?"

"Eight-hundred silver dollars."

"We are not talking about a lot of money here. Why doesn't she just borrow it from someone?"

"It may not be much to you Americans. It is more than I can make in a year. Between the two of us, we could only come up with six hundred. They give her two weeks to come up with the other two hundred…" Jasmine paused. "It is all my fault. I shouldn't have told her."

"Told her what?"

"I told her that the Paramount was short of girls during the Chinese New Year, and she knew how much I could make during the holidays."

"She thinks she can make that kind of money too?"

"Yes. She is fresh and pretty, and men like that."

"What does she have to do?" Jack inquired apprehensively.

"I told her that all she has to do is to sit with the customers, talk, and make them buy more drinks. In a few weeks, she can make the two hundred dollars and then quit."

"That's all?"

"Yes…I don't want her to do what I do," she said self-mockingly, smoke reeking from her mouth.

"I see. I wish she had told me...I could lend her the rest." Jack said quietly, but he was secretly glad that he was her first and only customer. "Do you know where she is now?"

"She is staying with me. She is too embarrassed to see you. That is why she didn't show up at the church. She likes you, and she does not want you to think badly of her."

"Oh, please tell her that I don't think badly of her at all…" Jack stammered. "I wish I can talk to her. Is she coming here tonight?"

"Mr. Wells! Of course not. I've already told her not to work here no more. Borrow or steal; I will do whatever I can to get the rest of the money for her."

"Jasmine." Jack patted lightly on her hand. "You are okay. Can you tell her that I haven't told my parents about any of this? Her secret is safe with me."

"Thank you, Mr. Wells. I will tell her."

"Also, please tell her that if she needs any help on that $200, I can help her out."

"Thank you; I will tell her." She cracked a small smile. "Mr. Wells, you are okay too."

The empty dance floor started to stir as other cabaret girls began to take their usual seats by the side of the stage.

"I need to go," Jasmine said sadly as she slowly got up from the booth. "I will tell Lily what you told me."

"Please do that. Jasmine, thank you."

"Leaving so early, sir?" asked the club manager.

"Yeah, you got a problem with that?"

"No, no problem, sir."

Jack stepped out of the Paramount Club as the cold breeze from the East China Sea whipped across his face. He hurried along the sidewalk, hardly noticing that a rickshaw man had been trailing behind him.

"*Lau Ban,* want a ride, cheap!" he cried out, pattering in his straw sandals.

"I don't want any ride."

"*Lau Ban,* want girls? I know lots of beautiful girls." The man trotted closer to the curb.

Jack turned around angrily. "No, I told you I don't want any ride, and I don't want any girls!"

Running beside him, he saw this bantam of a man, an emaciated figure dry as a windswept tree. His shriveled body looked like a bag of bones wrapped in leathery dark skin, but his ingratiating smile had that vague look of well-bred gentry. Perhaps once upon a time, he might have been a shopkeeper or a village school teacher. The idea that such a puny man was going to pull a 190-pound American on his back began to feel obscene to him; but for a few coppers, he was willing.

Abruptly Jack stopped, took out his wallet, and threw a whole dollar bill into the backseat of his rickshaw. "No ride tonight. Thank you anyway."

"Shie-shie, Lau Ban! Shie-shie, Lau Ban! Thank you, thank you, Big Boss!" Bowing, the rickshaw man thanked him profusely as he trotted away.

"You are welcome," Jack murmured, watching a gaunt image flickering past the fancy shop windows before he disappeared into a dark alley; just like the tens of thousands of other wretched souls, these cruel Shanghai streets had just swallowed him, and nobody even knew his name.

CHAPTER 15

Shopping at Wing On

Jack couldn't concentrate on his work, what happened over the weekend still fresh on his mind. After that talk with Jasmine, he could not stop thinking about Lily. As he absentmindedly flipped through a thick file when the telephone on his desk suddenly rang.

"Jack, Lily is back!" his mother hollered on the other end.

"Oh, that's great news, Mother!"

"Miss Helen Richardson has agreed to give her an interview this Friday. Is that great news or what?"

"Yes! I hope she can get in."

"Of course, she can get in. I hope she can also get a scholarship."

"I hope so." Jack was glad that he had that talk with Jasmine.

"Jack, are you busy later today?"

"I will be free after work. Why?"

"I am going to Nanking Road to do some shopping. I want to get Lily a new dress for her interview."

"Oh…I think I need a new lighter."

"Then we will meet you at Wing On around four on the second floor. You know where it is, right?"

"Yeah, I know where it is."

Blond-haired mannequins, sporting the latest Parisian fashions, greeted Jack as he rode the squeaking wooden escalator up to the second floor of the Wing On Department Store.

"Hi, Jack, we are here!" Jack saw his mother and Lily standing by a wall of colorful silk shawls amidst throngs of shoppers perusing bolts of Chinese silks and racks of crepe de Chine.

"Hi, Mother!"

"Jack, I have an idea what you should get for Joann's birthday—an embroidered silk shawl."

"Mother, I don't know she would like that kind of thing."

"All women like pretty things. Am I right, Lily?"

"Yes, Mrs. Wells," she replied whisperingly pretending to examine a bolt of silk.

"Lily, do you think green goes with blond hair?"

"Yes, Mrs. Wells," she said without looking up. Lily had changed back to her white cotton blouse and black pants.

"What do you think of this?" Jack's mother held up a silk shawl with a green sphinx in white clouds.

"It looks okay," Jack shrugged.

"Let me try it on her...Lily, you look just like a China doll!"

"It is very nice, Mrs. Wells." She quickly unwrapped it from her shoulders.

"Lily, would you tell the sales clerk that I'll take two for five dollars each?" She picked up another shawl with golden flowers on a dark background.

"Mother, I think one is enough. I'm not even sure where Joann can wear that in New York."

"The second one is for me, dear." She stuffed a few dollar bills into Lily's hand.

Lily soon returned with the change.

"Jack, just one more stop. I want to look for a dress for Lily's interview. It shouldn't take long."

"Okay." Jack watched them disappear into the lady's dress section. When he saw them again, Lily was wearing a white pleated skirt and a matching white satin blouse with puffed sleeves and a fluffy bow. Discreetly, he watched her preen in front of a three-sided mirror, swiveling her body this way and that; her demeanor was full of little swaggers, quite a departure from the way she looked before. *No wonder women like shopping,* Jack mused.

"Jack, doesn't she now look just like an American girl?"

"It looks nice on her." Jack nodded approvingly.

"Lily, do you like it?"

"I do. I like it a lot, Mrs. Wells."

"Then, it will be a present from the Reverend and me. It is our appreciation for all the work you have done for us."

"Oh! Are you sure? Mrs. Wells, I can pay you back." She put her hand over her mouth.

"Yes, I am sure. We want you to wear something nice for your interview, just like all the other rich Shanghai girls."

"Thank you, Mrs. Wells."

"You are quite welcome. Then, we are all done. Jack, you see, shopping is not that bad."

"It is okay."

"Jack, didn't you say that you want to buy a lighter? Why don't you two young people run along? I have to meet Mrs. Spencer at the

Park Hotel for tea. They are organizing another charity ball for the Chinese orphans. I'd better be running along."

"Mrs. Wells, thank you and the Reverend for the dress."

"Lily, you are quite welcome. I am sure Miss Richardson will be impressed."

They watched her go down the wooden escalator, and then Lily said softly, "Mr. Wells, I hope we didn't bore you with all that shopping."

"No, you didn't bore me at all. This store is amazing."

"Mr. Wells…I want to thank you."

"For what?"

"For not telling your parents." Lily blushed.

"I hope you are not mad at me for the way I've treated you."

"No, I'm not mad. I was actually glad that you were there, Mr. Wells…Oh, God! I am so embarrassed." She started running up the escalator.

"Lily, where are you going?"

"I thought you wanted to buy a lighter." Lily waited for him at the landing. "They sell cigarette lighters over there."

"Okay, show me where it is." Jack eagerly followed her down a corridor crammed with lamps and electric fans.

"*Chien-wen, Ye men mai da hoa ji ma?* Do you sell cigarette lighters?" Lily approached a man behind a glass counter.

"We sell American lighters, German lighters, and even Japanese lighters. How many do you want?"

"I don't want to buy any. This American gentleman would like to see what you have." She waved Jack to come closer.

"Can you show me some Zippo lighters?"

"Which one you like?"

"How about that one on the left? The one with the white flowers."

"That's their top model. You got good taste." He reached under the counter.

"What kind of flowers are they?"

"Lilies."

"It looks nice; I'll take it."

"Thank you for shopping at Wing On. Please come back again." The doorman held open the door.

"Mr. Wells, I will see you at the church. Again, I want to thank you."

"Don't mention it…where are you going now?" Jack looked around the crowded Nanking Road.

"I'm going to Jasmine's place."

"Want to grab a cup of coffee?" Jack saw her pulling on her thin coat.

"Thank you, Mr. Wells. I don't drink coffee."

"Do you want to get something to eat? It's past six; you must be hungry."

"A little bit." Lily nodded.

"I know this place that serves very good chili."

"What kind of food is it?"

"American food, of course. It is really good. Did you ever have chili before?"

"Eh…no." She shook her head.

"Wanta give it a try?"

"Eh…If you are not too busy."

"No, I am not too busy."

"Hey, Jack, back again?" The proprietor grinned when he saw them walk in.

"Hey Jimmy, how is it going? A table for two."

"Just grab any seat."

"Sure. How about giving us two bowls of chili and two beers?" Jack pulled out a chair.

"Mr. Wells, I don't drink."

"Okay, ever had milkshake before?"

"No." Lily shook her head.

"Hey, Jimmy, make it two bowls of chili and two milkshakes," Jack hollered. "Have you ever been in here before?"

"I walked by here many times but never been inside."

"Why not?"

"I don't know…I see only Americans in here." Lily shifted uncomfortably in her chair as she looked around the room and then said quietly, "Mr. Wells, Jasmine got me a new job teaching ballroom dancing."

"Jasmine told me that you are a good dancer."

"Thank you."

"So, where do you teach?"

"At the Majestic Hotel."

"I didn't know that Western ballroom dance is so popular here in China."

"It is very popular with the Shanghainese crowd. They all want to know how to waltz or do the fox-trot."

"Why?"

"Because they want to be Westernized."

"Try the milkshake." Jack watched the waiter put down their food.

"Okay." Lily took a small sip from the straw.

"You like it?"

"Mm, I like it." She nodded.

"Try the chili."

"Okay."

"What you think?"

"Mm…it is very good." She took another spoonful, savoring the spicy taste with her tongue. "It is scrumptious."

"Wow, that's a big word."

"Your mother taught me that word." She blushed.

"My parents told me that you were helping Pastor Henderson delivering his Sunday sermons just after one year of learning how to speak English."

"Not really. My English was not that good then. He helped me with my English and did all the Bible translations for me. He was a very nice man," Lily said pensively. "Why did God have to take him away so soon."

"Lily, I don't mean to bring up your past."

"It is okay.

"My parents told me that you met him on the street in Chapei…" Jack stopped.

"Yes." She slowly put down her spoon.

"Lily, they told me that you ran away from an arranged marriage you hated. It must have been very hard for a young girl all alone in such a big city."

"Yes, I have eaten some bitterness, but my little brother is still paying the price for my freedom." Her voice faltered.

"Lily, why do you blame yourself? I thought it was your own father who had sent you away."

"But I didn't know the bargain he had made with the House of Zhou."

"Lily, how old were you then?"

"I was barely fifteen. One day my father just told me that he was going to send me to live in the big House of Zhou in a small town near our village. But he had never told me that he owed them a lot of money and an arranged marriage was his way of paying back his debt." Lily paused as if she was reliving her past. "He drove me there in an ox-drawn cart, and that was the last time I ever saw my father again. While I was there, I rarely saw the boy I was supposed to marry because he was attending some foreign school in Shanghai. I wanted to run away, but there was no place for me to go. After I turned seventeen, I came to Shanghai with the old mistress because she wanted to buy her son an English suit and me a white Western wedding dress at Wing On. This boy, his name is Zhou Hsiao-ming, was not happy to see me at all. He just stared up at the ceiling pretending he didn't even see me, and after a while, he suddenly whispered in my ear, 'Lee Li-wha, I don't want to marry you! I don't want to marry a peasant girl! I am giving you the freedom I know you have always wanted. Go!' So, I started to run; I ran out of the store, I ran across the Thibet Bridge, and I slept in the streets in Chapei until one day, I bumped into this foreign priest."

"Reverend Henderson?" Jack was mesmerized.

"Yes, Reverend Henderson. He took me to a place called the Door of Hopes for many runaway Chinese girls, and later on, he sent me to the Sung Tak Girls School to study English. And after that, I went to work for him as his assistant and translator. Not long after, he passed away. And you know the rest of the story." Lily said softly. "I just wonder where is my little brother now. I don't even know he is dead or alive."

"Lily, I am sorry about your brother. I've got some money saved up. I can help you out."

"Thank you, Mr. Wells, but it will take me a long time to pay you back."

"Hey, I got an idea! How about you give me some dance lessons so you can pay me back sooner? I am always free every Saturday afternoon."

"I thought you already know to dance."

"No, not really. I only know how to slow dance."

"I charge one dollar for a two-hour lesson."

"Let's see, at that rate, I will have to take two-hundred lessons from you, but don't worry, I need a lot of lessons."

"Mr. Wells, you don't think it wouldn't look kind of funny to see a Chinese girl teaching an American man how to waltz or do the jitterbug? People would be watching us."

"No. Tell you what, if it makes you feel any better, when I am dancing with you, I will pretend that I am a Chinese boy." Jack flashed a disarming grin.

"Mr. Wells, you are so funny." Lily giggled.

"Please call me Jack. No more of that Mr. Wells business, okay? It makes me sound so much older than you are. I'm only twenty-five."

"I am nineteen, but according to the Chinese calendar, I am actually twenty," she said softly, avoiding his gaze.

CHAPTER 16

Pomp and Circumstance

Now, after work on Saturday, Jack would change into a white leisure suit then dash to the Majestic Hotel on the Bubbling Well Road for his dance lessons. Often he would be the only foreign face on the dance floor in the hotel's Winter Garden Tea Room, but he didn't care. With a pretty Chinese girl in his arms, Jack was content to whittle away the afternoon-tea hours with his dance lessons and scotch and soda.

"Lily, is waltz hard to learn?" Jack looked around the Shanghai smart-set on the crowded dance floor.

"No, it is the same as the four-step or Cha Cha; you lead, and I follow."

"Okay, let's give it a try." Jack crushed out his cigarette.

"Okay…first, you move your left foot forward with your body leaning a little toward me, and I'll move back; then you step up with your right foot slightly to the side and turn your body this way."

"I think I got it."

"Then you move your left foot back. One, two, three; and one, two, three." Lily gently pulled and pushed on his big frame.

"One, two, three; one, two, three." Jack looked down at his feet.

"Jack, just listen to the music and follow the beats."

"Alright, one, two, three…one, two, three. Lily, the waltz is harder than it looks." Jack stumbled around the clover-shaped fountain, occasionally grinning back at the curious stares and polite smiles.

"Jack, the waltz is not that hard; just imagine you are dancing in the grand ballroom in Vienna. Feel the music, and follow the beats as you glide your lady around the floor. One, two, three; one, two, three," Lily urged him.

"Lily, have you ever been to Vienna?"

"No."

"Then how do you know how the Vienna Ballroom looks like?"

"Jasmine and I often see lots of foreign movies at the Carlton Theatre…one, two, three, and one two three. Jack, I think you've got it. You just need a little more practice."

"Lily, you are a good teacher. Maybe you can teach me how to do tango next week." Jack beamed as they headed back to their table.

"This place is all booked up for parties next week." She dabbed the sweat off from her face.

"What parties?"

"Jack, have you ever heard someone named Mrs. Wallis Simpson?"

"Of course, she is going to marry King Edward VIII. So, what does she have to do with this place?"

"Do you know that she once stayed at this hotel and danced on this very floor?"

"Really?"

"Yes. Everybody now wants to come here to have parties in the Winter Garden and stay in the same room where she had slept before."

"Mm, very interesting...I didn't know Chinese followed this kind of thing."

"Jack, this is Shanghai, and many people are interested in what is going on with the British royalty, especially when an ordinary American woman is about to become a Duchess. It is like a fairytale come true."

"Lily, do you know that he has to abdicate his throne to marry her?"

"Yes. His brother will become the new king," Lily said knowledgeably.

All the pomp and circumstance accorded to the Coronation of King George VI and Queen Elizabeth were on full display in this far-away outpost of the British Empire. Elaborate decorations and glittering lights went up on all the buildings along the Bund, and every British expatriate living in China was invited to the coronation party at the British Consulate. To fill up their reception hall, they had also invited some of the officers and staff at the Hongkong and Shanghai Bank. For such a special occasion, Jack went out and bought himself a white tuxedo.

"Mr. Wells, you look quite smashing today." Mary pinned a pink carnation onto his lapel.

"You don't look too bad yourself. Just like a proper English lady," Jack said approvingly.

"I have to look the part." Mary, decked out in a powder-blue evening gown, struck a studied pose. "You don't get invited to a coronation party every day, you know."

"This is a first for me too. Mary, I've invited my friend Mr. Bobby Ferguson to come with us. He will be here in a few minutes."

"Oh." Her voice suddenly went flat.

"Have you ever met him before?"

"No, but I've talked to him many times on the phone," she replied indifferently.

"I think you'll like him…there he is." Jack saw Bobby rush through the brass door. "Mary, allow me to introduce you to my good friend, Bobby Ferguson." Jack gently pushed her toward him. "Bobby, this is Miss Mary Lane, my secretary."

"How do you do? Mr. Ferguson, we've spoken on the telephone before." She nodded politely.

"Yes, of course. It is a pleasure finally to meet you." Bobby eagerly extended out his hand. "Now, I can put that proper English accent to a pretty face."

"I am flattered, Mr. Ferguson. Now, I can put a face with your voice too, and I must say you look just the way I've imagined."

"Do I look okay?"

"Yes, you look just fine," she replied haughtily, *a cowboy in a double-breasted suit.*

"Mary, you look much younger than I had imagined."

"Oh? I didn't know I projected such a prudish image over the telephone." She cracked a strained smile.

"No, no, you just sound very professional over the phone." Fumbling for words, Bobby found himself drawn to this unapproachable woman.

"Mr. Ferguson, for a man of your position, you look quite younger than I first thought." Mary returned his compliment.

"Now that you two have met, shall we get going?" Jack interjected.

"Jack, are we going to walk there?" Bobby asked.

"I don't mind. The British Consulate is just down on the other end of the Bund."

"Okay, shall we?" Bobby rushed to hold open the door.

"Thank you."

"Mary, would you like one?" Once outside, Bobby quickly took out his cigarettes.

"Sure." She took one and leaned over his lighter. "Thank you, Mr. Ferguson."

"You are welcome, Miss Mary Lane."

Mary blew out her smoke and tilted her head up at the glowing Shanghai skyline. "Isn't that pretty?"

"The Brits are pulling out all the stops for this coronation business. The whole place now looks like Coney Island at night." Bobby flipped closed his lighter.

"I have never been there. Is it as pretty as Hawaii?"

"No, but it is a lot of fun."

"Mr. Ferguson, what do you think of Edward VIII marrying one of your American women?"

"Miss Lane, all I know is that this is the first time a British king marries a commoner—a divorcee, no less."

"Mr. Ferguson, I presume that you don't approve of their marriage."

"Miss Lane, I reckon the man, at his age, should know better than letting a married woman hoodwink him into abdicating his throne. For Heaven's sake, that Mrs. Wally Simpson ain't no spring chicken," Bobby said scornfully.

"What do you think, Mr. Wells?"

"Mary, I don't know. Maybe he loves this woman more than he loves power."

"He must. I hope they will live happily ever after."

"But life ain't a fairytale."

"Mr. Ferguson, you are quite right; life is not a fairytale." His blunt remarks made Mary smile, profane and rough on the edges, quite a departure from the polished, lyrical tongues she was used to hearing at the bank. Mary shared a small apartment with two other Eurasian girls somewhere on the backside of Shanghai. She had no contacts with either the English or the Chinese side of her family. She had never spoken to her father after he went back to England, and the connection to her Chinese half was long lost after her mother died. Even though she spoke Chinese, the locals regarded her as a foreigner because of her blue eyes. The Shanghailanders didn't accept her because of her Chinese blood. Neither Chinese nor British, she was persona non grata, a lone traveler in life, looking for a home.

As they approached the British Consulate, Jack could see that the choir boys from the Holy Trinity Church had already gathered under the brightly lit veranda, and a well-dressed crowd anxiously awaited by the entrance. He could hear the crackling broadcast sounds emanating from a large table radio at the door: "From henceforth, George VI is the King of Britain and the Dominions of the British Commonwealth and the Emperor of India…."

"That is the Archbishop of Canterbury delivering his benediction on BBC Broadcasting," a passerby whispered as "Pomp and Circumstance" started to blare inside the reception hall and a long procession of British dignitaries led by Scottish pipers in kilts began to take their seats.

"Miss Lane, don't you love all these pageantries?" Bobby whispered. "You must be very proud to be British at this moment."

"Mr. Ferguson, I am not British. I am just someone looking in from outside," Mary replied flatly.

"I thought you were."

"Can't you tell?" Mary pointed to her eyes with a hint of bitterness in her voice.

"Your dad is British, right?"

"Yes, but I hardly remember him."

"I am sorry."

"Don't be sorry. These people have nothing to do with me. I don't remember any of them ever inviting me into their homes."

"Hey, if you don't want to stay, we can get out of here as soon as this thing is over."

"I want to stay for their roast beef."

"You never had it before?"

"No. I have only heard my boss talk about it. I want to try it."

"You have any plan after that?"

"No, I have no plan."

"You want to grab a drink at the Cathay Hotel?"

"Sure, Mr. Ferguson." She nodded.

"Mary, just call me Bobby."

"Okay, Bobby."

"You like jazz?"

"I love jazz. I have a few Benny Goodman records."

"Me too. You like to dance?" Bobby wasted no time.

"Mm, love to dance."

"Can you do the Texas Two-Step?"

"I don't know that one. Mr. Wells, do you know how to do the Texas Two-Step?"

"No, not really. I've just started to take ballroom dance lessons a month ago."

"Jack, I didn't know that."

"Bobby, remember Lily? She is teaching me."

"Who is Lily?"

"She works for Jack's father."

"Is she an American?"

"No, she is Chinese."

"Mr. Wells, why don't you invite her to join us?"

"Yeah, Jack, why don't you give her a call?"

"Bobby, I don't think she has a telephone."

"I got a car, and we can swing by her place."

"Bobby, I don't know her that well. It is not like I can just drop by her place and ask her out or something," Jack fretted, thinking back to where she lives in Chapei. "Maybe next time."

"Okay, maybe next time."

Standing outside of the British Consulate, Bobby looked up at a full moon hanging over the Shanghai Harbor. "Hey, you guys want to take a walk? The night is still young."

"Sure, I'd love to. It is so nice out," Mary quickly agreed.

"Why don't you two go?" Jack demurred. "Have a good time."

"Mr. Wells, are you sure?"

"Mary, I'm quite sure. Goodnight."

"Good night, Mr. Wells...thank you." Mary placed a light peck on Jack's cheek.

CHAPTER 17

A Double Date

Before Jack even had a chance to hang up his coat the next Monday morning, Bobby was already on the phone. "What's up?"

"Hey, buddy, I owe you one." A grateful voice came over the line.

"What do you owe me?"

"I like her. She is very nice."

"Good for you. I am glad that you two have hit it off." Jack smiled, looking out of his office; Mary's face had a little glow that was not there before. "Bobby, I think she likes you too."

"You think so?"

"Yes, I know so."

"Jack, got any plan for this Saturday?"

"Just my dance lesson with Lily."

"Mary would like to meet her. We could all go to the Cathay Hotel, grab a drink, and listen to the Filipino Jazz Band. We could even do a little dancing over there. And after that, I would like to take Mary up to their roof-top restaurant. She's never been up there before. Whaddya think?"

"When?"

"How about this Saturday after work?"

"Alright, I will ask her, but no guarantee, okay?" he said hesitantly. He knew Lily would worry about what the church ladies might think of her if they ever found out that she was going out with the Reverend's son.

When Jack entered the Cathay Hotel lobby, Bobby and Mary were already waiting.

"Where is Lily?" Mary saw Jack came in alone.

"She said she would meet us here."

"Here in the lobby?"

"Yeah. Maybe she is a little late."

"Mr. Wells, I'll bet she is waiting for us outside."

"Why? I told her that we would meet here at the hotel."

"Mr. Wells, this place frowns upon a Chinese woman coming in here all alone…they might think she is a…."

"I understand. Let's wait for her outside then."

As they walked through the revolving door, Mary quickly spotted a Chinese girl standing primly on the sidewalk. "Is that her?"

"Yeah, that's her."

"She is kind of young. How did she become your dance teacher?" Mary raised her eyebrows.

"I'll tell you later." Jack rushed over. "Hi, Lily!"

"Hi, Jack." She waved. "I wasn't sure where you wanted to meet."

"Lily, let me introduce you to my secretary, Mary Lane." Jack gestured.

"Hi, I'm Mary."

"Hi, I am Lily."

"Lily, you have already met Mr. Bobby Ferguson."

"Yes, it is nice to meet you again, Mr. Ferguson."

"Same here...you look different." Bobby tried to remember how she looked on that night.

"I like your dress. Where did you get it?" Mary took a glance at her chiffon dress.

"It is not mine. I borrowed it from my friend," she replied shyly, clutching a small handbag in front of her.

"Lily, you look very nice." Jack was a little surprised that she got all dressed up.

"Welcome back!" The hotel concierge smiled at them expectantly. "Will you all be needing a room tonight?"

"No, we are just going to have a drink at your Jazz Bar."

"We still have a few rooms available in case you change your mind."

"Is the Filipino Jazz Band playing tonight?"

"They are there now."

"Great! We picked the right time."

"Welcome to the Jazz Bar. How many?"

"Four." Bobby put up his fingers. "Can you give us a table close to the dance floor?"

"Certainly." The waiter started toward the back.

"This Filipino Jazz Band is pretty good. When I first heard them playing, I couldn't believe that Chinamen could blow horns like that."

"I thought you said they were Filipinos." Mary saw four older Oriental men in black tuxedos and white bow ties busy setting up their instruments.

"I don't know; they all look the same to me." Bobby took out his cigarette. "You have never heard them play before?"

"No. This is my first time."

As they waited for their drinks, Ira Gershwin's "Summertime" started to flow up in the air, and the Filipino Jazz Bar began to fill with the lingering notes of the saxophones and the brassy sounds of the trumpets.

"You like it?" Jack turned to Lily.

"Yes, it is very pretty." Lily watched intently as the four old musicians bounced up and down in their chairs, tossing around the notes with bravado.

"Mary, would you like to dance?"

"Sure, Bobby, I'd love to."

Jack stood up and watched them move onto a small dance floor, holding hands. "Lily, would you like to dance?"

"Yes." She followed him to the dance floor.

Jack held out his hands. She moved closer and waited for him to make the first move. Without hesitation, Jack started to swing her around, arms waving up and down, and feet stomping back and forth.

"Hey, Jack, you dance pretty good!" Bobby hollered through the music.

"I've got a good teacher." Jack beamed.

And by the time they finally returned to their table, they were all perspiring and smiling.

"Jack, want another round?"

"Sure, why not."

"Yeah, I would like to have one more glass of wine." Mary raised her glass.

"Mary, after we finish here, let's go up to their Tower Restaurant. I want to show you girls Shanghai night from high up there."

"Care for another round, sir?" The waiter rushed over.

"Yes, of course, and after this, we want to go upstairs to have dinner at your Tower Restaurant. Can you tell them to have a table ready for us around 8:30?"

"So sorry sir, the Tower Restaurant is all booked tonight for a private party."

"How about your Roof Garden Restaurant?"

"It is solidly booked too."

"Heck, it never ceases to amaze me how many rich people there are in Shanghai."

"Bobby, we can go somewhere else," said Mary.

"Nah, I want to show the girls a good time. Something different. Jack, have you ever had Japanese food before?"

"No. Where can you get Japanese food in Shanghai?"

"In Little Tokyo."

"Where is that?"

"In Hongkew, on the other side of the Soochow Creek. Mary, you like sushi?"

"What is that?"

"It is a piece of raw fish and rice wrapped in seaweed. You want to try it?"

"Sure, why not, I never had raw fish before."

CHAPTER 18

The Little Tokyo

They left the Jazz Bar in a taxi. As they went over the Garden Bridge and past the gray Astor House Hotel, shop signs in Japanese and paper lantern began to appear along East Broadway; Japanese men and women in kimonos and split-toe wooden sandals started to gather on the sidewalks.

"Jack, did you know that over 30,000 Japs live around here?" Bobby saw him glued to the window.

"No wonder they call this place the 'Little Tokyo.'" Jack turned to Lily. "Do you come here often?"

"Sometimes. I come here with your mother to shop at their Hongkew Market."

"Maybe we can all go over there to shop after we eat," Mary added enthusiastically.

"Sir, can you pull over in front of that restaurant?" Bobby pointed out the window.

A Japanese man in a blue cotton kimono called out when he saw them getting off the taxi. "You and your lady friends eat inside? We have very, very fresh fish, just from Japan this morning."

"Jack, this place is pretty good. I've eaten here a couple of times before. Wanta try it?"

"Sure. How about you ladies?"

"Bobby, you decide."

"We have Sukiyaki too, cooked not raw." The Japanese man gestured ingratiatingly toward a paper screen door.

"Okay, let's go in." Bobby led them into a quiet, almost serene space surrounded by an oasis of blond wood and subdued lighting.

"This is a pretty nice place," Mary whispered as they waited on the cool slate floor.

"*Irasshaimase!*" a kimono-clad hostess greeted them as she shuffled over in her slit-toe wooden sandals.

"*Konnichiwa,* table for four." Bobby put up his fingers.

"No table tonight, only tatami rooms." She gave an indifferent glance at Lily.

They quietly followed the hostess toward the back, passing groups of Japanese men in dark business suits and brown military uniforms sitting along a long oak counter. Looking over their shoulders, Jack could see sushi chefs in white kimonos and blue headbands working intently on slabs of fresh fish.

"Please take off your shoes." The hostess bowed.

"Sure." Bobby quickly took off his shoes, and others soon followed. Without much talking, they walked behind the waitress down a narrow hallway lined with glowing paper screens on both sides.

"Mary, these are called shoji screens. The Japs use them even for their bedrooms," Bobby whispered.

"Please." The kimono-clad waitress stopped in front of a sliding shoji screen and bowed.

"Ladies?" Bobby followed Mary and Lily into a small room with wall-to-wall straw mats on the floor and a low-slung wooden table in the center.

"I don't see any chairs." Jack looked around.

"This is how you sit." Bobby plunked down on the mat.

As they watched him struggle with his stiff legs, another waitress entered. "Welcome to Akashio."

"*Konnichiwa!*"

"Would you like to see the menu?"

"Jack, you want to see the menu?"

"No, why don't you order for us."

"Okay, let me order…for our appetizers, one sashimi, and one sushi combination plate and four tuna hand-rolls, and for our main course, a large Sukiyaki for four, with everything in it and four bowls of rice."

"Would that be all?"

"For now. Mary, what would you like to drink?"

"A glass of white wine."

"Mary, I don't think they serve wine here. How about trying some of their warm sake? It tastes like a sweet wine. Jack, you wanta try some of their Japanese beer?"

"Sure."

"Two warm sakes and two Sapporo."

"Thank you very much." The waitress quietly slid off the tatami mat, closing the screen door behind her.

"Bobby, how do you know so much about Japanese food?" Mary asked adoringly.

"I go out with some of them Mitsui Trading guys a lot, and I learned to eat what they like to eat."

"I am glad you've suggested this place. I never had Japanese food before." Jack took out his cigarettes.

With muffled rustlings of kimonos, the screen door slid open again; two waitresses returned with their drinks and food. They watched the waitresses placing the colorful plates of thinly sliced fish on the low-slung table.

"They look so pretty."

"Mary, would you like to try a piece of tuna?" Bobby picked up a slice of pink fish with his chopsticks and dipped it into the soy sauce.

"Sure, thank you."

"Lily, would you like to try one too?"

"I have never eaten raw fish before." She hesitated.

"It's considered a delicacy in Japan. Try a piece," Bobby urged her.

"Okay, there is a first time for everything." Lily slowly put it into her mouth.

"What do you think? Good?" Bobby asked anxiously.

"Not as fishy as I thought. The flavor is a little bland but subtle." Lily quickly took a sip of her warm sake.

"I will try one too." Jack picked up a piece with his fork.

"Mr. Wells, what do you think?"

"It is pretty good...Mary, we are not at work anymore, so we all should be on a first-name basis. Let me make a toast." Jack raised his beer. "Lily, Mary, and Bobby, to our friendship!"

"To our friendship! Let's do this more often!" Bobby said giddily, knocking back his beer.

With the soft twanging of the samisen playing outside the screen doors, they quickly lost track of time as a blanket of hazy warm air filled their tatami room.

"*Domo arigato.*" The lady in a white kimono bowed.

"Thank you very much. I enjoyed it. My compliment to the chef." Jack took out his wallet, and just then, from the corner of his eye, he saw a man at the sushi bar suddenly swing around on his chair and call out, "Mr. Jack Wells, is that you?"

Jack didn't know what to make of this man in a brown military uniform; he did not know a single Japanese person in Shanghai.

"Jack, it's me, Akira Tanaka." He strutted toward him.

"Akira? What in the world are you doing here in Shanghai?" Jack finally recognized him.

"I'm on military duty."

"What are you doing in the military? I thought you went back to Japan to practice medicine."

"They called up my conscription." He let go of his hand. "I am now a doctor in the Japanese Imperial Army."

"Akira, you look pretty sharp in that military uniform."

"Thank you. So, what are you doing in Shanghai?"

"I am working for the Hongkong and Shanghai Bank. Wow, what a small world!"

"Yes, indeed. How is Joann? Is she here with you?"

"No, she is still in New York," Jack replied haltingly. "What about you? I heard you were engaged. When is the wedding?"

"I am afraid my duty to my country comes before my personal affairs." His shoulders straightened up a bit. "I would love to have you and Joann come to my wedding."

"Sure, just let me know when."

"As soon as my military tour is over. Perhaps next spring."

"I'll look forward to it. Akira, we must get together soon." Jack noticed his military buddies were all staring at them from the sushi bar.

"Yes, yes, of course. Where can I reach you?"

"You can reach me at Hongkong and Shanghai Bank on the Bund, not too far from here."

"Okay, I will look you up. I am glad to see you again. Please give my regard to Joann."

"Sure, I will."

"And don't forget to invite me to your wedding. I would love to see Joann again. You two make such a perfect pair. Sayonara, my good friend."

"Goodbye, Akira."

"*Arigatou gozaimasu,* thank you very much." The hostesses bowed as they walked out of the restaurant.

"Thank you." Jack nodded.

"Hey, you guys want to grab some nightcaps?" Bobby asked. "We can all go back to my place."

"Thank you for a lovely evening, Mr. Ferguson. I think I better get going." Lily held out her hand.

"What are you talking about? The night is still young. Let's go back to my place."

"Lily, are you sure? Bobby doesn't live too far from here."

"Mary, it's nice meeting you, but I think I should get going. Jack, why don't you go with them?"

"It wouldn't be much fun without you. Lily, we all can go back to the Jazz Bar and do more dancing, if you want."

"Mary, why don't you three go without me. I can go home by myself. The tram stop is just across the street."

"Why? Lily, are you sure?"

"Yes," she nodded.

"Okay, Jack will take you home."

"Mary, it's okay. I can take the tram."

"Lily, please let Jack take you home. That is the proper etiquette for a gentleman to escort a lady home."

"It is okay, Mary. I will take the tram." Lily started walking away.

"Where do you live?" Mary suddenly asked her in Chinese.

"I live in Chapei," she replied in Chinese.

"It is not too far from here. I can go with you."

"Mary, *tsai-jian*." She started running across East Broadway before Mary could say another word.

"I don't understand why she doesn't want us to take her home." Bobby looked puzzled. "Is she mad at us or something? Jack, did you say something to piss her off?"

"No, I don't think so. Everything was fine just a few minutes ago."

"Jack, I did notice she became a little quiet after we ran into your Japanese friend. He said something about you and Joann getting married. Who is Joann?"

"She is…she is my girlfriend."

"You have a girlfriend! And she didn't know?" Mary bristled; she had always assumed that Jack was detached.

"She knew."

"Are you two engaged?"

"Eh…no."

"But your Japanese friend seems to think you are. He said something about coming to your wedding."

"Eh…Mary, I am not planning on any wedding."

"Now I understand why Lily suddenly acted that way." Mary shook her head.

"Mary, don't be so hard on Jack. I asked him to invite her. I don't think it is such a big deal to go out just to have a drink."

"Maybe because you're a guy," Mary replied indignantly. "But a girl needs to worry about her reputation, especially here in Shanghai."

"C'mon, Mary, I am sorry. I didn't it mean that way." Bobby nudged on her arm.

"Man, of all the places, I got to run into Akira here in Shanghai." Jack shook his head in disbelief.

"Mr. Wells, that's not the point, is it?"

"Mary, I don't know what else to say," Jack pleaded.

"She trusted you. You should have at least told her that you are about to get married, so she would know what she is getting into," Mary snapped. For the moment, she seemed to have forgotten that Jack was her boss.

"Mary, I am not about to get married. Really, I am not." He fidgeted with his cigarette.

"Mr. Wells, you must understand, Lily is taking a chance by hanging out with you."

"But why?" Bobby asked casually.

"You guys don't know how the Chinese think. Whenever they see a Chinese girl go out with a foreigner, right away, they will think she is his mistress or worse, a whore; and her friends, family, and neighbors would shun her. Now I understand why Lily didn't want you to pick her up at her place."

"Mary, I like her, and I would never treat her that way." Jack stared at the empty tram station across the street.

"Mr. Wells, what do you expect her to think after she heard about you and Joann? She will think you just want her as your mistress and nothing more."

"Mary, please believe me. I have no intention to treat her as my mistress," Jack said earnestly.

"My mother believed that my father wouldn't treat her as his mistress too, but he abandoned her anyway because he was already married." She struggled to control her tears.

"Hey, baby, are you okay?" Bobby squeezed her hand.

"I am okay," Mary replied quietly. "I remember the tiny room in Chapei, and no one ever came to visit us because all her relatives thought my mother deserved what was coming to her."

"Mary, I am not about to get married…really!"

"Not yet anyway…Mr. Wells, after you and Joann get married, what would that make her? A foreigner's whore, just like what they called my mother."

"Mary, I won't do that to you. I am not married." Bobby tried to hug her. "I hope you are not mad at us, or anything."

"No, Bobby, I am not mad at you guys. I just feel bad for her. It is sad, isn't it? This is her country, and she has to act like a second-class citizen in front of you two Americans," Mary said ruefully.

CHAPTER 19

The Little Moscow Café

It had been a long week since he saw Lily last. As he walked toward the Majestic Hotel, unsure if she would be there. When he saw Lily standing underneath the hotel canopy, holding her little green parasol, Jack felt relieved. "Hi, Lily. I am so glad you are here! Shall we go in?"

"Mr. Wells," Lily saw him approaching. "If you don't mind, I would like to skip your dance lesson today."

"Okay, I don't feel like dancing either." Jack sensed a distance between them that was not there before. "Lily, I owe you an explanation."

"Mr. Wells, you don't need to explain. I just don't feel like teaching dancing today. Maybe next week." She popped open her parasol just as the soggy summer mists suddenly turned into a steady drizzle.

"Okay, I will take a rain check. No pun intended."

"What?" she snapped and started to walk away.

"I thought you knew about her." Jack followed her out into the rain.

"I did…but I just thought…anyway, I just don't think it is appropriate for me to go out with a married man."

"Lily, I am not married!"

"Just the same. Mr. Wells, maybe I will see you at your next dance lesson." She started running across the street.

"Lily, where are you going?"

"Not your business!"

"Lily, please don't be mad at me. I-I just don't know what is going on between us."

"Mr. Wells, nothing is going on between us," she said coolly.

"Lily, please, give me a chance. I like you a lot. I swear to God; I won't do anything to hurt you."

"Excuse me; I have to meet Jasmine at the Little Moscow Café."

"I haven't seen Jasmine for a long time. How is she doing? Is she still teaching dancing?"

"No, she does not have to teach dancing anymore."

"Why not?"

"She has a new boyfriend, a university student. His father is very rich. Excuse me; I have to go to their sit-down discussion."

"What is a sit-down discussion?"

"Just a bunch of university students sitting around the table talking to their professor."

"Can I come? I don't live too far from there."

"You won't be interested. It is going to be very boring. Jack… Mr. Wells, I think we should keep our contact just to dance lessons. If you don't mind."

"Lily, do you know that when I was living in Greenwich Village, I often went to some of these 'sitting down' discussions to talk about how to make the world a better place."

"I thought you lived in New York City."

"The Village is a part of the city. A lot of progressive college students live there, and I used to hang around with them a lot."

"When was that?"

"Not that long ago; when I was attending Columbia…Lily, I'm only twenty-five. Remember?"

"Mr. Wells, these university students are going to talk about the problems facing China. You Americans wouldn't be interested."

"Lily, I am very interested. I have often heard my parents talk about the many issues China is facing today. Maybe some of your university students want to hear what we Americans have to say. Lily, can I come? Please. I could use a cup of strong Russian coffee on such a rainy day."

"I think you will find it very boring." She wavered.

"Lily, I like to hear what these students have to say." Without hesitation, Jack put his hand on her parasol and held it above her head as raindrops fell on his broad shoulders.

"Oh, Jack." She slowly put her hand into his elbow.

Dodging the puddles, they scurried along the crowded Avenue Joffre, hardly noticing that by the time they reached the Little Moscow Café, the drizzle had already tapered off.

"Hey, Lee Li-wha!"

"Hey, Zheng Ting, why aren't you inside?"

"We just got here." She spun the raindrops off her pink parasol.

"Hello, Jasmine." Jack waved.

"Hi, Mr. Wells. This is my friend, André Chung."

"How do you do?" A bookish young man with wire-rimmed glasses and a French beret extended his hand.

"Hi, I am Jack Wells."

"It's nice to make your acquaintance. I am glad you can come to our political discussion."

"I am here just to listen. I don't speak Chinese."

"Don't worry, Mr. Wells, I speak English. I can translate for you…shall we go in?"

"Sure."

"Good afternoon." A White Russian in a white sash blouse and black Cossack boots greeted them at the door, gesturing with one hand and holding a violin in the other. "We serve some of the best Russian food in Shanghai." He saw Jack looking at the handwritten Cyrillic menu on a little blackboard.

"We are here for a meeting." André Chung cast his eyes about the empty restaurant.

"Follow me." The man said curtly as he started toward the back, passing a large painting of an onion-domed Russian Orthodox Church on the wall. He stopped in front of a nondescript door, watching them all go in before he slammed the door shut. While not happy to see so many Chinese in his restaurant, but he let them meet here anyway. It was a slow afternoon.

"Hey, everybody! Let me introduce you to an American friend, Mr. Jack Wells," André Chung announced loudly.

"Welcome, our American friend!" All heads turned in their direction.

"Where you from?" someone shouted.

"I am from New York City."

"Yes, I know, the Empire State Building, the tallest building in the world."

"Mr. Wells, this is our Professor Kao. He teaches Chinese history at Fudan University." André pointed toward an old Chinese man in a blue gown and black pants. "Professor Kao, this is our American friend, Mr. Jack Wells."

"How do you do, Professor?" Jack leaned over to shake his cold hand.

"American, eh? You speak Chinese?" The professor arched his eyebrows.

"No, but I took a world geography course in college. I understand that China has one of the longest continuous civilizations in the world, more than three thousand years."

"Five thousand years, not three."

"Of course. I meant recorded history, Professor," Jack replied diplomatically.

"Three thousand, five thousand, what is the difference? America has less than two hundred years of history, and it is already much stronger than we are!" one of his students said loudly.

"Mr. Wells, how did America become so strong in such a short time?" another student in a suit and tie asked.

"Well, …we are a democratic Christian nation. We have a capitalistic economic system." Jack looked around the smoke-filled room as he struggled to come up with a good answer.

"Who vant beer?" A middle-aged Russian woman with brassy bleached blond hair suddenly wedged her plump body between him and a skinny Chinese student.

"I could use a beer." Jack raised his index finger.

"I will have one too," said André.

"Do you have any tea?" Lily raised her hand.

"Only Russian teas, no Chinese. Anyone else vant beer?"

A few more hands went up. As they waited for her to count the heads around the table, André Chung took out a piece of crumpled onion paper from his satchel. "Mr. Wells, can you read something I wrote?"

"Okay, let me see."

"André Chung is our resident poet." Someone offered from the other side of the table.

"Why don't you read it? It is your poem."

"My English is not so good. I have a heavy accent."

"Alright, I will give it a try." Flashing a self-conscious smile at Lily, Jack cleared his throat, and started to read:

A Mirage by the East China Sea
By André Chung

Oh, Shanghai, the Pearl of the Orient,
Or should I call you the Whore of the Far East?
From afar, they came; in their images they built
a city of stones, but a place I cannot call my own.

Wide boulevards and tall buildings, but I know
only dark alleyways and squalid dwellings.
A city of wines and flesh, but I see
only a place of starvations and deaths.

Careless gaieties and endless parties, but I see
only battered souls and broken bodies.
In your white bosom, I saw a new dawn, full of hope.

At your cold feet, I cried over my crushed dreams, full of despair.

Oh, Shanghai! You are a city without a country; a city without pity.
You are illegitimate, but you are so beautiful.
As much as I hate how you were born,
in your dazzling lights, my heart is torn!

"*Hen hao, Hen hao!* Very good, very good! Hey, André, one day you may become as famous as Lu Xan," someone shouted.

"*Shie-shie, Beu gan don, beu gan don.* Thank you. I don't deserve such praise. I am humbled just to have my name mentioned next to such a famous writer." André clasped together his folded fists and bowed.

"André, I like how you portray Shanghai, just like the *Tales of Two Cities*." Jack handed back his poem.

"Yes, one Oriental and one Occidental...It was the best of times, and it was the worst of times." André recited. "Charles Dickens is one of my favorite authors."

"Shakespeare is my favorite author." Someone from the back of the room yelled out.

"I am reading Adam Smith's *Wealth of Nations*," another student in a double-breasted suite quickly added.

"Good for you. I am impressed." Jack sat down, but from the corner of his eyes, he could see the Chinese professor shake his head disapprovingly.

"What about studying a little more of our ancient text and see how they have influenced the world!" he grumbled.

"Professor Kao, we all have read the Four Books and studied the Five Classics. The ancient texts taught us about China as it was, but we want to study about China as it could be," André countered.

"Professor Kao, we have not forgotten China's glorious past. We just want to move on with its future. We are a nation of peasants! China must become industrialized! We must learn from the West and adopt their modern technologies and scientific methods! We must do what the Japanese did!" another student said loudly.

"China should also get rid of its rotten feudal Confucianism and adopt the Western democracy!" Still, another shouted.

"You young men seem to think that every idea coming out from the West is superior, but before you abandon your past and rush to copy what the Japanese did, just remember that for millennia, our Celestial Kingdom was most advanced and prosperous country on earth! Shoguns from Japan, Malaccan sultans from Malaysia, and even potentates from Arabia came to learn from us and pay us respect!" the professor said proudly. "Long before the Greeks built their Parthenon or the Romans their little aqueducts, we Chinese had already built the 4,000-mile Great Wall and dug the 1,000-mile Grand Canal! Long before the British ever left their tiny islands, Admiral Zheng Ho's armada of giant ships had already sailed around the Horn of Africa; and long before Adam Smith wrote his book on free trade, we had been trading with other nations for over one-thousand years!" The professor paused to take another long drag on his Great Wall cigarette, which he held between two stained fingers. "I am sure that you all have heard of the Silk Road."

"Yes, Professor Kao, we all know what China had accomplished in its past," the student in the double-breasted suit said calmly. "It is true that we have invented gunpowder, but the West has invented tanks and airplanes! We may have sailed around the world in big junks, but the West is now prowling the Seven Seas in their steel warships! And some of them are pointing at us right now in the harbor!"

"Young man, don't be frightened by the West, or by those Japanese bandits. Even Genghis Khan's mighty empire couldn't conquer us! In the end, they all eventually became like us. Do you know that Kublai Khan spoke Chinese?"

"Professor Kao, that is all well and good, but why do you keep bringing up dead history? Just look at China now!"

Even though Jack didn't understand a lot of the things they were saying, he could feel the emotional intensity in the air. He glanced at Lily's face, flushed and focused; she too got caught up in this little "sit-down" discussion.

"What do you think, Mr. Wells?" André Chung saw him looking in her direction. "Do you think China one day can become as strong as America?"

"I do not doubt that one day China will rise again. We Americans want to help China become a democratic Christian nation just like ours."

"I love everything about your country; I wish China could be like America one day," the student in the double-breasted suit said sincerely.

"Young man, you might love America, but it might not love you back!"

"Why do you say that, Professor? America is our friend."

"You are all too young to know." The professor sighed as his finger slowly traced around the rim of his teacup. "Twenty years ago, when I was an adjunct professor at Peking University, I too believed that everything Western was good and superior; I too wanted to change China in its image. But when the Allied Powers sold China out after World War I by giving away the former German-occupied territories in Northern China to Japan, I began to see the true nature of the so-called democratic West," the old professor said grimly as he took another loud sip of his green tea. "The West likes to take the moral high ground for their beliefs. They preach democracy and freedom, but they don't practice them on other people they have colonized. As I reflect on China's sad history over the past one-hundred years, I see not the West's superiority but its hypocrisy. In the name of free trade, the West drugged our bodies with opium. When we protested, they sent in their troops to teach us a lesson; they ransacked our palaces and forced us to sign unequal treaties, cede our land, and pay ruinous retributions. In the name of love, they poisoned our minds with their religion; and if you don't believe in their God, they'll tell you that you will be condemned to hell. What kind of love is that?" The old professor slammed down his teacup on the table, knocking his Great Wall cigarette to the floor.

The smoke-filled room suddenly turned somber, and his students looked a little chastened as if they were being scolded by their own father.

"Professor Kao, we have not forgotten what the foreigners did to us!"

"How did China fall so far? Everyone looks down on us!" a student cried out in pain. "Even a lowly uneducated English policeman thinks he is better than our esteemed professor!" another shouted.

"Don't despair, young man. Just remember the blood of our Yellow Emperor runs through our veins! It is in our language; it is in our food; it is in our poetry, and it is in the ways we live and die. China is not just a state; it is a state of mind! Born a Chinese, you will always be a Chinese!"

"Professor, not everyone in China is a Han Chinese."

"But if you are, then you should be proud of being Chinese!" the old professor shouted, saliva splattering from his mouth.

"Professor Kao, we are not ashamed of who we are, but at this point of our history, there isn't much we can be proud of!"

"We want to see China become strong again!"

"We all do...we all do." The old professor suddenly slumped into his chair, looking tired and defeated. "China had thirty-six dynasties throughout its long history; I have seen the last dynasty ended in my lifetime and I just hope China will not end in yours."

"Professor Kao, I think if it weren't for that wicked Empress Dowager Tz'u-hsi, China would not be defeated by the British and the Japanese!" Someone in the room said angrily.

"We lost Manchuria because of her! She was weak and incompetent. That woman had no business in governing China!"

"How true." The professor nodded in agreement. "If only we had a good emperor, China wouldn't be in such a sorry state today."

"Ai Yo! Why do we women always get the blame!" Until now sitting quietly at the end of the table, Jasmine unexpectedly burst out, and all eyes abruptly turned toward her.

"Young lady, women cannot be good rulers. That has long been proven!" the professor said patronizingly.

"Why do you say that, Professor?"

"Our ancient adage has a saying: 'When a woman rules, there will be chaos in the land.' It is so because men ruled by intellect and women by emotion. Men want to change things as they should be, but women want to preserve things as they are. Just like the forces of yin-and-yang in the universe, men are stronger, and women are weaker. Fathers will be fathers and sons will be sons, and only then there be harmony under Heaven."

“Zheng Ting, our professor is right.” André Chung looked at her askance. “Empress Dowager Tz’u-hsi did not have Heaven’s Mandate to govern China! She is not even Chinese; she is a Manchu! She was more interested in palace intrigues than in government affairs. Instead of building up China’s navy, she squandered our national treasury on her fancy jewelry and sumptuous Summer Palace, while letting the foreign powers walk all over us!”

“Queen Victoria is a woman,” Jasmine persisted.

“True, but she was there just to keep the throne warm for a male heir.”

The room burst into laughter.

“Queen Victoria ruled England for thirty-nine years, and Empress Dowager Tz’u-hsi ruled for forty-seven, longer than many Chinese emperors could! She was not wicked or ruthless; she was just smarter than most of the men who served under her!” Jasmine rankled.

“Those men were eunuchs, a bunch of yes-men,” André smirked.

“Correction! They were not just yes-men; they were half-men!” The room again broke out laughing.

“That may be so, but how can we be the little women when all we have here are just a bunch of little men?” Jasmine didn’t miss a beat.

“Ha! Ha! Ha! André Chung, your girlfriend has a sharp tongue.”

“She is Shanghainese; what do you expect?”

“Who vant more beer?” The plump White Russian waitress suddenly reappeared.

“No more beer for us.”

"What about you, Amerikun boy?"

"I am with them." Jack just smiled at her.

"You want to eat somethin'? We serve real Russian food, not like those sheety noodle stuff." She stared at him with a bored vodka-drowned expression. Her sullen blue eyes still sparkled behind her false eyelashes, but the weight of living in Shanghai had long squeezed the joy out of her.

"Love to try it sometime."

"Ya, you come back without those cheap Chinamen…You vant a girlfriend?" the Russian waitress winked.

"No, not really."

"Not me; I am too old for you. I know a nice White Russian girl, very beautiful, blue eyes and blond hair. She is a countess."

"A real countess?"

"Yeah, her father used to be a Duke under Tsar Nicholas."

"Really?" Jack mused, *Only in Shanghai.*

"You vant to think about it?" she persisted. "I can bring her here so you can see how beautiful she is. She can be your girlfriend if you can take her to America."

"It sounds very tempting, but no thanks." Jack followed others out of the room.

Outside the Little Moscow Café, dusk had already blanketed the city with a warm glow, and colorful neon began to blink on the wet pavements.

"Mr. Wells, thank you for reading my poem." André Chung shook his hand.

"Thank you for having me. I've enjoyed it."

"Lee Li-wha, I'll see you tomorrow. Bye-bye." Jasmine waved.

"*Ming tian jian*. See you tomorrow." Lily watched them walk away. "Jack, I am glad that you've enjoyed their political discussions. What do you think of Professor Kao?"

"Lily, to tell you the truth, I think he is stuck in the past, and he cannot accept the fact that the world has long since changed and China has not changed with it."

"Yes, China has many problems, and no one seems to know how to solve them…I just wish there was something I could do."

CHAPTER 20

The Marco Polo Bridge Incident

In his suit and tie, Jack tried to cool off in front of a wall-mounted air-conditioner when Mary walked in with a neatly folded *North-China Daily News.*

"Mary, is it always this hot in July?"

"Yes. It will get even hotter in August. We are fortunate—at least we have some air-conditioning in this building. How is Lily?"

"She is doing fine."

"Jack, I think she likes you."

"I like her too." He took the paper from her moist hand.

"Jack, it is not business. But if you ever want to get serious with her, you better keep it discreet around here. Bank policy, you know," Mary said sarcastically.

"Thanks for reminding me."

"Jack, if you need anything else, I will be outside."

"Mary, I'm okay for now." Jack settled into his chair, snapped open the paper, and the bold headline read: "Fighting Breaks Out Between Chinese and Japanese Soldiers on the Marco Polo Bridge!"

"What!" Jack bolted up and tore open the page.

> *Last night, for reasons still unknown, the Chinese and Japanese soldiers started shooting at each other on the Marco Polo Bridge. The Chinese Nationalists were quickly driven off the bridge. Using this incident, the Japanese Imperial Army is now poised to pour down from Peking. Shanghai will be within their reach in ten days...*

"Good morning, Jack." Spencer suddenly appeared at his door.

"Have you seen this?" Jack asked alarmingly.

"Have I seen what?"

"It says here that the Japanese Imperial Army is marching toward Shanghai!"

"Yes, I have heard. Awful, isn't it? I just hope this will not be another 1932."

"What happened in 1932?"

"In 1932, the Japanese used another minor incident involving one of their monks as an excuse to send their Imperial Navy into Shanghai to teach the Chinese a lesson."

"That was just five years ago!"

"Yes. Fortunately, the Japs had the good sense to withdraw from the city after they annihilated Chiang Kai-shek's Nineteenth Route Army."

"Mr. Spencer, what do you think will happen this time?"

"I don't know. But coming on the heel of their recent victories over the Chinese in the North, I am afraid that the Japanese might use this Marco Polo Bridge incident as another excuse to send more troops into China and eventually take over the whole country."

"Mr. Spencer, it says here that Chiang Kai-shek is sending 20,000 of his best German-trained soldiers from his 88th Central

Division to defend Shanghai. Why doesn't he just send them straight up north?"

"Good question. The Generalissimo's army is no match to the mighty Japanese Imperial Army. Many of his Nationalist soldiers are not worth the uniforms on their backs, and some of them are mere boys," Spencer scoffed. "If he picks his fight with the Japs in Peking, he would certainly be wiped out. He is counting on you Americans to do some of the fightings for him."

"I don't understand. What do you mean?"

"Jack, by putting his troops so close to our International Settlement, he is hoping that the Japs might accidentally drop some of their bombs on us foreigners, and then we would have no choice but to get involved in his war."

"That's pretty devious of him."

"A rather brilliant military strategy, if I may say so. Jack, with us fighting on his side, the Generalissimo is hoping that he could preserve his men to crush the Communists in the countryside and kill his sworn enemy, Mao Tse-tung."

"I have heard of that name lately."

"Mao is now the leader of the Chinese Communist party." Spencer puffed on his pipe. "Chiang Kai-shek fears this Mao character because he has millions of angry Chinese peasants willing to die for him. He was often quoted saying that Mao is the disease of the body, and the Japanese are mere superficial wounds of the skin."

"What do you mean?"

"It means that he would rather trade time with space to preserve his armies, so he could first get rid of the disease."

"You mean this Chiang character would rather let tens of thousands of his countrymen die so he can kill just one man?"

"Precisely! This Generalissimo Chiang is a quintessential Chinese warlord. His whole mindset is rooted in Chinese history, where struggles between emperors and rebellious Chinese peasants are the stuff of legends. For one new dynasty to be born, the old one must die a violent death, and Chiang Kai-shek is deathly afraid that this might happen to him." Spencer paused on his pipe and said somberly: "I can still see those half-starving bodies lying in front of our bank. The 1932 refugee problem was bad enough, but I am quite sure this time would be worse. I pray there won't be another war, for the Chinese sake." Without another word, Spencer thrust his pipe back into his pocket and walked out.

The Marco Polo Bridge Incident had put Shanghai on edge. Jack could see fears in the streets and on people's faces.

"Lily, you look worried." Jack rushed over as she stepped off from the tram.

"All my neighbors are very scared. They remember what the Japanese did to them in 1932."

"Were you here then?"

"No, I wasn't, but I can still see some of the burnt-out houses around Chapei. Jack, I am scared too."

"Do you want to skip our lesson today?"

"If you want."

"What do you want to do then?"

"I don't know," Lily stared blankly into the street.

"You want to get something to eat?'

"Alright." She nodded.

"How about we go to the Little Jimmy's? I could use some spicy chili."

"Okay." She followed him across the busy Thibet Road.

As they were making their way along the crowded sidewalk toward French Town, Jack suddenly heard someone shouting. "What is going on over there?"

"I don't know. It looks like some sort of demonstration."

They walked closer, and Lily suddenly gasped, covering her mouth as if she had just seen a ghost. "Oh, my God! It can't be him!"

"Lily, what's the matter?"

"I-I think I know him!"

"Who?" Over a sea of fedoras and black hair, Jack saw a Chinese man thrusting his fist in the air as he shouted into a bullhorn.

"That boy! That man!" She pointed toward a young man pacing back and forth on the park bench, shouting at the crowd surrounding him. "His name is Zhou Hsiao-ming, the boy I was supposed to marry. He looks so different from the way I remember him."

The Number One Son of the House of Zhou had changed a great deal. His body was now fuller, his face was harder, and his voice was angrier. In a well-worn blue cotton Chinese robe and a red armband on his sleeve, he looked more like a union organizer than the rich man's son that he once was.

"My patriotic countrymen," he shouted, tamping down the excited crowd with his palm. "At this moment as I speak, the Japanese Imperial Army is sweeping down from the North toward Shanghai! China's very survival is now in question!"

"Down with the Japanese Imperialists!"

"Down with the Japanese devils!"

Even though Jack didn't understand what the young man was saying, or what the crowd was shouting about, but he could feel the anger in their words.

"My patriotic countrymen, despite his promises, Chiang Kai-shek continues to pour our national resources into his Bandit Extermination Campaign against the Communists while allowing the Japanese Imperial Army to take control of over one-fifth of China and rape tens of thousands of our women! If we let this tragedy continue, China as we know it will soon cease to exist!"

"Chinese must not fight Chinese!"

"Down with Chiang Kai-shek!"

"My countrymen, China is now on its knees! Our cowardly Kuomintang government has done nothing to fight back the Japanese bandits! But I will fight them with my last breath!" He punched his clenched fist into the air.

"I will fight them with the last drop of my blood," an old man cried out wildly.

"I want to kill the Japanese with my bare hands!" another shouted, full of animus.

"Your friend is pretty good at stirring up the crowd," Jack whispered.

"I can't believe it is him." Wide-eyed, Lily shook her head.

The young man surveyed the galvanized crowd, waited, and then said gravely. "My fellow countrymen, as China faces its existential crisis, it is no longer enough to just talk about fighting the Japanese. Now, each of us must choose between the love of yourself and the love for your country, and some of us will have to die so China can live!"

"What can we do? We don't even have guns!"

"We don't know how to fight."

"Yes, this is true; all you intellectual bourgeois know is how to talk a good talk and shout patriotic slogans," he said, staring down contemptuously at a group of university students. "There are things we all can do to resist the Japanese invasion!"

"Like what?"

"You can teach shop owners how to boycott Japanese goods, or you can go to the countryside to help peasants organize guerrilla resistance, or you can go north to Yenan to join Mao's forces. Whatever you choose, you must not stand idly by as our China is being conquered and raped!"

"Young man, you've got to be very careful about urging us to join the Communists. Even if the Blue Shirts don't catch you, the French police might turn you in. I would hate to see your head hung on a lamppost tomorrow," warned an old man.

"The Blue Shirts are Chiang Kai-shek's special secret police," Lily whispered.

"Like Hitler's Gestapo?"

"Something like that. They are everywhere in Shanghai. They will kidnap and murder anyone they suspect is a Communist."

"Even here in the International Settlement?"

"Even here. It makes no difference to them, because they know the English and French police, and even you Americans, will look the other way."

"Whoa, I didn't know practicing politics is such a dangerous business here in Shanghai."

"Jack, Shanghai is not Paris."

"You can say that again." Jack shook his head.

"Jack, I think I hear something." Lily suddenly fixed her ears on a siren approaching from afar. "I think I heard the police siren."

"Me too." Jack watched the nervous crowd began to disperse, pushing them backward.

"Where did he go?" Lily stared at the empty park bench.

"I think he has split. Maybe you will run into him again," Jack draped his arm around her. "Lily, do you still want to go to the Little Jimmy's?"

"What?" she replied absent-mindedly as she cast her eyes about the empty sidewalk. "I wish I had a chance to say hello to him."

"I said do you still want to go to the Little Jimmy's?"

"No. I feel like having a bowl of Chinese noodles," Lily murmured.

"Okay, but you gotta tell me where to go for that."

"Have you ever been to the Great World?"

"What is the Great World? A Chinese restaurant?"

"No. It is a place with lots of restaurants and shops, all under one roof."

"It sounds interesting. I don't mind giving it a try. Why don't you lead the way?"

CHAPTER 21

The Great World

Everything in this Chinese part of Shanghai was so different from the French Town, just a few blocks away. Negotiating their ways past heaps of wet vegetable stands and steaming food stalls, Jack followed Lily into a noisy brick building, teeming with farmers in straw hats, fortune tellers in black skull caps, and barbers with their wet aprons. Packed tightly on the wet concrete floors, loud fish mongers, pushy grain peddlers, and whining vegetable vendors were all hawking at the top of their lungs, drowning out the nervous chirping of farm chickens and the babbling cracking of the caged ducks.

"Wow, this place is wild!" Jack still had that surprised tourist look on his face as they picked their way through swarms of shoppers.

"Jack, many people like to come here to shop, eat, and have fun."

"Do you come here often?"

"Sometimes. I come here with Jasmine to shop. They have lots of little small and cheap stores here."

"What are those?" Jack pointed to a basket of lumpy creatures shaped like crooked cucumbers.

"Sea cucumbers."

"You eat that?"

"Yes, stewed-sea cucumber is a very famous Shanghainese dish," Lily said matter-of-factly.

"I see they sell live crabs here too." Jack walked past a bunch of bamboo baskets.

"Jack, you know what those are?" Lily pointed.

"No, what are they?" Jack leaned over a wooden bucket full of glistening creatures slithering on top of each other. "They look like snakes to me."

"They are eels. Not very pretty to look at, but very delicious. Jack, did you ever have eels cooked in garlic sauce before?"

"Are you kidding me! They look so slimy."

"Want to try it?" Lily taunted him with a sly smile.

"I-I don't think so."

"Your mother doesn't like them either. Jack, let's go upstairs." She pulled on his arm toward a dimly lit stairwell. Curious shoppers stopped on their way down, surprised to see a foreign face in this part of the city. Jack nodded and smiled as he walked up the dirty concrete stairs. *Maybe eating here was not such a good idea. Too late now.*

The smells of cooking permeated the second floor. Jack quietly followed Lily down a long corridor lined on either side with small restaurants and noodle-and-rice shops, each claiming their regional specialties with white banners hung above their doors. In front of a tiny noodle shop, Jack stopped to watch a burly man swinging a long piece of soft dough into the air, stretching it, and then twisting it into what looked like a large pretzel. "What is he making?"

"Shanghai stretched noodles."

"How many?" asked a stout woman, holding two steaming bowls in her hands.

“Two.” Lily put up her fingers.

“Please sit; please sit.”

They followed her into a narrow room where mismatched tables and chairs were strewn on a well-worn linoleum floor, and bare lightbulbs hung from a dark ceiling. Jack looked uneasily around as they waited for the lady to take away the eaten noodle bowls and used chopsticks.

“Not too many foreigners come here.” Lily noticed him shifting uncomfortably on the wobbling chair.

“I can see that.” Jack looked down at a pair of chopsticks placed haphazardly on the table.

“Jack, do you know how to use chopsticks?” Lily picked out another pair from a bamboo holder.

“Lily, do they have a fork?” Jack clumsily held his chopsticks with his fingers.

“I don’t think so, but I can ask. What would you like to eat?”

“Can I see the menu?”

“I don’t think they have any menu.” Lily pointed to strips of red paper hanging on the wall.

“They are in Chinese.” Jack stared at the cursive writing. “I will have whatever you’re having.”

“I want their Shanghai stretched noodles.”

“Okay, I will have the same. Lily, can you order me a beer?” Jack uneasily glanced around the dingy space, and suddenly he spotted a man sitting by the kitchen door. “Lily, don’t look, but I think your friend is back there.”

“Oh, my God, it is him.” Lily slowly turned around. “I have to go over there to say hello to him.”

"I don't think he wants to—"

"Zhou Hsiao-ming!" Lily called out in a restrained voice.

The man abruptly looked up, startled.

"Zhou Hsiao-ming, it's me, Lee Li-wha!" She moved closer.

"Lee Li-wha!" He finally recognized her. "What are you doing here?"

"I saw you at the demonstration," Lily whispered.

"You did?"

"Yeah. I thought I would never see you again. Eh, I am really happy to see you!"

"Ni hao ma?" He gazed at her.

"Hen Hao, I'm well. Have you eaten yet?"

"Just finished. Their noodles are pretty good..." He struggled to find words. Standing in front of him, he saw a pretty and polished young woman, not the same peasant girl he remembered. "Lee Li-wha, I can see you have done well."

"Yes, I am doing okay. I am really glad that I bumped into you because I want to thank you for what you did for me."

"For what?"

"For letting me freed."

"Bu yao shie. You need not thank me. Lee Li-wha, I am just sorry about what happened to your brother. Have you heard anything from him? I haven't been back home for a while."

"People said that he joined the army."

"Which army? The Nationalists or the Red Army?"

"I don't know which one. How are your father and mother? Are they in good health?"

"Not so good. The imported Japanese silks have killed much of my father's business." He sighed. "And he had lost all his land because of some bad investments he made in Shanghai."

My father almost lost his land too, Lily thought. "So, what are you doing now? Are you still attending university?"

"No. I had to quit. I am now working at the Commercial Press in Chapei."

"I live in Chapei. How come I have never run into you?"

"I work at night."

"Hsiao-ming, I could have never imagined that you would become a factory worker. You look pale."

"I am okay. I have found that working with my hands gives me so much more meaning in life; now I have many proletarian friends. I am now a member of the Shanghai Workers' Union."

"I work at the New Hope Church in Hongkew."

"Really? What do you do over there?" He sounded almost disappointed. "Are you religious?"

"Yes, I am now a Christian. I help out at the church and do some translations for Reverend Wells. Hsiao-ming, I am not too far from where you work. Why don't you drop by if you have some time?"

"Sorry, I don't believe in their God."

"Hsiao-ming, you don't have to believe everything our Reverend has to say. He is here to help China."

"Did he have anything to do with it?" He looked past her.

Lily turned around and saw Jack walking toward them. "Oh, don't worry; he is an American. He was at the demonstration too."

"Is he your boyfriend?"

"Jack, this is Zhou Hsiao-ming." Lily quickly turned around.

"How do you do? I'm Jack Wells." Jack extended out his hand.

"How do you do?" Zhou Hsiao-ming nodded.

"Hey, I saw you at the demonstration. You were pretty good."

"Thank you."

"I want you to know that we Americans are all rooting for China."

"I am glad, but I am afraid your American government is supporting the wrong man," he replied curtly.

"Really? I've heard that your President Chiang is now bravely resisting the Japanese up in the north."

"What you have heard is just propaganda by the Kuomintang government. Instead of fighting the Japanese, Chiang Kai-shek is using the weapons sent by your American government to fight Mao Tse-tung in the west and kill many innocent Chinese people in the process," Zhou Hsiao-ming said flatly.

"That is not what I've heard."

"Of course not. All your Western governments are on his side… Mr. Wells, perhaps we can have this discussion at another time. This place is crawling with Chiang's spies. I don't want them to notice me standing here talking to you." Zhou Hsiao-ming abruptly grabbed his hat off the table. "It's nice meeting you…Lee Li-wha, *tsai jian;* until we meet again."

"Hsiao-ming, drop by whenever you have some time. *Tsai jian.* Take care of your health." She watched him hastily walk out of the crowded noodle shop.

"Lily, he doesn't like us Americans, does he?"

"I don't know; he seems to be a different person from the way I remember him."

"Lily, by the way he looked at you, I think he might be regretting that he didn't marry you."

"Jack, that was a long time ago. We all have chosen our separate paths in life," Lily said pensively.

CHAPTER 22

Bombs Over Shanghai

As Chiang Kai-shek's elite troops started to set up defensive posts around the North Railroad Station in Chapei, the Japanese Imperial Navy also began to send more battleships into the Shanghai Harbor. Even though no fire had been exchanged, everyone dreaded the inevitable.

"Good morning, Jack." Mary walked into his office with his morning tea.

"Good morning, Mary. You are rather chirpy today," Jack said glumly.

"What can we do? We all have to go on living," Mary replied casually. "Jack, Bobby and I are going to see a movie. Would you like to join us?"

"What movie are you going to see?"

"*The Good Earth*."

"I've heard it is very good. It got rave reviews back in the States. Have you read Pearl Buck's book?"

"No, not yet. I want to see the movie first. Why don't you ask Lily to come with us? I think she should see it. It is about China."

"I will ask her. When do you guys want to go?"

"How about three-thirty this Saturday? We can all meet up in front of the Grand Theater. Do you know where it is?"

"Sure, I know where it is."

From the other side of the Nanking Road, Jack looked up at the noble Chinese peasant faces of Paul Muni and Luise Rainer glowing on the Grand Theater's marquee. "Lily, I heard the movie is very good. I think you will like it."

"Jasmine saw it with her boyfriend, and she thought it was pretty good too, but she doesn't understand why Miss Anna May Wong did not play O-Lan; she was born in America, and she speaks fluent English and Chinese. Have you seen her in *Shanghai Express*?"

"Is she the one who played next to Marlene Dietrich?"

"Yes. I think they should have given her a chance."

"The Hollywood studio might have their reasons; I don't know…I think I see them." Mary saw them approaching.

Jack quickened his steps.

"Hey, guys, I've got bad news for you. The four o'clock show is sold out, but we got the seven o'clock tickets," Mary hollered.

"Jack, I told her if she wants to see a movie about China, we can all just drive out of Shanghai and see the real thing," Bobby quipped jokingly.

"Bobby!" Mary gently nudged his arm. "Do you see all these Chinese people? They all want to see this movie too."

"Just joking. Hey, we got three hours to kill, how about we go get a drink? Cathay Hotel is not far from here."

"That sounds good. I could use a drink," Jack agreed heartily.

"Lily, how about you and I go shopping and let the men go drinking?"

"C'mon, Mary, it wouldn't be any fun without you girls."

"Okay, Bobby. I hope their Filipino band is still playing there."

Despite the threat of war—or perhaps because of it—Nanking Road was packed with motorcars, rickshaws, and anxious shoppers.

"People are scared," Lily whimpered.

"Are you okay?"

"Mm, I am okay…I just hope there won't be any war."

"I hope not."

"Jack, what is going on over there?" Lily suddenly looked up and saw something flying in the sky.

"Don't know. Maybe it's an air show." Jack squinted.

"I think that's a Northrop," Bobby looked up at the four propeller airplanes buzzing up and down over the harbor.

"What is a Northrop?" Mary cuddled in his arm.

"It's an American airplane, one of the best planes they've ever made."

Then, they heard loud cheers and boos as a tall plume of water shot up in the middle of the Whangpoo River.

"What are they doing? Are they fighting?" Lily became alarmed.

"I don't know…I don't think so." Jack strained his eyes to get a closer look. "Oh, my God! I think they are trying to sink the *Izumo* cruiser!"

"Holy shit! You are right!" Bobby cried out.

"Bobby, I think we'd better go back!" A frightening realization came over Jack: the much-anticipated war between the Chinese and Japanese had just started, right in front of their eyes! But before he had a chance to pull Lily away, he saw two of the Northrop planes inexplicably start to bank toward them, and he could even see the red and blue sunburst of the Chinese Nationalist flags painted on the plane's tails as the popping sounds of the propellers buzzed louder and louder toward them. And then he spotted four black dots hurtling down toward them from the blue skies. "Jesus Christ! They look like real bombs!"

"Shit! Those are real bombs!" Bobby was flabbergasted.

Screaming erupted all around them as the spooked weekend shoppers, foreign tourists, and office workers looked up with sheer terror in their eyes. Before anyone could run, in an instant, incendiary explosions blew everything into their faces. Shards of window glass showered down from above; pieces of shattered bricks crashed down on their heads; hats, shoes, and torn limbs flew up into the air. A pleasant Saturday afternoon had unexpectedly turned into a pandemonium of terror, and the breezy summer air quickly thickened with the dense smoke of explosions and pungent smells of burning flesh. Shiny foreign motorcars smoldered in orange fire, wounded men and women moaned in pools of bright red blood, and desperate wailing for help echoed between the crumbling walls. Hundreds of Chinese and foreigners alike lay side by side, wounded or dead.

Jack fell onto the ground, and for a moment, he wasn't sure if he was wounded or not. He looked around the carnage and tried to move away from a maimed body when he saw Lily was lying a few feet away. "Lily, are you okay?"

"Yes, I am alright…I think," Lily sat up in a daze, wiping the dust off her face.

"Old Man Heaven! Why are you doing this to us?" a Chinese woman pleaded on her knees.

"In God's name, what's the bloody meaning of this?" an Englishman shouted into the skies as if the airplanes could hear him.

Wheezing and coughing, Bobby staggered up. "Goddamit, I'm bleeding. Mary, are you okay?"

"Yes, I think I am okay." She sat near a mutilated Chinese woman with her dead child lying beside her.

"For the love of God, where is my husband?" an American woman shouted.

"Sweet Jesus, what the hell just happened?" an English woman screamed, staring at her companion's blood splatter over the sidewalk.

"The Japs just dropped their bombs on us!" someone yelled out amidst the chaos.

"No, it is the Chinese! I saw them with my own eyes."

Then, Jack heard another ominous buzzing overhead and saw two more bombs flying towards the nearby Palace Hotel. He jumped up, grabbed Lily's hand and started to run. Bobby and Mary quickly scrambled after them toward the Cathay Hotel. A doorman lay dead at the front door, and the hotel manager stood inside blocking the terrified Chinese begging to get in.

"My goodness! Are you people okay?" The manager cracked open the door, letting them in, one at a time, and then quickly locked it behind them. "Sir, I am afraid we don't have any staff to serve you at this moment. We don't even have a chair for you to sit down."

"It's okay; thank you, Freddy. We only have some nicks and scrapes, nothing serious. Just go take care of the more seriously wounded," Jack mumbled, shaking off the debris from his hair as he crumpled down on the marble floor next to the crowded reception desk.

"Have you heard?" A man in a bloodied white flannel plopped down next to him. "They have just bombed the Great World; over a thousand Chinese were killed! I simply cannot fathom why they would do such a thing to their people."

"I think they are trying to drag us into the war," Jack recalled what his boss had said just a few days ago.

"This Chiang Kai-shek fellow is bloody mad!" Wiping the blood off his face, the man called out to the frazzled hotel manager. "I say, my good man, would you be so kind as to give me a glass of bubbly and a telephone?"

"So sorry, sir, I am afraid all our telephone lines are dead."

"Oh, then a glass of bubbly will do."

"I hear the sirens of fire engines. I think the bombing has stopped. Let's get the hell out of here!" Bobby jumped up, reaching out for Mary's hand.

"Yeah, let's go." Jack helped Lily struggle on her feet.

They scrambled out the hotel, scampering under the shadows of the bombed-out buildings, where the broken walls looked like scarred faces and shattered windows empty eye sockets. The bustling Bund stood still, crowded trams abandoned and sidewalk cafés deserted.

"In my wildest dream, I could not have imagined what had just happened! Guys, I think we have just witnessed the beginning of the war," Jack said grimly, standing in front of his apartment building.

"Man, I feel sorry for those people. Just like that, they are all dead." Bobby shook his head. "What a day! Are you guys gonna be okay?"

"Yeah, we are okay."

"I am glad that none of us are hurt. Lily, I am sorry we dragged you guys into this."

"Mary, it is not your fault." Lily wrapped her arms around Mary, their cheeks wet with tears.

"Goodnight. See you guys tomorrow." Bobby waved.

Lily nervously followed Jack into the building. For the first time in her life, she found herself standing in a man's apartment, all alone.

"Lily, would you like to have a cup of tea?"

"Okay."

"I don't have any Chinese teas, just English Breakfast or Earl Grey."

"Any tea would be fine."

"I need to boil some water first. The bathroom is down the hall. Would you like to take a shower?"

"No! I just need to wash off all this blood," Lily answered tensely.

"The towel is behind thc door."

"Okay." She dashed into the bathroom and locked the door behind her. A few minutes later, she emerged in the same dirty clothes.

"Here is your tea." Jack handed her a porcelain cup.

"Thank you."

"Sorry I don't have any clean clothes for you to change into."

"It is okay, Jack." She put her lips to the cup, supping loudly.

"What a day. I am glad that you weren't hurt."

"I am glad you are okay, too."

"Lily, I think you'd better stay here for the night. I don't think it is safe for you to go back to Chapei…"

Silence.

"I will sleep on the sofa." Self-consciously, Jack led Lily into the living room. As they approached the window, they saw a squadron of Japanese airplanes buzzing in the distance and orange flames shooting up on the other side of Soochow Creek.

"Oh my God! They are dropping bombs over Chapei!" Lily gasped, putting her hand over her mouth.

"Oh, my God! You are right!" Jack could not tell where Chapei ended and where Hongkew began, but he immediately feared that his parents might be in danger. Abruptly, he ran toward the telephone. "Operator! Can you connect me to the New Hope Church in Hongkew? Hurry!"

"I'm sorry, sir, all the lines into Hongkew and Chapei are dead," an unflappable female voice calmly answered.

"You don't have any telephone line into the area at all?" Jack asked urgently.

"Not as far as I know. So sorry."

Then he heard a click on the other end. "Shit!"

"What happened?"

"All the lines into Hongkew are dead. Lily, I gotta go over there to check up on my parents." Jack grabbed his jacket off the sofa.

"Jack, it is a long walk from here. Why don't you give Bobby a call? Maybe you can borrow his car."

"I just hope Bobby's phone still works." After a few rings, Jack heard his voice. "Hey, Bobby, can I borrow your car? I gotta go over there to check up on my parents."

"C'mon, Jack, the Japs ain't stupid. They are not gonna drop bombs on their own people."

"But from where I am standing, I can't tell."

"Jack, from my window, I don't see any fireballs on the Hongkew side. I think they are just trying to bomb Chapei."

"Bobby, I just want to make sure my parents are okay."

"Okay, come over. I am gonna drive you there."

CHAPTER 23

Chapei in Ruins

"Mary! Jack and Lily are here! I'm gonna drive them to the New Hope Church," Bobby yelled out as he opened the door.

"Okay, be careful...Hi, Lily, you need to change out of those dirty clothes. I think I have something that might fit you." Mary emerged from the bathroom, brushing her wet hair.

"Thank you, Mary. I am going to the church with Jack."

"Lily, why don't you stay here? Bobby told me that the Shanghai Volunteer Corps has already started to put up barricades over the bridge. If you don't have a residence pass, they might not let you back in."

"Mary, don't worry; she is with me."

"Jack, you don't want to take the chance."

"Mary, there is no point for me to stay here. The Reverend might need my help."

"Lily, are you sure? You want me to go with you?"

"Why don't you girls come along?"

"A friend of mine has just told me that the Japs have taken over Nantao, and they are shooting at any Chinese man who looks like a

Nationalist soldier. This reminds me of 1932 all over again," Bobby said somberly as he drove down the Avenue Joffre.

Outside of their car windows, they could see all the crossroads and alleyways leading into the French Town from the Chinese City of Nantao were being hastily sealed off with barbed-wire fences. Jack could see French policemen, with rifles slung on their shoulders, standing alertly by the wooden barricades. The invisible border that separated the foreigners' Shanghai and the rest of China was now ever so apparent. They looked on in silence as masses of frightened Chinese men, women, and children pressed their desperate faces against the barbed-wire gates, frantically pleading to get in.

"Lily, are you okay?" Jack saw Lily slumped into the backseat, almost too ashamed to look.

"Where are you people going?" A red-turbaned Sikh policeman in brown khaki stopped their car as they approached the Thibet Bridge.

Bobby rolled down his window. "We are going to Hongkew."

"Sir, I hope you people are aware of the fact that on the other side of this bridge there is a war going on. I advise you to stay here until things settle down a bit."

"I know, but we are not going to Chapei; we are going to the New Hope Church in Hongkew. I don't think there is a war going on over there."

"Is that young Chinese lady going with you?"

"Yes, she is."

"Does she have a residence pass?"

"Eh…no, but she is with us."

"Sir, can you see those Chinese on the other side of the barricade? They all want to get over to our side, and she wants to leave, but why?"

"Lily, are you sure you want to go?" Bobby turned around.

"Yes."

"Young lady, you better listen to your man. The whole International Section is now sealed off from the Chinese who don't have a residence pass."

"I know," Lily whimpered.

"Suit yourself. Make sure you come back with these two nice Americans, or else I won't let you in." The Sikh policeman waved them to move on.

"Jack, remind me to get her a residence pass next time," Bobby grumbled as he stepped on the gas pedal.

In disbelief, they looked on at the destruction of Chapei unfolded along the Thibet Road. As they slowly drove past shuttered storefronts and abandoned rickshaws, they could see fireballs flaring up from burning houses, and they could hear the machine-gun sounds echoing in the alleyways. Helpless men carrying their family belongings on their shoulders, frightened women with babies wrapped on their backs, and kids without their parents, all wandered aimlessly in the street, hoping to find a place to sleep or to sit down.

"This is bad…this is gonna be worse than 1932." Bobby shook his head.

The situation at the New Hope Church was not much better. They soon found themselves standing in the middle of a noisy crowd of old Chinese parishioners and their families, lying in the aisles and sleeping on the pews; their belongings were strewn everywhere on the floor.

"Jack, I am glad you are here." Jack heard his mother's voice as he gingerly stepped between the tired bodies and grungy cloth bundles. Her neatly coiffed hair was out of place and her face smeared with dirt.

"Mother, are you okay?" Jack grabbed her arms.

"I am at my wit's end!"

"Where is Dad? Is he okay?"

"I don't know; he is trying to get in touch with other churches to see if they can help, but all the lines are dead. We have too many wounded, and we don't even have a doctor here. We need food, medicine, blankets," his mother said rapidly.

"Ma, I will see what I can do."

"Mrs. Wells, I am Bobby Ferguson. I have a car. I can go back to get some food and medicine for you." Bobby stepped up to shake her hand.

"Bless you, Mr. Ferguson. That would be a tremendous help."

"Hi, I am Mary. What can I do to help?"

"Bless you all; I don't even know where you can start." She sounded flustered. "Jack, why don't you go see what your father might need."

Just then, Jack saw his father walk in from the garden.

"Are you okay, Dad?"

"As okay as I can be, Son." He looked tired and weary.

"Reverend, I'm Bobby Ferguson. I am fixin' to get some food and medicine. Is there anything else you might need?" Bobby shook his hand.

"I don't know. Mr. Ferguson here's two hundred dollars. That's all I have; get whatever you can." He thrust a stack of dollar bills into Bobby's hand.

"It's okay, I got money," Bobby said, pushing back the Reverend's hand.

"Dad, I got a thousand bucks saved up."

"Son, by the looks of it, I may need every dollar I can get," he said glumly.

"Reverend, I'm Mary Lane. I have some money too."

"Thank you all." The Reverend then turned to Lily. "I think you better stay here with us tonight. Mrs. Lin told me that just about every house in your neighborhood had been burnt down. Chapei is in total ruins."

"Oh, my God!" Lily cried out.

"Lily, don't worry. Reverend and I will make you comfortable in our study." Mrs. Wells stroke gently on her arm.

"Thank you." Lily wanted to cry—she was homeless again.

"Lily, I have slept in that room before. It is not that bad." Jack moved closer.

"Lily, you can always stay with us," Mary volunteered.

"Thank you, Mary. I will see you guys tomorrow." Lily tried to hold back her tears.

"Are you going to be okay?" Jack wanted to hug her.

"Mm." She nodded, "Are you coming back tomorrow?"

"Yes, I'll be back tomorrow." Jack squeezed her hand reassuringly.

Safely back in his apartment, Jack poured himself a tall scotch and took a long swallow as he stood by the window watching the burning fires still raging over Chapei. He could hear the dull explosions in the distance and smell the gunpowder coursing through the air. Jack felt like he was standing on an island surrounded by a sea of violent storms; but she was out there, all alone. For the past few months, Jack had found himself thinking about Lily more often than he ever thought about Joann. He began to miss her long before his Saturday dance lessons. In his heart, Jack knew that he was falling for this Chinese girl. He drained his scotch, sat down at his desk, and began to write.

Dear Joann,

By now, you probably already know that there is a war going on here in Shanghai, and many people have been killed...even though we foreigners are not involved in their war, Shanghai is no longer safe for you to visit. I think you better put your trip on hold. I don't know how all this will end. I am sorry that this unexpected event has changed our plan....

CHAPTER 24
Escaping from Shanghai

The fighting between the entrenched Chiang Kai-shek's 88th Division and the Japanese Imperial Navy dragged on from summer into autumn. 1937, the Year of the Ox, had turned into a year of merciless killings. With their tanks relentlessly shelling on the ground and airplanes pelting from the air, most of the 100,000 of Chiang Kai-shek's elite German-trained soldiers stationed around Shanghai were slaughtered. Many in the West condemned the Japanese brutalities, but no one came to China's aide. To eulogize these brave men, Mme. Chiang Kai-shek—now hiding in Chungking, a thousand miles inland—was quoted in the *North-China Daily News,* saying: "They must die so that China can live."

But the imminent Japanese victory didn't bring any joy to General Suzuki; he was incensed because he was not able to crush Chiang's army in just one month as he had confidently predicted. Now, he was hell-bent on teaching these insolent Chinese soldiers a lesson. He ordered 10,000 more fresh troops from Japan to finish the job. Soon the Japanese blue-legged marines began to roam the streets of Chapei, randomly shooting anyone they thought might be an escaping Chinese soldier. Shots often rang out in the dead of night.

The killings had become so routine that people went on with their sleep, pretending not to hear the last gasping cries of these Chinese soldiers. Standing on the Thibet Bridge each morning, people would stare in mournful silence at the lifeless bodies drifting below, floating against the algae-covered embankment until they were gathered up by the Chinese coolies hired by the Shanghai Municipal Government.

Despite the barricades, desperate Chinese refugees, by the thousands, began to pour into the International Settlement as Shanghailanders looked on with hostile stares at these haggard Chinese men, women, and children wandering on the crowded Bund, scrounging through garbage cans during the day and hunkering down on the well-manicured lawns at night. The big cruise ships had long since departed, and the tugboat whistles had gone silent; only a few intrepid sampans remained in the harbor, darting in and out beneath the gray Japanese warships, trying to sell snacks and souvenirs to the sailors. The bright lights along the Bund dimmed, the careless gaieties turned somber, and even the once late-night-hopping nightclubs shut down early.

At work, Jack often gazed out at the gray Shanghai Harbor as he recalled the first time when he set his eyes on these once bustling waters.

"I see you couldn't concentrate either." Spencer walked in, arms folded.

"How can I?" Jack pointed to a row of Japanese battleships moored in the middle of the harbor.

"Good heavens, I think they have added a few more ships since last night," Spencer gasped. "Jack, do you know they are also moving some of their battleships up the Yangtze River toward Nanking as we speak?"

"Really? I didn't know that."

"The Japanese are planning to attack Nanking from all sides with their army and navy. They want to finish off Chiang Kai-shek once and for all."

"This war is going from bad to worse." Jack shook his head. "I guess his strategy of trading time for space didn't work."

"It doesn't look like it, does it? Jack, Nanking is the seat of his government, and if the Japanese ever conquer it, he is finished, and China is finished," he intoned gravely.

"I just hope Chiang Kai-shek's army would put up a good fight before that happens."

"Jack, I am afraid that is unlikely. Chiang and his generals have already fled to Chungking. What a bunch of cowards!"

"Is there anything we in the West could do?"

"Like what? I am afraid that the Chinese have to fight out this one on their own. Oh, by the way, how are your parents managing their refugee problems at the church?"

"As well as they can, I guess. It is getting harder and harder to find any food to buy around the city. Many Chinese farmers are now afraid to come into the city, and the only place I can get some fresh vegetables is at the Hongkew Market in Little Tokyo."

"Just as I've always feared, things are getting from bad to worse. Jack, I think 1937 might turn out to be the beginning of the end for China," Spencer said gravely.

As the fighting between the Japanese and Chinese ground into late fall, Jack began to spend more and more time with Lily. On weekends, he would go with her to the Hongkew Market to pick up bags of rice, bundles of vegetables, and a few pounds of meat to help his parents feed the hungry parishioners and their families living in the New Hope Church. Even though Jack had never liked shopping, now he actually looked forward to spending his Saturdays watching Lily picking up this vegetable and examining that piece of pork. And after shopping, they would share a big bowl of stir-fried noodles in the car, just like a married couple.

On this Saturday, as Jack slowly pulled up the black Ford next to the church, he saw four Japanese Bluejackets dragging two young Chinese soldiers out of the front door. Then he heard a few loud pops. Two lifeless bodies slumped right in front of him. Jack froze as he watched the Japanese soldiers blithely drove away with his father running after them, waving his fist: "They are mere boys! What kind of Godless people are you?"

"Dad, are you okay? What happened?" Jack rushed toward him.

"I tried to hide these two young soldiers in the church, but they found them...I wish I had the power to stop them." his father shook his head feebly.

"Dear, you did your best. I will get someone to bury the bodies." Jack heard his mother's stoic voice.

"Mother, are you okay?"

"Jack, this is not the first time they did this. The Japanese are hunting down these poor Chinese soldiers like animals. They have no more places to hide." His mother gritted her teeth as she tried to ease his father back into the church. "Dear, shall we go in?"

"God bless their souls." His father mumbled.

"Mrs. Wells, do you need any help?"

"No, Lily. I can manage," she replied numbly. "Why don't you and Jack go get the groceries?"

"Okay." Lily nodded. She slowly walked back to the car and popped open the trunk. Suddenly, she heard a whispering voice coming from a crack between the church wall and an old house.

"Psst...are they gone?"

"Yes." She abruptly turned around and saw a man crouching behind a piece of loose board.

"Good, Lee Li-wha."

Frightened by the stranger calling out her name, she stood still for a moment and then she heard him calling out again, "Lee Li-wha, it is me."

"Zhou Hsiao-ming?" She saw a figure slowly crawl out from the shadow, and she recognized his bloody face. "What happened to you?"

"Mei guan-shie. It doesn't matter." He staggered toward her, almost stumbled.

"Lily, what are you doing over there?" Jack rushed over. "Oh, my God, another wounded soldier!"

"No, Jack, this is Zhou Hsiao-ming."

"Who?"

"You two have met before."

"We have?" Jack took a closer look at him. "Oh, yes, of course, your friend."

"Hsiao-ming, you are bleeding. You need to see a doctor."

"No, no doctor." He struggled to stand up straight.

"Lily, we better get him inside quick before anyone sees him."

"Where did he come from?" The Reverend sounded relieved; *at least this one is still alive.*

"Reverend, this is Zhou Hsiao-ming, the boy I was supposed to—"

"Oh, yes, yes, that young man.... The Japanese marines were just here. I am so sorry I couldn't do anything to help your friends."

"Lee Li-wha, are they all dead?" His eyes fixed intently on her.

"Yes, Hsiao-ming, I am sorry."

"I shouldn't have told them to come out from their hiding. I told them that this foreigner's church would be safer. It is all my fault...it is all my fault."

"I am Mrs. Wells. Let me see your head." Jack's mother walked up, lifting off his cap. "You got a big gash behind your left ear, and I can see your bone. You are lucky the bullet didn't hit your brain." Like an experienced nurse, she gently started to remove the dried blood from his tangled hair.

"Dear, you had a lot of practice lately," the Reverend said affectionately.

"Let me go find some bandages. You may have to see a doctor." She stood up, brushing back her hair from her forehead.

"Thank you, but no doctors," Zhou Hsiao-ming mumbled in English.

"We don't even have a bottle of iodine left, and I hate to see your wound get infected."

"Hsiao-ming, are you sure you don't want to see a doctor?"

"Lee Li-wha, I'm okay. There are many Japanese spies around here." He tried to stand up when one of the parishioners suddenly burst in, shouting breathlessly: *"Bu Hao Na! Bu Hao Na!* Bad news! Japanese devils!"

"Quick, Jack, help me hide him under the pulpit!" The Reverend jerked him up violently as he raised his other arm. "Be calm! Everyone, please sit down!"

"Please sit down, everyone! Let's pretend to pray," Mrs. Wells shouted.

"Son, let's hide him under here!" The Reverend lifted the white cloth cover, just in time before a group of Japanese sentries appeared at the front door, waving their rifles.

"Gentlemen! Please have some respect for the sanctity of the house of worship!" the Reverend barked sternly in his booming voice. The soldiers halted their steps as their commander, dressed in a brown military uniform, forcefully barged in between them, brandishing a pistol. "Someone said he saw another wounded Chinese soldier!"

"No more wounded soldiers, Honorable Captain," Reverend Wells replied ingratiatingly as he slowly walked away from the pulpit.

"Search!" The captain waved his pistol, his eyes boring into the frightened parishioners as the soldiers fanned out of the room and into the garden. They didn't find any more Chinese soldiers, just an old man skulking behind the rock cropping.

"As I have told you, Honorable Captain, there are no more Nationalist soldiers hiding here," the Reverend said calmly.

"We will be back again! If I ever find another Chinese soldier hiding in your church, I will shut it down! Understand, Reverend!"

"Horse feather!" Mrs. Wells angrily pushed him aside. The harsh tone of this matronly, mild-mannered white woman surprised the captain. He blustered something in Japanese as he took another harsh glance around the room, hoping someone would squeal. "If any of you tries to help a Chinese soldier escape, I will shoot you! Understand!"

"Dad, thank God they didn't come up here." Jack could hear a collective sigh of relief after all the Japanese soldiers left the church.

"Son, I am sure they will be back again. I feel sorry for those poor Chinese soldiers. The Japanese are hunting them down like animals, and they have no place to hide."

"Let's see how he is doing." Jack's mother quickly lifted the cloth cover, extending out her hand. "Young man, you are quite fortunate they didn't search up here."

"Thank you." He staggered to his feet.

"Hsiao-ming, you don't look too good."

"Lee Li-wha, I am okay. Please thank them for their help…I will leave as soon as it gets dark."

"But where can you go?"

"I will go back home. I think I will be safe there."

"Hsiao-ming, that's eighty li from here!"

"Young man, I don't think you can travel anywhere in your condition. You need to stay in bed for a while." Mrs. Wells seemed to have understood what they were saying.

"Mother, he can stay in my apartment for a few days," Jack volunteered.

"But how can you get him out of here without someone noticing him?"

"I can hide him in the trunk." Da Tu stepped up.

"That sounds like a good idea."

"Son, you think you can get him across the bridge without them searching your car?"

"Dad, I have crossed the Thibet Bridge many times before, and some of these guards know my name. Besides, they usually don't search us Americans anyway."

"Jack, call us as soon as you get back to your apartment."

"Mother, don't worry. I'll call you. Da Tu, why don't you get the car? We will meet you around the back."

"Mrs. Wells, I will go with Jack in case he might need some help."

"You two be careful. Come back as soon as you can."

CHAPTER 25
Going Up to the Mountains

As their car slowly came to a stop at the foot of the Thibet Bridge, Jack could hear the guttural voices of the Japanese sentries, barking orders at a group of well-dressed Chinese holding their residence passes.

"Don't worry; you're with mc." Jack squeezed Lily's hand.

"Out! Out!" One of the sentries peeked into their black Ford, motioning for Lily to get out.

"What are you doing? I am an American, and she is with me!" Jack shouted from the other side.

"Does she have a residence pass?"

"Yes, yes, I have a pass." With both hands, Lily presented him with a piece of folded paper. The young Japanese sentry abruptly grabbed her hands, smiling at her lustfully. "Very soft, just like a geisha girl."

"Hey, get your hands off her!" Jack quickly ran over, fist clenched, ready to take a swing.

"You ought to be very careful not to punch one of our soldiers, my American friend." A Japanese officer came up from behind, slapping his heavy hand on Jack's shoulder. Instinctively, he swung around.

"I recognize you!"

"You are?" Jack softened his stand.

"I'm Captain Akira Tanaka's friend, and I saw you two talking in the Akashio Restaurant a while back."

"That's right; Akira is a very good friend of mine."

"His friend is my friend too." The captain smiled. "Open the gate!"

"Thank you, sir! Thank you, sir!" With shooting cap in hand, Da Tu made several quick bows before getting back into the car. As he slowly drove away from the barricades, he looked into the rear-view mirror. "Boss, so happy they don't open trunk."

"Me too."

As their black Ford inched up to his apartment, Jack spotted two French policemen, rifles slung over their shoulders, slowly walking toward them. "Man, this doesn't look good." He quickly got out of the car and greeted them cheerfully. "Bonjour, officers."

"Bonjour." They smiled without stopping.

"Have a good day, sirs," Jack tried to sound casual as he watched them walk past him. He quickly slipped back into the car. "I don't think they suspect anything."

"Jack, does your apartment have a garage?"

"No, it doesn't."

"What shall we do now?" Lily glanced at the back window.

"Maybe we can let him out in some back alley."

"Okay, boss. Where?" Da Tu put the car in gear.

"But we still have to take him back here, and these two policemen might still be here."

"What do you suggest?"

"Maybe we can let him out somewhere outside of the city and wait in the car until it gets dark."

"Lily, where is his home again?"

"It's about eighty li or sixty miles west from here…Jack, you are not thinking of driving him there right now?"

"Why not? Since we have to wait a few hours before it gets dark anyway."

"Uncle Tu, is that okay with you?"

"No problem, Miss Lee."

The dust began to kick up under their tires as the city began to recede behind their black Ford.

"Uncle Tu, how much longer?" Lily asked impatiently

"Miss Lee, not too far now. We left the city. Country over there." Da Tu pointed as he carefully maneuvered the car around potholes on a dirt road.

"Good. I don't want him to suffocate."

"Boss, police!"

Jack abruptly sat up and saw two policemen in dark blue uniforms and black-rimmed caps standing behind a white painted line, where the International Settlement territory ends, and China proper begins.

"They are Chinese policemen." Lily looked out the window.

"Lily, you think they would search our car?"

"I don't know."

"Boss, I take care of it." Da Tu quickly got out of the car and started toward the two Chinese policemen, smiling and bowing before he slipped something into each man's palm.

"Lily, I saw him just bribe those two Chinese policemen. Why does he have to do that?"

"Jack, out here, Chiang Kai-shek's men are in charge. Sometimes, they will make troubles just to squeeze a few coppers out of you… Uncle Tu, thank you."

"*Mei guanxi,* it is okay. It is only a little money. Miss Lee, your friend is a hero. China needs more of them." Da Tu stepped on the gas pedal, leaving the two Chinese policemen in a plume of dust in the rearview mirror. With them safely out of sight, he pulled up next to an abandoned wooden shack. "Boss, we stop here."

"Good! It's about time." Lily jumped out of the black Ford and popped open the trunk.

"*Shie-shie,* thank you." Zhou Hsiao-ming staggered out, wheezing.

"Hsiao-ming, are you okay?"

"Mm," he mumbled.

"Let's get him into the car." Jack slipped his limp body into the backseat as Lily tried to brush the blood stains off his tangled hair.

"You don't look good; you need food." Da Tu handed him a metal canteen. "Steamed dumplings I made myself."

"Hsiao-ming, eat, eat. It looks like you haven't eaten for a while." Lily stuffed a dumpling into his mouth.

"It is very tasty, Uncle Tu," he whimpered.

"*Gan quai zhi*, eat quickly."

"Uncle Tu, you Northerners know how to make good dumplings."

"I make bad dumplings," he replied modestly, watching him gobble down another. "How do I call you?"

"Zhou Hsiao-ming. Everyone calls me Hsiao-ming, Uncle Tu."

"*Bu gan don*. You are too polite. Just call me Da Tu."

"Uncle Tu, we young people can't call our elders that way," Lily said. "It is disrespectful."

"Miss Lee, it is okay. I like to be called Da Tu."

"Why?"

"Miss Lee, my family name is Zhu, and back home, people called me Lau Zhu, Old Pig, but the Reverend could not pronounce Zhu, and so he calls me Lau Tu. But it sounds like 'old country pumpkin.' So, I asked him to call me Da Tu."

"Jack, do you know what 'Da Tu' means in Chinese?"

"No. What does it mean?"

"It means Number One Disciple."

"That fits. My father told me that he was one of his first Chinese converts in China. Lily, what does your name mean in Chinese?"

"My family name is Lee, and my first name is Li-wha, which means beautiful flower."

"Mm, that's a very interesting name."

"But your mother likes to call me Lily because it sounded more American."

"Then, I shall call you Beautiful Lily," Jack said playfully.

"Lee Li-wha, what do you want me to call you?"

"Hsiao-ming, you still can call me Lee Li-wha."

There were no tall buildings or any foreign motorcars in sight as they drove along the rutted country road. All Jack could see were miles of rice paddies and straw-roofed farmhouses on both sides. More than an hour later, he finally saw a cluster of gray-tiled roofs in the distance. "Is that the town?"

"I am not sure." Lily looked out.

"Uncle Zhu, can you stop over there?" Zhou Hsiao-ming slowly sat up as they drove closer.

"Over there?" Da Tu pointed to an old wooden building with a banner flying over the door.

"Hsiao-ming, that's not your father's house." Lily still remembered the gated walls of the House of Zhou.

"This is my uncle's restaurant. My father is in the next town, but I want to stop by to say hello and treat Uncle Zhu to a delicious bowl of Zhejiang noodles."

"Oh, I love Zhejiang noodles. Haven't had them for a long time."

"Jack, we are going to stop at that restaurant. Is that okay?"

"Sure, I'm hungry too."

As their car moved closer, an old man, squatting by the door, quickly stood up and disappeared inside.

"*Qing wen, Zhou Xian-seng zai ma?* May I ask is Mr. Zhou here?" Zhou Hsiao-ming shuffled slowly into the restaurant.

"*Lau Ban Yung*, the Old Proprietress, is in the back. Let me go get her," the waiter answered curtly.

"What you want?" A small woman emerged from the kitchen, casting a suspicious glance at his bloody hair. She then burst into a wide grin. "Ai Yah, Hsiao-ming, I almost didn't recognize you! What happened to your head?"

"Just a small accident." He shrugged. "Aunty, are you all well? Is Uncle Zhou in the kitchen?"

"He is not here anymore; he passed away."

"So sorry, aunty, I didn't know. I was in Shanghai."

"No matter. My old man had eaten much bitterness. In this day and age, dead or alive, the same thing. I hope Old Man Heaven will treat him better in his next life." She sighed.

"Aunty, you must have eaten a lot of bitterness yourself." He gazed at her wrinkled face.

"*Mei guanxi,* no matter; let bygones be bygones; let's not talk about the past. Sit down, sit down. Let me cook your favorite noodles." She tugged on his arm.

"Aunty, these are my friends." He gestured for them to come closer.

"Aunty Zhou, how are you? I'm Lee Li-wha." Lily bowed politely.

"*Ai Yo,* Hsiao-ming, your girlfriend is so pretty!" She grabbed her hand.

"We are just friends." He was glad that she didn't recognize Lily was his former betrothed. "Aunty, this American is her friend too."

"How do you do? I'm Jack Wells." Jack stepped forward.

"What did this foreigner say?"

"Aunty, he asked you how you are."

"*Hen hao, hen hao*. Very good, very good."

"Lau Ban Yung, Old Proprietress, I am Da Tu. Your nephew said you cooked some of the best Zhejiang noodles. Can we have some taste of them?"

"Of course. That was my old man's specialty. You all sit down. Don't be so polite. You want something to drink, a pot of Jasmine tea?"

"Sure, that would be fine." Zhou Hsiao-ming gestured for everyone to sit down.

Four bowls of piping hot noodles with pieces of fresh vegetables soon appeared on their table.

"Mm, I can tell this is going to be delicious." Da Tu eagerly picked up strings of white noodles with his chopsticks and slurped them loudly into his mouth.

"Jack, I'm sorry they don't have a fork." Lily watched him struggle with his chopsticks.

"It's okay; I can manage," Jack replied gamely.

As Jack worked on his noodles, five haggard soldiers suddenly appeared at the front door; they would have been mistaken as beggars, if not for their torn military uniforms.

"Are they Chinese soldiers?" Jack whispered.

"I think so." Lily took a quick side glance at the door.

One of them, apparently in charge, tentatively approached the kitchen and in a humble voice, asked, "*Lau Ban Yung*, Old Proprietress, my men have not eaten since yesterday. Can you spare some food for them? But we don't have any money."

"You soldiers have suffered enough. What is another meal for them? You all come in and be my guest. I'm going to cook them some Zhejiang noodles."

"*Shie-shie, Lau Ban Yung.*" The man waved his men to come in.

"You can all sit over there." She pointed.

Wearily, the Chinese soldiers put down their guns and backpacks in the far corner as they silently took their seats around the table.

"Hsiao-ming, do you think they might be those Nationalist soldiers from the 88th Division?" Lily tried not to stare.

"I don't know, but I will go find out." He slowly walked over. "Hello, Comrades, where is your unit?"

The soldiers stared blankly back at him and said nothing.

"Who are you?" The man-in-charge looked at him suspiciously.

"Captain, I am Zhou Hsiao-ming. I work at the Commercial Press in Chapei."

"You don't look like a factory worker."

"I have helped some of your brave soldiers escape after their commanders abandoned them."

"Our commanders are cowards!" one of the young soldiers cried out.

"Shut your trap!" the man-in-charge yelled out sternly. "So why are you asking us about our unit? That's not your business!"

"Captain, I understand, but in this small town, your men stood out. I am just afraid they might catch the eyes of some Japanese spies around here."

"Who are your friends? What are you all doing here in this small town?" The captain glanced at them distrustfully.

"They are taking me back to my hometown to nurse my wound."

"What wound?"

"Right here." He pointed to his head.

"That's nothing!" he snickered.

"I want to go home!" a boy soldier whined. "Do you think your American friend can help us?"

"I don't think he can do much for you," Zhou Hsiao-ming said flatly.

"Then what shall we do!" the young soldier cried out. "I don't want to be captured by the Japanese devils!"

"They will kill us all!"

"Don't whine like a baby. Be a man!" the man-in-charge growled.

"Captain, please don't be too hard on your men; they are all too young to be soldiers."

"You don't think I know that? None of them volunteered for this," he groused. "But I still need to lead them back to rejoin their unit. Otherwise, they all will be branded as deserters."

"I've heard that Chiang Kai-shek's generals have already fled Nanking!" the old man who was sitting by the doorway interjected.

"Are you sure? Where did you get your information?"

"Captain, I've my sources."

"Then, it is hopeless." The captain sighed. "Now there is no way we can rejoin our unit even if we wanted to."

"Captain, your men can't go forward or backward. It seems to me that the only way to go is north," the old man urged.

"Where north?"

"Yenan, of course. Your men can join up with Mao Tse-tung's Eighth Route Army."

"Sorry, sir, we are not Communists. We are loyal Nationalist soldiers." He shook his head.

"But if you stay here, the Japs will have you all shot or beheaded," the old man said gravely.

"But If we go north and get caught by Chiang Kai-shek's men, we would be executed as deserters." The captain sounded like he wanted to cry too.

"Captain, you and your men are not deserters," the old man said perceptively. "Just think of all the heroes in the book *The Water Margins*. They were forced to go up the mountains to join the rebels because their corrupt generals had first deserted them. The situation your men are facing is not much different from what those heroes had to face eons ago."

"Old man, we are not heroes; we are just foot soldiers," the captain retorted agitatedly. "We just want to go back to our families!"

"Captain, no one is born a hero, but sometimes, one must rise to the occasion. You and your men are caught between forces that are beyond your control. Now you must choose between certain death and a chance to fight back and save China, a worthy cause to die for," the old man counseled him.

"He is right, captain." Zhou Hsiao-ming nodded.

"I guess I don't have much of choice then, do I?" The captain pondered for a long moment. "Let me first talk it over with my men."

"Captain, if your men decide to go to Yenan, can I have the honor to join you?" Zhou Hsiao-ming quickly asked.

"But why?" The captain cast a skeptical glance at him.

"I want to kill the Japanese devils too."

"You go back to your friends. Let me think about it."

A few minutes later, the captain walked over to their table. "Mr. Zhou, we all agree to go north, and you can come along. We need you to help us get a boat so that we can cross the Yangtze River."

"Great! Captain, it is an honor." Zhou Hsiao-ming grabbed his hand.

“Hsiao-ming, where are you going in your condition?” Lily asked, surprised and concerned.

“Lily, I’m going to Yenan with them.”

“Are you going to join the Communists?” she asked alarmingly.

“Young man, you are not made of iron,” Da Tu said. “In your condition, you will be lucky if you can cross the Yangtze River.”

“Uncle Zhu, if the Eighth Route Army could cross ten thousand li of swamps and climb ten thousand chi of icy mountains, then so can I,” he declared with bravado.

“Hsiao-ming, why are you doing this?” Lily asked.

“Li-wha, many of my friends have already gone to Yenan to help Mao Tse-tung fight the Japanese. I think it is time for me to put my money where my mouth is.”

“Hsiao-ming, you are in bad shape; you need time to recuperate.”

“Li-wha, even if I don’t make it all the way, at least I can help these soldiers cross the Yangtze River.”

“Would you like me to go with you?” Da Tu moved closer.

“Uncle Zhu, are you going with him too?” Lily was surprised.

“If they want me.” He then turned to the captain.

“Of course, the more, the merrier.” The captain patted his shoulder.

“Uncle Zhu, who is going to drive us back?”

“Boss, can you drive Miss Lee back? I go fight the Japanese.”

“Are you sure about what you’re doing?” Jack was taken aback by the sudden turns of events around him.

“I’m sure, boss. I want to save China.”

"Okay, you gotta do what you gotta do. Da Tu, after you finish fighting, please come back. My dad certainly could use a darn good driver like you."

"Tsai-jian, Miss Lee! I'm going up the mountains to join the rebels!" Da Tu shouted giddily, grabbing his shooting cap off the table.

"Aunty, I'm going now. Please pass the word to my father that I don't know when I will see him again."

"Hsiao-ming, you do us Chinese proud. I will tell your father that he has a patriotic son."

"Hsiao-ming, be careful. Take care of your health." Lily nudged closer.

"Li-wha," he looked at her hopefully, "would you like to come with me?"

"Hsiao-ming, I am not as brave as you are. I don't know what I could do in Yenan." Lily drew back a little.

"You could be a nurse, taking care of the wounded soldiers. There are many girl students already in Yenan."

"I-I don't know." She took a side glance at Jack.

"I understand!" Zhou Hsiao-ming abruptly pulled away. "Mr. Wells, I want to thank you. Without your help, I probably would still be stuck in Shanghai. At least now I have a chance to help my country. Thank you."

"You are welcome. Good luck."

"Hsiao-ming, tsai-jian, take care of your health." Lily watched him dash out the back door.

CHAPTER 26

Soldiers of the Rising Sun

"*Tsai-jian,* Aunty Zhou!" Lily waved as she followed Jack out of the restaurant. "Jack, do you know how to get back?"

"I think so." Gripping tightly on the steering wheel, Jack stared down at a winding dirt road. "Don't worry; I know where I am going."

Soon it began to get dark. As their headlights darted in and out of the shivering willow trees and bounced off the glistening rice paddies, Jack suddenly saw two bright headlights staring at them from the other end of a desolate country road. "What the hell is this?"

"I-I don't know. I think it is another car," Lily said nervously.

Slowly, they saw a military jeep emerge from the dark. It screeched to an abrupt stop, and three Japanese soldiers jumped out.

"Well, well, what do we have here?" A Japanese officer, dressed in a crisply pressed military brown uniform, strutted impetuously toward them.

"He looks like an American, sir!" One of the soldiers clicked on his heels.

"American?" the man-in-charge repeated.

"Yes, I am an American. My name is Jack Wells."

"Colonel Yamashita-san, there is also a Chinese girl in the car."

"I can see that." The Colonel peeked into the car window. "And who is this pretty Chinese girl?"

"Eh, she is my secretary," Jack answered hesitantly.

"I see," the Colonel smirked. "What are you two doing out here so late at night?"

"We are on our way back to Shanghai."

"Is that so?" he said doubtfully.

"Can we go now, sir?"

"I am afraid not."

"Why not? I've just told you, I am an American."

"Yes, I already know that. Normally I would have let you two go. But unfortunately, your car is blocking our China Expedition Forces on our way to Nanking."

"Sorry, sir. We will get out of your way." Jack was somewhat surprised that he spoke such good English.

"Too late now, I can't let you go back to Shanghai so you can tell the whole world what we are doing out here."

"Sir, I don't know what you're doing out here. We won't say a thing. Promise."

"My American friend, I am afraid you might have to come with me."

"No, really, Colonel, I have to get back to Shanghai. I work for the Hongkong and Shanghai Bank. My boss is expecting me," Jack pleaded.

"Your boss just has to wait, then." The Colonel ignored him. "Perhaps you two may want to see Nanking, the ancient imperial capital of China. I've heard it is almost as beautiful as our imperial city Kyoto. I can't wait to see it myself."

"Please, Colonel, we don't want to see Nanking. We don't have time." Jack and Lily exchanged an alarmed look with each other.

"Perhaps you may have to make some time. Put them on the truck! Sayonara." He hopped up into his jeep and sped ahead.

"Man, this can't be happening." Jack shook his head as he and Lily huddled in the back of a military truck filled with sleepy Japanese soldiers.

"Where are they taking us? I am cold." Lily wrapped herself tightly with her arms.

"I think we're heading toward Nanking; that was what the man said."

"Jack, I got a bad feeling about this. I am scared." Lily could feel the soldiers' gleeful eyes on her.

"How are you, little China doll?" a young soldier sitting next to her suddenly reached out to touch her face.

"Hey, buddy, don't do that!" Jack glowered, putting his hand in front of her. "Lily, they don't dare to touch you as long as I am here."

"Jack, I know." She snuggled closer, trusting him implicitly.

For hours on end, their truck rumbled along on the dark country roads before it suddenly came to a stop in front of a Japanese command post. A man in Western attire climbed in, chirping, "Good morning, Soldiers! I hope you all have slept well."

"Who are you?" one of the soldiers asked groggily.

"I am Shigeo Masuda from Asahi Shimbun. I am here to report all your glorious victories in China!"

"Why are you waking us so early? It is still dark out there," he griped.

"You are going to be the first Japanese soldiers ever to set foot in the imperial capital of the Ming Dynasty. Aren't you all excited?"

"Wake me up when we get there," the soldier mumbled.

"I see you are wounded." The reporter wasted little time, pointing at his legs. "Where did this happen?"

"In Shanghai."

"He meant in Chapei."

"Whatever, but I killed many Chinese soldiers," the sleepy soldier boasted, still not fully awake.

"How long have you been serving in our Imperial Army?"

"Almost one year now."

"Did you volunteer?"

"No. My father received the red conscription notice paper just one week after I graduated from the Nagasaki Commercial School."

"How did your father feel about sending his son to fight for his country?"

"Oh, he is very proud, of course! All our neighbors praised him. They even put up lots of banners in his honor."

"What kinds of banners did they put up?"

"The patriotic kind, of course."

"Such as?"

"Such as 'We Will Remember Your Sacrifice!' or 'May the Yamato Damashii Keep Your Son Safe!'"

"How does your mother feel about you going into the service?"

"You ask too many questions," he grumbled. "Eh…she cried, of course, but she said it is my duty to serve our Emperor."

"What about you, young soldier?" The reporter turned to another fresh face sitting close by.

"I am from the Nagasaki Prefecture too, Masuda-san! I volunteered even before they called my conscription."

"Why? You look too young to serve in the army. What do your mother and father think about that?"

"My parents are very proud that I am willing to fight and die for our Emperor, sir!" He stood up.

"Why?"

"Because…eh, because our Emperor is the head of our Japanese family tree and every Japanese, now and forever, is a part of that family tree!"

"You are not afraid to die?"

"No, sir! It is my sacred duty to die for our Emperor." The young soldier took out a copy of the Imperial Rescript to Soldiers and Sailors. "According to this sacred book, a soldier's paramount duty is his loyalty to the Emperor unto death; a soldier's duty is weightier than a mountain, and his death is lighter than a feather. If I die in battle, my death will be just like the spring cherry blossom falling onto the ground still in its full glory!" he gloated.

"Beautifully said, beautifully said. I wish Japan had more young men like you." Shigeo Masuda was almost moved to tears.

"Masuda-san, aren't you proud of our soldiers? They all have the Bushido Spirit. They will fight and die like a true samurai! Right, soldiers?"

"Yes, Captain! We will fight and die like a true samurai!"

Now all of the soldiers were wide awake.

"Thank you, thank you all for your supreme sacrifices. You have made our Yamato race very proud!" The reporter from Asahi Shimbun beamed as the early morning breeze from the Yangtze River brushed across his face. "Soldiers, you all will remember this momentous day for the rest of your young lives because you are about to make history!"

"Masuda-san, please take a picture of us. We must memorialize this precious moment. We want our fathers and mothers to see what their sons are doing in China for our motherland!"

"Can I have a copy of the picture so my father can show it off to his neighbors?"

"Can I have one too?" another clamored.

"Of course." The reporter from Asahi Shimbun happily complied. "I am sure that all your fathers and mothers will be very proud of their brave sons!"

As the soldiers moved closer for a group picture, he noticed that Jack and Lily were huddling in the back of the truck. "What do we have here—an American prisoner already? But we are not even at war with America. I don't understand." He put down his camera and asked in English, "My American friend, what is your name and what are you two doing here?"

"My name is Jack Wells." Jack immediately took him to be college educated, probably in America. "Your colonel has no right to hold us here! I hope you understand international laws better than he does."

"Masuda-san, our Colonel said that he had helped some Chinese soldiers escape."

"They said that you have helped some Chinese soldiers escape. Is that true?"

"It is not true!" Jack protested.

"Mr. Wells, if there is some misunderstanding, I am sure we will straighten it out once we get to Nanking. We Japanese have nothing but the greatest respect for you Americans."

"That's nice to hear. Then can you talk to the Colonel?" Jack asked hopefully.

"Don't worry, my American friend, our soldiers will treat you well in Nanking." The Japanese reporter started to move away, ready to snap the group portrait.

"Thanks for nothing." Jack watched the Japanese soldiers move together for a group portrait, and suddenly, he heard one of them yell out. "Look at those pathetic Chinese soldiers!"

Soon, others began to boo and jeer at something outside of the truck.

"We took them as real soldiers. They don't deserve to wear military uniforms!"

"They are not real soldiers; they are just a bunch of farmers!"

"They all deserve to be chopped down like a piece of lumber!"

"Those Chankoros disgust me! They all deserve to be killed like pigs." The young soldier who stood close to Jack spat out of the truck.

"At least the real pigs are edible," another added.

Laughter erupted in the truck.

Through the cracks of the side panels, Jack could see a motley group of confused Chinese Nationalist soldiers, prodded by bayonets, stumbling around in an open field. They looked like homeless people in torn blue uniforms and tattered cotton coats, carrying white flags in their hands and straw mats on their backs.

"Jack, what is going on?" Lily asked fearfully.

"I don't know. I just saw a bunch of Chinese war prisoners." Jack watched these hapless men being goaded into a small circle.

"Are they Nationalist soldiers?"

"I think so."

"What are they going to do to them?"

"I don't know. I think they…" Jack then heard a sudden burst of rapid machine-gun fire ripping through the chilly morning air, and those Chinese soldiers began to tumble to the ground like whacked weeds.

"Oh, my God! Oh, my God! Jack, why, why do they have to kill them?" Lily jumped up to her feet, gripping her throat and hyperventilating as if she was shot.

"According to the Geneva Convention, they are not supposed to kill their war prisoners," Jack stammered, jaw dropped, and eyes widened.

"Old Man Heaven! Why? Why?" Lily collapsed onto the floor, tightly wrapping herself in a ball, shaking and weeping uncontrollably.

Jack watched in disbelief as the Japanese soldiers in the truck cheered on their comrades in the bloodied field. Not long ago, these young men were just office clerks, factory workers, and college students, but now, in their muster-brown military uniforms, they had become something else. The sight of these dead Chinese soldiers seemed to have taken hold of them; their faces glowed with excitement, and their eyes widened with lusts, the savages in them awakened, and evil spirits unleashed. With those beastly eyes, they looked like an army of killer ants, jubilantly singing as they headed toward Nanking.

Our swords are sharpened
and our arrows are drawn.
We are ready to fulfill our sacred duties!
We will be glad to die in His Name
with honor and joy.

CHAPTER 27

The Kempeitai Headquarters

As the pale morning sun began to peek through the early morning mists, the reporter from Asahi Shimbun suddenly shouted pointing his camera at a Japanese flag fluttering high on top of a tall drum tower. "Look, everyone! We are about to enter the ancient imperial capital of China! This is truly a historic day for Japan!"

Lily jumped up. In the distance, she could see a group of Japanese soldiers waving their rifles triumphantly on top of a huge crenelated city wall, and she could hear them shouting, "Banzai! Banzai!"

And all around her, the Japanese soldiers started to pump their rifles in the air, joining their comrades with ecstatic cries. "Banzai! Banzai!"

"I can't believe Nanking has fallen!" Lily crumbled back onto the floor, sobbing.

Slowly, their truck rumbled into Nanking under the tall arch of the Taiping Gate. The noisy soldiers soon grew quiet as they watched the spoils of their victory passing in front of them—abandoned household belongings strewn in the streets, burning wooden houses smoldering in the alleyways, and heaps of dead Chinese men, women, and children, some still with their shoes on, slumped by the doorways.

"Old Man Heaven, what have we ever done to them?" Lily looked up into the sky in a daze, too numbed even to cry.

Jack could not find another word to comfort her as he looked on grimly at the horrors happening in front of him. "I don't understand why the Japanese hate the Chinese so much."

Moving behind a convoy of military vehicles, minutes after painful minutes, their truck finally screeched to a stop in front of a large Tudor-style mansion.

"Goodbye, soldiers, may the Yamato Damashii keep you all safe!" The reporter from Asahi Shimbun waved as he jumped off the truck.

"Meet you at Yasukuni, Masuda-san!"

"Where are we?" Lily struggled up on her feet as the soldiers emptied out the truck.

"I don't know."

"Out! Out!" A Japanese man in a police uniform goaded them to get off.

"Jack, I think this is a police headquarters." She looked up at a large Japanese sign perched on top of a tall wrought-iron gate.

"I think you are right." Jack saw a "Japanese Military Police Headquarters" sign in English by the side of the main door.

"Inside! Inside!" The policeman unceremoniously shoved them into a spacious room appointed with Chinese carpets, leather sofas, and Art Deco lamps; it looked like a rich man's living room except for a large Japanese sunburst flag on the wall. With sentries staring at them in each corner, Jack and Lily looked at each other in fear, not knowing what would come next.

Suddenly, a beefy Japanese officer pranced in. "Welcome to Japanese Kempeitai Headquarters. I am Colonel Taro Yamashita in charge of the military police for the 16th Division of our China Expedition Force."

"Colonel, you've got us here, can we go now?" Jack watched him gingerly putting down his sword on a carved-walnut desk.

"Mr. Wells, besides your girlfriend, who are the other two Chinese men in your car? Or should I say, were in your car?" the Colonel asked gruffly as he plunked down on a large swivel leather chair, rubbing his hands over the armrests. "I like this chair. I hope whoever used to own it doesn't mind if I use it for a while."

"What are you talking about? There were just two of us… nobody else." Jack cast a worried look at Lily.

"Really?" The Colonel looked over his wire-rimmed glasses. "The report says here that there were five Nationalist soldiers in that restaurant, not counting the two in your car. Mr. Wells, I am very upset that they all left before I could send a welcome party to meet them," the Colonel said sarcastically.

"Colonel, as I told you before, we were on our way back to Shanghai—"

"Yes, yes, you had told me that, Mr. Wells, but as I asked you before, what were you two doing in the middle of nowhere when there is a war going on?" He narrowed his skeptical eyes.

"We were on our way back from a business meeting. I have documents to prove it."

"Show me," the Colonel demanded.

"I think they are still in my car."

"Heh…heh…heh! Mr. Wells, please tell me the truth."

"What do you mean? I am telling you the truth." Jack grinned self-consciously.

"Please don't insult my intelligence. We have already searched your car and found nothing besides some blood stains in the backseat. How do you explain that?" Incessantly, the Colonel drummed his fingers on the desk.

"I-I must have left the documents in the restaurant then."

"You're lying." He slammed down his palm. "Mr. Wells, we didn't find any bank documents, but we did find a Bible and some papers that belonged to the New Hope Church in the car."

"Really?"

"Really." The Colonel flashed a smug smile. "I know that your father, Reverend Jonathan Wells, is the pastor at the church." He slowly swiveled around in his chair. "Mr. Wells, I also know that there was a young man in your car who was wanted by Chiang's Blue Shirts because he is a union organizer and a Communist sympathizer, and I think he was the one who had left the blood stains in the backseat."

"I don't know what you are talking about, sir." Jack feigned ignorance, but a chill began to run down his spine. *This guy knows everything.*

"Mr. Wells, like everyone else, we too have our own eyes and ears in Shanghai. Because you and your girlfriend helped him along with five other Chinese Nationalist soldiers escape, we consider you two as our enemy combatants, and according to our Military Penal Code, it is punishable by death!"

"Whoa! Colonel Yamashita, what the hell are you talking about?" Jack's straight posture began to hunch a bit. "Colonel, we don't have anything to do with this...really, I am telling you the truth."

The Colonel seemed to take some pleasure in watching the young American sweat. He kept swiveling around in his leather chair before he finally spoke again. "Mr. Wells, I will overlook all this on account of your father's good reputation."

"Thank you, sir." Jack felt relieved.

"Jack, go home and don't get mixed up with the Chinese. It is not worth it. It is our war, not yours," the Colonel advised as he peeked through his wire-rimmed glasses.

"Thank you very much, sir. Can we go now?"

"Yes, you can go." He waved his hand petulantly.

"Thank you, Colonel. Thank you very much. Lily, let's go!"

"Just you, Mr. Wells. She stays."

"What are you talking about, Colonel? She goes with me!"

"No, no, no." The Colonel waved his forefinger. "My American friend, she is Chinese, not American, and we will have to treat her accordingly."

"Hey, buddy, she goes with me! You understand?" Jack said emphatically.

"No, no, no, you don't understand, Mr. Wells. I am not your buddy. You go, and she stays. That is final!" Colonel Taro Yamashita's voice suddenly turned guttural and threatening.

"Why are you doing this? Colonel, please."

"Mr. Wells, don't worry, I am not going to harm her. She is too pretty to be wasted like other Chinese girls. General Ito Honda is a connoisseur of pretty young girls, that old fox." The Colonel flashed a creepy smile under his small mustache.

"Jack!" Lily wailed, struggling to free herself from the two Japanese sentries.

“This is egregious! You can’t...” Jack took a step toward him before a rifle rammed in front of his chest and a pistol pointed at his face.

“I can’t what?” the Colonel smirked.

“You can’t do this! You can’t keep her here!” Jack shouted.

“Mr. Wells, I can do whatever I want with her. She is our prisoner now.”

“You can’t do that to her! You Goddamn Japs!”

“Mr. Wells, if you were not an American, I would cut you in half with my sword right now!” The Colonel jumped to his feet, but something stopped him. “Next time I won’t be so nice.”

“Colonel, please, I didn’t mean to insult you, but I won’t leave here without her.” Jack softened his stance.

“Suit yourself.”

“Please, Colonel, she hasn’t done anything wrong. I’ll take full responsibility for what happened.”

“Oh, by the way,” the Colonel ignored his pleas as he picked up his pistol and sword from the desk, “I am afraid that your car has to stay too. It is now officially the property of our Imperial Japanese Army under the international rules of engagement.”

“That’s bullshit! You can’t confiscate my father’s car! We’ll see about that when I get to the U.S. Embassy,” Jack bristled.

“Mr. Wells, your embassy was closed a few days ago. Your ambassador has fled to Chungking with that cowardice Chiang Kai-shek. Nobody is here to protect you now,” the Colonel said harshly. “And for your safety, Mr. Wells, I think you had better stay here for the night. It is too dangerous to travel at night without a car. As I said, this is our war, not yours, and I don’t want to see you get killed, causing an international incident.”

"Okay, Colonel Yamashita, you can keep the car, but please let her go."

"Mr. Wells, I am afraid our accommodations are not going to be as good as the Cathay Hotel. I hope you don't mind," the Colonel said facetiously.

"Let me go! Let me go!" Lily kicked and screamed, trying to free herself from the Japanese sentries.

"Lily!" Jack lurched helplessly toward her, almost touching the sharp point of the bayonet.

"Jack, help me! Jack, help me..." Lily's voice gradually faded into the hallway as she was dragged away.

"Where are you bastards taking her?" Jack yelled out impotently.

"Mr. Wells, go back to Shanghai while you still have a chance. The last boat will be leaving Nanking tomorrow. I hope you have a safe trip back. Sayonara, my American friend." The Colonel grinned, waving with the back of his hand dismissively.

CHAPTER 28

The Killing Field

Jack soon found himself standing in a dark and damp cell. "This is fucking unbelievable!" He shook his head as the metal door slammed closed behind him with a loud bang.

"Hi, there! You must be American." A man slowly rolled out from the shadow.

"Who the hell are you?" Jack could barely make out his face, but he recognized his American accent.

"Walter McDaniel, Associated Press." The man stood up from his metal bunk bed.

"I'm Jack Wells…where are you from?"

"Originally from Missouri. And you?"

"New York City."

"That is a long way from home."

"You too. So, what are you doing in here?" Jack felt a little better. At least there was someone familiar sharing this small cell with him.

"The Japs wanted to make sure that I catch the last boat back to Shanghai before I can take more pictures."

"Come again? I don't get it."

"The Japs want me to leave Nanking by tomorrow. They caught me taking pictures of things they don't want the world to see. They smashed my camera and almost cracked my head. So much for freedom of the press."

"I am sorry to hear that." Jack took out his Camels. "Want one?"

"Sure." He eagerly took one. "So, what are you in here for?"

"My lady friend and I were on our way back to Shanghai when we ran into their China Expedition Forces, and this colonel from their military police was afraid that we might expose their secret. So, he brought us here."

"Jack, have you seen what these Japs are doing to the Chinese since they took over the city?"

"Yes, I have...I saw them execute hundreds of Chinese soldiers on my way here. I thought the Geneva Convention prohibited the execution of war prisoners."

"The Japs don't give a shit about the convention. Just in the last two weeks, they have slaughtered tens of thousands of Chinese soldiers and raped thousands and upon thousands of Chinese women, often in broad daylight!" The AP reporter took a few more puffs on his smoke.

"I thought they had already conquered Nanking. Why do they still have to kill so many innocent people?"

"The Japanese want to terrorize the Chinese into submission and revenge for their dead comrades. I have heard that their Command Headquarters has even issued an explicit order to their soldiers just to do that. Have you ever heard of their 'Three All's Policy: Loot all; Burn all, and Kill all?'"

"No, I haven't."

“The Japanese are a sadistic bunch. They seem to enjoy killing and torturing innocent people. I have seen them bury some Chinese men alive, or behead them and then dump their bodies into the Yangtze River. I have even seen a Japanese soldier cut off a woman’s breasts off after he raped her! I’ve caught them in the act with my camera, and that’s why they want me out of here by tomorrow.” He blew out another smoke.

“What is going on with these Japanese soldiers? Why haven’t any of our Western governments condemned their atrocities?”

“I don’t know. Maybe the whole world has not yet seen what these Japs are doing here in Nanking.” He paused and whispered, “Fortunately, I still have a couple of rolls of film hidden in my coat. I hope these pictures will shock the world into action.”

“I hope so. We in the West have gotta help these poor people.” Jack stared out the steel-barred window.

“Jack, do you see that misty mountain yonder?”

“Yeah.”

“That is the famous Purple Mountain.” The AP reporter pointed with his cigarette.

“Why is it famous?”

“That is where all the Chinese emperors of the Ming dynasty were buried. Their tombs are in huge underground caverns protected by big stone animals at the entrance. Not in a million years could these Ming emperors have imagined that these soldiers from a little island nation, once their vassal state, would now be trampling on their graves. They all must be furious as hell.”

“I could only imagine.”

“Three-hundred years of glorious Chinese history are all buried up there. You ought to go see it before the Japs ransack it.”

"If I ever get out of here," Jack said despondently.

"Jack, do you know that Dr. Sun Yat-sen, the founder of China's first Republic, was also buried up there?"

"No, I didn't know that."

"He too must be rolling in his grave right now. Jack, there is a saying here in China: 'When the Purple Mountain burns, China is lost.'"

"I would have never thought that China would fall this way."

"Neither did the Chinese…anyway, I am going back to sleep. Gotta get up early tomorrow." The AP reporter crushed out his smoke on the floor.

"Goodnight." Just as Jack was about to move away from the cell window, he saw a group of Japanese soldiers swarming around a military truck parked outside the compound. "What is going on over there?"

"Don't know."

They watched the truck's tailgate slam open with a loud bang, and a bunch of dejected Chinese men in ripped cotton shirts and torn pants jumped off. Goaded by bayonets and barking orders, they were forced into a tight circle on the damp ground. Upon a small hill, a group of Imperial Japanese Army officers, all dressed resplendently in sharply pressed military uniforms, slowly emerged from a tent. They chatted casually as they took their seats on the folding chairs.

"What is going to happen to these poor guys?" Jack asked tensely.

"Whatever it is, it doesn't look good."

Jack then saw another Japanese officer, with a samurai sword strapped by his hip, strutting out from a side door. "Speak of the devil!"

"You know him?"

"He's that colonel I've told you about."

They watched him taking a bow in front of his superiors before turning to the young Japanese soldiers standing around the terrified Chinese men. As if on cue, two of the soldiers violently yanked out an old man, dragged his limp body toward a wooden post, and tied his hands around it.

"Are they going to shoot that poor old man?" Jack was aghast.

"I-I think so."

"No! They are gonna bayonet him alive!" Jack cried out when he saw another young soldier reluctantly move toward the old man, hands shaking as he raised his bayonet blade. "Jesus Christ! I don't believe what I am seeing!" Mortified, Jack watched the young soldier inch closer, and after a brief hesitation, Jack heard a loud guttural cry, full of combative rage and burning hatred. The young soldier yelled out savagely before thrusting his glistening blade into the old man's chest. A gush of blood spewed out, his head lurched forward, and his impaled body slumped to the ground.

"Oh…my God!" Jack watched with revulsion as the young soldier pulled out his blood-stained blade, stumbled backward, but then quickly regained his composure. His nervous face looked relieved, but his fearful eyes now darkened with death as he took a deep bow toward his commanding officers. Colonel Yamashita smiled and nodded approvingly, pleased with what this young soldier had just done: he was now officially initiated into the Japanese Imperial Army.

"This is unbelievable! They are using Chinese as live target practice!" Jack pounded his fists on the window bars. "This is beyond barbaric! They are a bunch of sadistic animals!"

"I've heard the Japanese Imperial Army used Chinese prisoners for live bayonet practice before, but this is the first time I saw it with my own eyes. I wish I still had my camera." The AP reporter gritted his teeth, trembling.

"For the life of me, I can't understand what possessed him to do that! He is young enough to be the poor man's grandson!" Jack cried out hoarsely.

"These young Japanese soldiers probably have never killed a human being before. Their generals want to desensitize their nerves so that they can kill on the battlefield without any hesitation."

"But…but, you don't use real people for target practice!"

"Jack, they were trained to think of the Chinese not as people but as some sort of pig, or a dog, or just a piece of wood."

"How in the world could they think like that?" Jack was incredulous. "What kind of people are they!"

"Jack, because of their samurai ethos, sometimes death doesn't seem to matter to these Japs. But still, it has never ceased to amaze me what these little yellow men are capable of. The inhumanity of it all!" He shook his head from side to side. Even as a veteran reporter of many wars, he couldn't stomach what he had just witnessed. Slowly he walked away from the window, muttering, "I wish I still had my camera."

As dusk settled into their cell, there were no reprieves outside. As hours dragged on, Jack could hear more guttural rages, followed by more barking orders.

"Walter, they have turned the backyard of their police headquarters into a killing field. I can't take this anymore. I think I am gonna throw up." Jack recoiled and fell on the cold concrete floor, cigarette dangling from his mouth, succumbing to all the deaths taking place outside of their cell window.

"Jack, you know what day it is?"

"No."

"It is Christmas Eve."

"Oh? I almost forgot."

"Jack, I have been in China for a long time. I have never felt homesick until now."

"Me too." Jack suddenly remembered the last Christmas Eve he spent with his parents. He could feel the glowing warmth of that night as an overwhelming sadness welled up inside him. Mournfully, he started to hum. "Silent night, Holy night, all is calm, all is bright…."

The sounds of rattling keys aroused Jack from his sleep. Standing in the doorway, Colonel Taro Yamashita was beaming. "Good morning," he greeted them cheerfully. "I hope you gentlemen have slept well. I have good news for you. The wind of Heaven has blown our way. Our Imperial Army is now in complete control of Nanking. No more fighting and dying. Now we will have peace!"

"Colonel, you don't need to keep us here anymore. Can we leave now?" The AP reporter walked over to the door.

"Of course, now you two can go, but make sure you go directly to your boat." He gestured graciously.

"Where is Lily? I won't leave here without her!" Jack demanded.

"Mr. Wells, like I told you, she will be staying with us a little longer, if you don't mind."

"Colonel, please let her go. You have no reason to keep her here anymore!"

"My American friend, consider your girlfriend very lucky. She won't be treated like other Chinese women, giving many sexual favors to our common soldiers. She will be living in a nice hotel doing nothing but making herself look pretty. Ha! Ha! Ha!"

"The hell she will! She is coming with me!"

"As I said, my American friend, I will take good care of your Chinese girlfriend. I will give her a thorough physical checkup before she leaves here. One can never be too careful with these Chinese women. You never know what kinds of diseases they may have on them," he said disdainfully.

"If you ever touch her...by God, I swear I will kill you!" Jack lurched forward, wagging his fingers.

"I wouldn't do that if I were you," the AP reporter mumbled.

Too late. The Colonel swiped his fist across Jack's face. "Get them out of here!"

Jack stumbled back a few steps, blood dripping from his mouth.

"Hey Jack, let's get out of here." The AP reporter pulled on his arm.

"No!" Jack steadied himself, then refused to move, anger surging inside of him. "Colonel Yamashita, you fancy yourself a samurai warrior, but you are nothing but a fucking pimp!"

"What, what? What did you call me?" The Colonel sputtered, saliva spattering.

"You heard me, Taro! You fancy yourself as an honorable samurai, but you are nothing but a fucking pimp for your boss!" Jack shouted into his face, full of uncontrollable rage.

"Jack, calm down!" The AP reporter nudged on his elbow. "You don't want to get this animal riled up. Remember, we are not in Shanghai anymore."

"How dare you insult an Imperial Japanese Army officer!" The Colonel became unhinged, one hand on the scabbard and the other on his samurai sword as his face turned crimson.

"Good morning, Colonel Yamashita-san, where is the Chinese girl you wanted me to look at?" A voice suddenly came from the end of the hallway.

"Captain Tanaka-san, you are just in time to prevent an international incident." Catching himself, the Colonel slowly let his sword slide back into its sheathing.

That voice sounds familiar. Jack jerked around and saw a young Japanese doctor in a white coat walking toward him.

"Akira! Is that you?" Jack yelled out incredulously.

"Jack? What…what are you doing here?" Akira Tanaka stammered, as his smiling face collapsed.

"Captain Tanaka, do you know this man?" the Colonel demanded.

"Hai, Colonel Yamashita-san!" Akira clicked his boots.

"From where?"

"I met him in New York City."

"Akira, where are you guys taking Lily?"

Akira didn't reply, looking pale.

"Mr. Wells, for your information, he is going to examine her to make sure she is clean before I send her to the Command Headquarters," the Colonel said matter-of-factly.

"Akira! Are you part of this shenanigan! My God, I don't believe this! Akira! Not you! How can you do this?" Jack blasted into his face.

Akira lowered his head and said nothing.

"Jack! Jack, help me!" Lily's voice burst out from one of the prison cells as she fought to free herself from the grip of two Japanese sentries.

"Lily!" Jack reached out toward her, but two cold bayonet blades held him in his place.

Akira turned his head, and his pale face now turned white.

"Captain Tanaka, do you know her too?"

"Hai, Colonel Yamashita-san!"

"Is that so? What a coincidence." The Colonel slowly stroked on his small mustache.

"Honorable Colonel Yamashita-san, please forgive me." He took a deep bow and held it.

"This is insubordination, Captain Tanaka! I could have you court-martialed!" The Colonel knew what he was about to ask.

"Colonel Yamashita-san, please forgive me for my brazen request. She is Mr. Jack Wells' girlfriend. Please reconsider your order." Akira bowed lower.

"Captain Tanaka, you are one of the best doctors serving in our imperial army. So why are you throwing away such a promising career for this Chinese girl?"

"Colonel Yamashita-san, so sorry." Tanaka took another deep bow.

"Captain Tanaka-san, if your future father-in-law was not a general in our Imperial Army, do you know what would happen to you?"

"Hai!"

"But I am afraid I can't change my order," he said icily.

"Colonel, please reconsider your order," Jack interjected. "Captain Tanaka is just trying to do an honorable thing for his friend."

"Mr. Wells, I am afraid that I can't change my order. Captain Tanaka, take her away!" he barked.

"Jack! Jack!" Lily screamed.

Jack shuddered at the thought of what they would do to her once she disappeared from his life. But, with two blades pointed at his chest, he couldn't move.

"Colonel, please reconsider your order." The AP reported stepped forward.

"My order is final!" the Colonel started to walk away.

"Colonel, have you ever considered the grave consequence if you don't let her go?"

"What consequence do I need to consider?" the Colonel smirked.

"Colonel, when we get back to Shanghai and tell the world what we saw here, I doubt any of your commanding officers would want his name to be associated with what you are trying to do for them. This kind of sordid things would make your generals look pretty bad in the eyes of the world! It would be very unbecoming of an Imperial Army officer even for your Japanese people," the AP Reporter said calmly.

"That's right! He will tell every newspaper that the Japanese Imperial Army is forcing many innocent Chinese women to become sex slaves, and you are their pimps!" Jack shouted into the colonel's expressionless face. "Colonel, Mr. McDaniel is an American newspaper reporter. He knows how to report this kinda thing. Once this unsavory stuff gets on the front pages of the *New York Times* or the *Herald Tribune*, just imagine what kind of damage would that do to that highly refined cultural image you Japanese are so proud of!"

"And not to mention the damage to your military career!" The AP reporter saw him wavering.

The Colonel's jaws tightened; it looked like he was about to become unhinged again. He flashed a threatening stare as his lips twitched, and without another word, he abruptly turned on his heels, waving angrily with the back of his hand. "Get them out of here!"

"Thank you very much, Colonel Yamashita-san!" Akira took a deep bow.

"Captain Tanaka, see me in my office! Now!" he barked.

"Hai!"

"Akira, thank you." Jack reached out to shake his hand.

"Jack, please take her away as quickly as you can!"

"Akira, if you ever are in Shanghai, let's get together."

"Tanaka-san!" the Colonel barked.

CHAPTER 29

The Nanking Safety Zone

"I don't ever want to see this place again…are you okay?" Jack looked back at the sinister Kempeitai Headquarters.

"Yes." Lily looked dazed.

"Young lady, you should count your lucky stars. If not for Jack here, I don't think that crazy colonel would ever have let you go."

"Jack, thank you for saving my life."

"Lily, I am just glad you are safe." Jack protectively draped his arm around her. "We should thank Mr. McDaniel here and also my friend, Akira. It was very brave of him to disobey the colonel's order."

"Jack, he did it for you, not for me."

"You think so?"

"I know so. I saw him taking away two women last night. They begged him not to take them away; one of them threw herself against the wall, and she died. I wonder what happened to the other poor woman."

"C'mon, let's get out of here. We need to go straight to the dock before our boat leaves Nanking."

"Walter, you lead the way."

"Follow me. This street will lead us straight toward the Yangtze River."

"Mr. McDaniel, you seem to know this city pretty well."

"I should. I have been living here on and off for the past ten years." The AP reporter strutted ahead, working his way around the panicky Nanking residents, all desperately trying to get close to the Yangtze River.

"I think all these people are trying to get to the boat."

"Jack, I don't think there are any boats for these people." The AP reporter shook his head. "They need a boarding pass."

"Do I need one?"

"No, Jack, your face is your pass. The boat is for us foreigners only."

"I don't have a pass," Lily said.

"Lily, don't worry. You are with me." Jack squeezed her hand reassuringly.

"Jack, I think you'd better say that she is your wife. A girlfriend wouldn't do unless she is rich and with connections."

"Lily, is it all right if I call you my wife?"

"Mm," Lily nodded.

"Is that a yes?" Jack grinned.

"Mm."

"Walter, how far are we from the river?"

"Not far. That's Nanking University Hospital, and the river is just a few blocks beyond that." He pointed to a cluster of brick buildings behind a black wrought-iron fence.

"How come I see a Japanese flag flying on top of that building?"

"The Japs took over the whole place a few days ago. I think your doctor friend may be working in there."

Staring up at the sunburst flag, Jack winced at the thought of what could have happened to Lily in there. He squeezed her hand more tightly as they hurried along the jammed sidewalks, passing shuttered stores and burned-out buildings. Just as they were passing a dark alleyway, he suddenly heard a young girl screaming wildly.

"Jiu ming la! Jiu ming la! Save me! Please save me!"

"*Shao gu yiang, nei chi na?* Little girl, where are you going?"

"Hey, you bastard! What the hell do you think you're doing?" Jack saw a disheveled Japanese soldier running after a hysterical little girl.

"*Shao gu yiang,* little girl, your daddy is here." The drunken soldier pulled on the little girl's pants.

"Please don't! Please don't! I am only twelve!" She balled up like a frightened kitten.

"Stop that! Stop that!" Lily started running toward them, but before she could reach the little girl, another Japanese soldier suddenly grabbed hold of Lily, tightening his arms around her chest.

"What the fuck do you think you are doing!" Jack swung his fist at the man, forcefully striking him in the face and broke his nose.

Reeling, the soldier staggered backward, pulling out his pistol from his holster and brandishing it in Jack's face. "How dare you hit me! I am going to shoot you, mother-fucker!" he cried out menacingly in Japanese.

"Hey, buddy, take it easy." The AP reporter stepped forward and pushed away his pistol.

"You two stop that at this very minute! They are Americans." A Japanese officer emerged from the back of the alley.

"You Chenkaro lovers! If you were not Americans, I would shoot both of you mother-fuckers!" The soldier with the broken nose turned to Lily. "Maybe you want to go back with me so I can finish my business."

"Go back to where you came from, you little weasel!" Standing a little taller than him, Lily stared back at the soldier with a hateful glare as blood dripped down his face.

"Get out of here, or I am gonna beat the shit out of you, you little Jap!" Jack stepped up between them, fist clenched.

"Let's go! That's an order!" his officer barked. "Let's not waste our time here. There are plenty of other women back in there."

Watching the soldiers stagger back into the alley, Lily knelt next to the sobbing girl. "*Shao-mei mei, bu yao pa.* Little sis, don't be afraid."

"*Jei-jei, bu yao le kia oh.* Big sister, don't leave me!" The little girl was beside herself.

"Don't worry; we won't leave you," Lily said soothingly, patting her hair. "*Shao-mei mei, ni zhu zai nali?* Little sis, where do you live?"

"*Riben ren...*Japanese soldiers, no home! Please take me to the foreigner's safe zone!" she cried out incoherently.

"*Shao-mei mei,* where is this foreigner's place?"

"Over there." She pointed with her shaking finger.

"Lily, I think she meant the Nanking International Safety Zone. It is on the other side of the Nanking University Hospital we just passed," the AP reporter said.

"Let's go then." Jack helped her up.

"Jack, we only have about an hour before our boat leaves Nanking." He tapped on his watch. "You don't want to miss it."

"Walter, I hear you but can we give it a try?"

"Jack, you don't have your car anymore. How do you plan to get back to Shanghai?"

"Lily, he is right." Jack looked back at her pleadingly.

"Jei-jei, big sister, please don't leave me here! I beg you. Please save me! Please save me!"

"Shao-mei mei. Shao-mei mei." Lily gently patted the little girl's head, tears welling in her eyes. She didn't know what else to say to console this frightened little girl.

"Jei-jei, big sister, please don't let them rape me! I beg you! I am only twelve!" The little girl wailed louder as she frantically kowtowed at their feet, banging her head again and again on the ground.

"No! I won't let them touch you!" Lily suddenly stood up and said in a strained voice, "Jack, I'll take her there."

"Miss, don't forget what almost happened to you back there. I am telling you, no Chinese woman is safe in Nanking at this moment."

"But we can't just leave her here. If we don't help her, then who will?" Lily cried out as she reached out for her little girl's hand. *"Shao-mei mei, bu yao pa.* Little sis, don't be afraid; you lead the way, I will take you there."

"Lily, I can't leave you here all by yourself. I will go with you. Little girl, we are going to take you to this foreigner's place."

"Jack, if you miss the boat, how the hell are you going to get back to Shanghai?"

"I don't know." He just shrugged. "But do I have a choice?"

"Oh, man." The AP reporter shook his head begrudgingly. "You better hurry up then. Just walk straight down this road. You can't miss it. And I will see what I can do to hold up the boat for you."

"Hey, thanks."

"You are welcome; just don't take too long."

The Nanking International Safety Zone did not look like much. It was just a few ordinary streets blocked off with a few makeshift fences and handwritten signs strung over some old ropes or nailed to the wooden posts. Behind the ropes, they saw every open spot was taken up by frightened Chinese women, children, and a few old men.

"Excuse me, Miss, she needs to see a doctor." Jack tried to get the attention of a Western woman wearing a Red Cross armband.

She walked over, and without a word or a smile, she let them in.

"Thank you. I am Jack Wells."

"I am Minnie Vautrin," the tall fiftyish American replied wearily. "Mr. Wells, please wait here, I'll see if the doctor is available to see her. We are very short-handed."

A few minutes later, a somber-looking man, with a big swastika medal hanging in front of his chest, slowly approached them.

"Hi, I am Jack Wells."

"I am John Rabe." The bald man extended one hand as he pushed up his wire-rimmed glasses with the other. "Dr. Robert Wilson is swamped with many wounded. I am afraid it will be a while before he can get to her." His face was wrinkled with stress, and his eyes were puffy from lack of sleep.

"Mr. Rabe, is this Dr. Robert Wilson the only doctor working around here?"

"Very much so at this moment. Only a handful of Western doctors are still here in Nanking. We are doing our best. Please be patient."

"Thank you, Mr. Rabe. We were on our way to catch our boat, and we saw this little girl was being attacked by—"

"You need to say no more. This sort of things happens every day now ever since the Japanese took over the city." The German shook his tired head. "Day and night, these soldiers maraud through the streets, barge into people's homes, and sometimes they even try to sneak in here to rape some of our nurses. Tens of thousands of women, some as young as eight or as old as eighty, have been raped, mutilated, and then killed."

"Sir, thank God you are here to protect them."

"There are just too few of us left here in Nanking. I have only twenty-seven Westerners here to look after 250,000 Chinese refugees. My swastika can only do so much to scare off those Japanese soldiers," he said grimly. "If their commanders don't rein them in soon, we will run out of space even for her to sit down."

"I hope you still have room for one more."

"Of course, Mr. Wells, but I am afraid the only accommodation I can offer her is a little straw mat shared by other women. She has to sleep in the street."

"Thank you, Mr. Rabe. It is still much better than outside." Lily gently pushed the little girl forward. *"Shao-mei mei, bu yao haipa.* Little sis, don't be afraid; this foreign uncle will protect you."

"Jei-jei, bu yao li kai wo! Big sis, please don't leave me!"

"Shao-mei mei, jei-jei has to leave now." Lily hugged the little girl tenderly.

"Jei-jei, I am frightened. Please stay with me!" the girl sobbed loudly.

"Jei-jei can't stay." On one bent knee, Lily gently touched her smudged face. *"Bu yao haipa, ah.* Don't be afraid, little sis. You will

be safe here. This foreign uncle will protect you. Ah, be a sweet little girl. I hope I can come back to see you again." Lily slowly stood up.

"I will ask Miss Minnie Vautrin to find a woman to take care of her." John Rabe reached for the little girl's hand.

"Mr. Rabe, thank you for taking care of her. It is very kind of you."

"You are welcome; Nanking has been my home for more than twenty years. I like living here, I like the people, but for the life of me, I just don't understand why the Japanese hate the Chinese so much," he said gravely.

"I've asked myself that same question many times."

"Miss, it breaks my heart to see your people suffer this way, and there is no one here to help them…what brought you two to Nanking during the worst possible time?"

"Mr. Rabe, it is a long story. Sorry, we have a boat to catch," Jack interjected.

"I understand. Everybody has left the city. Even your American Embassy has closed."

"Mr. Rabe, I wish there were something more we could do to help."

"Mr. Wells, there is something you can do."

"What do you want me to do?" Jack stared at the swastika dangling in front of his chest.

"I have two rolls of film I would like you to take back with you. Show all the newspapers what these Japanese soldiers are doing here in Nanking."

"I will, Mr. Rabe."

"People in the West must know what is happening here in Nanking, and see with their own eyes of the brutalities these Japanese soldiers are inflicting on the Chinese. Mr. Wells, please tell thc world that the Japanese Imperial Army is committing genocide in Nanking!"

"Yes, I will, Mr. Rabe. I will make sure that these two rolls of films get to the *New York Times* and all the papers. Mr. Rabe, you are a good man. Goodbye."

"Mr. Rabe, thank you so much." Lily stepped forward to shake his hand. "Without you, many more people would be killed, and women raped. From the bottom of my heart, I want to express my deepest appreciation for what you are doing for our Chinese people." Lily took a small bow.

"I just wish I could do more to help your people."

"We Chinese will never forget your kindness. Mr. Rabe, you are a living Buddha!" Lily bent her body lower and took another bow.

"Miss, under these tragic circumstances, I am just doing something any decent human being would do," he replied modestly. "You two have a safe trip back. Merry Christmas."

"Merry Christmas, Mr. Rabe."

CHAPTER 30
On the Yangtze River

"What is to become of her?" Lily looked back lingeringly. "I wish I could…"

"Lily, you did your best…what road were we on before?" Jack looked left and right, trying to get his bearing.

"Chungyang Road, I think."

"I don't know how to read the street signs."

"I think that one." Lily looked up at the Chinese characters on the lamp post.

"Okay, let's hurry! I think we still have time." Jack grabbed her hand as they slowly made their way along the narrow streets ensnarled with desperate people, all heading toward the Yangtze River.

"I think I see it." Jack sighed with relief when he saw a column of gray smoke billowing out from an old steamboat.

"We made it." Lily saw many foreigners standing around the dock.

As they hastened up the gangplank, a familiar voice came up from bchind them. "You guys better hurry up before the Japs start shooting at us!"

"Hey, Walter." Jack wheeled around. "Thanks for holding the boat for us."

"You don't need to thank me. The Japs won't let us leave until they make sure that no Chinese Nationalist soldiers are hiding onboard. Lily, did that little girl make it to the Nanking Safety Zone okay?"

"Yes," she nodded.

"Lily, you did the right thing. I just hate to think what would have happened to her if you hadn't done what you did."

"Thank you. I wish she could come with me."

Under the watchful eyes of two gray Japanese battleships anchored in the middle of the Yangtze River, their steamboat quickly slipped away from the dock, leaving thousands of desperate people howling on shore. But before their boat got very far into the river, someone suddenly cried out, "What is going on over there?"

Further downstream, Jack saw a bunch of Japanese soldiers barking orders and waving their bayonets at another group of Chinese soldiers kneeling on the wet riverbank. "Oh, my God, not again!"

"Oh, please! Please don't kill them!" Lily cried out.

Then they heard a burst of the rat-ta-ta sound of machine-guns. Streams of bullets began to ricochet off the water as the Chinese soldiers began to tumble over the riverbank; and some of them, still alive, started running wildly into the river as the Japanese soldiers calmly took aim at their thrashing bodies as if they were hunting down some sort of wounded animals. In just a few short minutes, the river turned red.

Numbed by the orgies of killings they had seen in the past few weeks, many passengers just stood there, stunned and speechless, as they looked on at the lifeless bodies drifting along the red currents as if they were following them back to Shanghai.

"Lily, I just wish there was something we in the West could do," the AP reporter mumbled.

"I hate them! I hate them!" Lily pounded her fist on the railing.

"Lily, I am sorry. I know how you feel." Jack gently put his arm around her, not knowing what else to do.

"I wish the Old Man Heaven would take revenge on these Japanese devils! There will be a price to pay on their souls!" Lily raised her fist toward the bleak skies.

"God help us all!" An American woman standing nearby pleaded for divine intervention and then added, "Why didn't these Chinese soldiers put up a good fight since they knew they were going to die anyway?"

"They have lost their will to fight. I have heard that their generals have deserted them and left them with nothing to fight with, no guns or ammunitions." Her companion said somberly.

"Our government must do something to help these poor people."

"What can our government do? I just don't think we Americans want to fight their war."

"I wish we could do something." The American woman mumbled as she slowly walked away from the railing.

"Lily, it is getting cold. Let's go inside." Jack nudged on her arm as he watched other passengers drifting away from the deck. And just as they were about to step inside the cabin, Lily abruptly stopped and perked up her ears. "Wait, I think I hear someone singing. It sounds like Chinese opera."

"I hear it too. It's weird. Why would anyone be singing Chinese opera at a time like this?"

"Can we go take a look?"

"If you want. Walter, you wanta come?"

"Sure, why not."

In the back of the boat and behind a circle of curious passengers, they saw a middle-aged Chinese woman twirling around and around on the polished teak deck as if she was performing on stage. Wearing a white *chi pao* and holding a green handkerchief in one hand, she stabbed her other two fingers into the air this way and that as if they were an imaginary sword.

"She looks familiar," someone whispered.

"I think she is that famous Chinese opera singer," another added.

"Lily, what is she doing?" Jack asked.

"I think she is singing the last scene from *Farewell My Concubine*." Lily peeked behind the crowd.

"What is that?"

"It is a famous repertoire from Peking opera."

"I see…." Jack remembered he had seen something similar at Mr. Zhou's Chinese New Year's party a few months back. "Lily, do you understand what she is singing?"

"Not every word, but you don't have to. Most Chinese know the story by heart. It is a classic morality play about a woman's honor and loyalty to her husband."

"Very Chinese," the AP reporter quipped.

"Yes, very Chinese."

"So, what is it about?"

"It is about a king who urged his favorite concubine to escape after his army was defeated. He didn't want the barbarians to capture her, fearing they would make her their sex slave." Lily listened intently as the lady in white sang in a quaveringly high-pitched falsetto voice.

> *Oh, my lord, as you enjoy the wine*
> *I will dance for you to relieve your worries.*
> *The Chin force has defeated your army and ruined our country;*
> *heroes have risen, and battle lines are drawn,*
> *but history has taught me a true lesson that*
> *winning and losing are common affairs in war...*
> *You have fought many brave battles and*
> *I have been by your side in all your campaigns;*
> *I've shared many of your glorious victories.*
> *Now, in your unfortunate defeat, I will stand by you.*
> *My Lord, how can I seek my own life,*
> *and let you face death alone?*
> *What would be the meaning of life without you?*
> *In life, and in death, I will be at your side.*
> *Oh, my Lord...*

"She is singing her heart out." Jack was mesmerized.

"Yes, I can hear the sadness in her voice; she is grief-stricken because she is about to lose her man and her country. Now she is doing the final sword dance to distract him, and in the end, she will use the sword to kill herself, so he does not have to worry about her after he dies," Lily whispered.

The lady in white spun faster and faster, and her quavering voice became more and more strident. She flailed up her imaginary long sleeve and stabbed her imaginary swords as she moved closer and closer to the guardrail.

"No singing here. Go back cabin!" A uniformed Chinese man with a dark, swarthy complexion suddenly appeared.

"Please, sir, let her sing." Lily stepped forward.

"Woman, you go back cabin too!" he glowered.

"Let the poor woman sing!" Jack shouted into the man's face.

"Not allowed. Our rule," he shot back with a vacant stare.

"Goddamit! What is the matter with you? China is your country too!" Jack stared straight in his eyes. The man, stunned by this tall foreigner's authoritative voice, slunk backward and a vague expression of embarrassment slipped across his face. He quickly loosened his grip on the lady in white, and in an instant, she ran toward the guardrail, climbed over it, and stood carelessly by the edge of the boat as she looked down at the churning white foam, oblivious to the gasping onlookers rushing toward her. After a brief hesitation, she plunged into the cold Yangtze River.

"Oh, my God, she jumped!" the crowd screamed, craning their heads over the guardrail, fixing their eyes at the churning white waves. They searched in vain but saw nothing.

"Oh, Sweet Jesus! What did she do that for?" the same American woman Jack saw before asked bewilderingly. "I would think she should feel fortunate that she has gotten on the boat with us. Is she crazy or something?"

"No. I heard someone say that the Japanese soldiers had raped her daughter and shot her husband," another passenger quickly explained.

"Oh…I am so sorry. My apology. I didn't mean to be so…." She quietly walked away.

"Another sad case of life imitates art," the AP reporter mumbled to himself as he stared out into the receding white foam. For all his experience in China, even he was not prepared for what he had just witnessed.

"Old Man Heaven, why are you so cruel?" Lily railed, her face contorted with pain and her knees buckling under the weight of the day as she fell into Jack's arms. "Why does she have to suffer such a tragic fate! What is becoming of China?"

"I don't know…I wish I knew," Jack mumbled.

"Jack, I think we've all had enough tragedies for one day. Shall we all go back inside?"

"Walter, why don't you go in first. I think she wants to stay here for a while."

And soon, the deck became deserted. Jack and Lily stood there alone as their steamboat forlornly slipped down the misty Yangtze River.

What she had gone through in the last few days had sucked everything out of her. Lily leaned into Jack's arms, feeling drained as she stared out at the deserted riverbanks. As their boat slowly drifted around the bend, she suddenly pulled away from him and ran toward the guardrail.

"What are you doing?" Jack yelled out alarmingly.

"Jack, do you see that wooden plaque over there?" Lily pointed to a piece of board that was half submerged in the water. "That's the Longjiang Shipyard!"

"What shipyard?" Jack rushed over.

"Longjiang Shipyard. That was where Eunuch Zheng Ho launched his armada to the Horn of Africa!" With a far-off look, she fixated her eyes on the last remnants of the ramshackle shipyard as if she could hear the echoing sounds of hammering in her ears and see the giant square-sails fluttering in front of her eyes.

"Is that it?" Jack recalled what that old professor had said about some giant Chinese junks that sailed to Africa three-hundred years ago.

"Hard to believe, isn't it?" Lily shook her head and then said with glints of pride dancing in her eyes. "Jack, do you know that when Marco Polo first came to China more than six hundred years ago, our streets were paved with stones and roofs glittered with gold. He could see young scholars in Mandarin robes reciting poetry on the balconies of teahouses and elegant ladies in flowing gowns browsing in the silk shops below. In the crowded squares, he could watch acrobatic troupes performing for the giggling children. At night, he could hear boisterous laughter in small noodle shops and the gentle Pipa playing in the fragrant gardens. In the Grand Canal, he could see bountiful boats moving up north loaded with grains, fish, and teas, and in this Yangtze River, big ships sailing out to faraway foreign ports, carrying silk and porcelains. Our Middle Kingdom was prosperous, people were happy, and land under Heaven was at peace. Whatever became of that China? Our ancestors could never have imagined that their descendants would now be wandering in these same streets in rags and being slaughtered like dogs by the Japanese bandits!"

"Lily, I am sorry. Now, I kinda appreciate why that old professor was so saddened by what is happening to his country."

"I am very saddened too," Lily said quietly as she watched the last piece of the rotten wood that was the Longjiang Shipyard slowly disappear.

"Lily, we all had a long day. Shall we go in?"

In the stillness of the night, Jack found himself reflecting on the first time he saw Lily in his father's garden; the first time he held her in his arms on the dance floor, and the many weekends they shared a bowl of noodles in his father's black Ford. Just a year ago, he never knew she even existed, and now she is sleeping soundly in his arms. Love begins, as it so often does, with that chance encounter or with that casual effervescent smile. "Lily, I think I am falling in love with you," Jack gently kissed her hair and closed his eyes. Soon, the incessant humming of the engine below his feet slowly lulled him into oblivion.

CHAPTER 31

In the Name of Our Emperor

Beneath the moonless skies, their steamboat quietly slipped down the Yangtze River, passing the ancient pagoda perched high on the Purple Mountain; the eerie silence interrupted only by the persistent humming below the deck and the occasional croaking of bullfrogs on the desolated riverbanks. Sometime in the dead of night, the engine suddenly sputtered and quit. Jack bolted up and saw swarms of flashlights waving around him and a cold bayonet pointing at his face. “Hey! Hey! What the hell are you guys doing?”

“Come with us! You are under arrest!”

“What? What are you talking about?” Bewildered, Jack struggled to free himself, but he seemed to be immobilized.

“You have committed a crime against our Imperial Army!” They wrestled him up from his seat. And soon he found himself in the back of a military truck with Lily sitting next to him; hands roped together.

“Jack, where are they taking us?”

“I think they are taking us back to Nanking.”

“But why?”

"I don't know. This guy kept on saying that I have committed some sort of crime. What crime? I don't understand."

"I don't want to see that colonel again."

"Don't worry, Lily. I am here." Jack tried to put up a brave front.

After rumbling throughout the night, their truck finally came to a stop in front of the same Tudor-style mansion back in Nanking, and Colonel Taro Yamashita was waiting for them by the front gate.

"Mr. Wells…Mr. Wells, I thought I wouldn't see you again," he said teasingly.

"Colonel, I didn't want to see you either. We were on our way back to Shanghai, but your men picked me up on some trumped-up charges!"

"Mr. Wells, I have fewer than twenty military policemen to watch over thirty thousand soldiers. I don't have time for this nonsense!" He abruptly swiveled on his heels. "See you in my office!"

"Colonel, I hope you won't keep us here for long." Jack watched the Colonel gently lay down his samurai sword and casually prop up his shiny boots on the desk.

"Mr. Wells, I let you go last time, but why do you have to push your luck?" he said in a gruff voice.

"Colonel, I haven't done anything. What are you talking about?"

"You've hit one of our Imperial Army soldiers in the face and broke his nose. Hitting our soldiers is a crime, punishable by death!"

"Whoa! What the hell are you saying, Colonel? Your soldiers were trying to rape a little girl, and one of them even tried to attack her." He glanced at Lily. "What do you expect me to do? Okay, I am sorry."

"No need to apologize, Mr. Wells. You did what a man should do for his woman, and I respect that, but unfortunately, the matter is out of my hands now."

"What do you mean it is out of your hands?"

"The soldier you hit came from another division; his superiors demanded your severe punishment. Because you're an American, our Command Headquarters has gotten involved." He stared at a black telephone expectantly.

"Sir, I am sure this whole thing is just a big misunderstanding," Jack said.

"Mr. Wells, it is too late to explain things to me. Now, I have to wait for my instruction from Headquarters on what to do with you and your Chinese girlfriend."

"How long do we have to wait here?"

"Frankly I have no idea. Mr. Wells, relax. Who knows, you might get lucky again." The Colonel took off his wire-rimmed glasses and slowly wiped them with his white handkerchief. Suddenly, he looked more like a college professor than a military man; his ramrod posture softened, and his face became thoughtful. "Mr. Wells, have you ever read Charles Darwin's book, *On the Origin of Species*?"

"Yes, I have studied it in college," Jack replied unsurely.

"His idea of survival of the fittest is so relevant to what is going on around the world today. Yes?" The Colonel thoughtfully picked up the hardcover book from his desk and pushed his glasses up the ridge of his nose.

"I guess so," Jack replied negligently, not sure where the colonel was going with this.

"Mr. Wells, I was not always a colonel, you know. Not long ago, I was teaching at Todai, the Harvard of Japan. Your friend, Captain

Tanaka-san, went there too. Of course, you already knew that. He was conscribed, while I volunteered. Unfortunately, I was too old to fight, so they put me in charge of the military police."

"Colonel, that's all very interesting. How long do we have to stand here?"

"Mr. Wells, be patient. It won't be much longer. I am sure my commanders have not forgotten about you." The Colonel casually picked up another book. "Mr. Wells, I am now reading this book, *Mein Kampf*. Have you ever read it?"

"No, I haven't had a chance to." Jack shrugged.

"If you have time, you should read this excellent book." He flippantly thumbed through the pages. "This Hitler fellow offers a very compelling argument about why the Aryan race is superior to all the Slavic and other non-Aryan races living around Germany. He explains why the superior races need more living space not just to survive, but to thrive so that they won't be overwhelmed by the sheer numbers of all these inferior beings. Survival of the fittest!" he declared forcefully.

Jack and Lily looked at each other and did not know what to say.

"Mr. Wells, do you know that we Japanese have the same belief?"

"But you are not Aryans."

"True, but do you also know that our Yamato race descended directly from the Goddess Amaterasu."

"If you say so, Colonel," Jack said perfunctorily.

"Just like this Hitler fellow, we too fear all the inferior races surrounding Japan. And just like Germany, we too need more living space!" Colonel Yamashita pulled down his wire-rimmed glasses as if he was lecturing his college students. "Mr. Wells, have you ever heard the word, *Lebensraum*?"

"No, I have not. What is that? Some kind of disease?" Jack replied facetiously.

"No, that is the word Hitler uses to describe the imperative need for us superior people to acquire more living space and more natural resources. Like Germany, Japan, too, needs more living space. But by some unfortunate historical circumstances, we are not blessed with either. We are essentially an island nation contending with a mere 142,270 square miles of mountainous land and rugged coasts, while you Americans have a whole continent with three million square miles of open spaces and fertile land."

"Yes, Colonel, we Americans are very blessed." Jack managed a small smile. "Can we talk about all this over a beer sometime?"

"Like America, China too has lots of land, and with a little cooperation from them, we Japanese can put these resources into more productive use and then we can all prosper together in the Greater East Asian Co-Prosperity Sphere—peacefully, without war!" the Colonel declared wistfully, as visions of Japan's glorious future danced in his eyes.

"With all due respect, sir, you are not talking about cooperation; you are advocating invasion, just like what Germany is doing in Europe."

"The word *invasion* sounds so harsh. Mr. Wells, have you ever heard of the Japanese Monroe Doctrine?"

"No, I haven't. Is that like our American Monroe Doctrine?"

"Yes, exactly! Just like you Americans like to think you are the natural leader of all the Americas. We Japanese like to think that we are the natural leader of the whole of Asia. Even your president,

Theodore Roosevelt, had once said that Japan is the only civilized nation in Asia capable of leading all other lesser developed countries into the twentieth century! It is not just our duty, but our destiny to lead our Asian brethren out of the dark ages!"

"Sir, I don't believe our president ever said that," Jack carped.

"Yes, he certainly did. Too bad he is no longer with us. Just the same. Your Western powers have occupied Asia long enough. We think it is time for us Japanese to lead our Asian brethren into a better future…look at what we have already done in Manchuria; we have built new roads, schools, and hospitals for the Chinese people, and we can do the same for China!"

"We don't need any of your help! And Manchuria does not belong to you!" Lily chafed.

"Young lady, China does need our help. For the past one hundred years, you Chinese haven't been able to reform yourselves. We don't call you Chinks the 'Sick Men of Asia' for nothing!" the Colonel said disdainfully.

"Why do you hate us so much?"

"We Japanese don't hate you Chinese. For a thousand years, we have been kowtowing to China because we thought you were a superior race. Imagine that!" He sneered, shaking his head as if he couldn't believe that Japan had been one of China's vassal states once upon a time. "China had its moment in history, but today it is a mere shadow of its old self. Like a good neighbor, we Japanese are ready to help you get back on your feet!"

"You have done nothing to help us! Your soldiers came to China to kill our men and rape our women! Japan has done nothing for us except leaving a long trail of blood on our soil!" Lily protested as anger seethed in her blood and hatred gnawed at her vitals.

"Colonel, I have seen it with my own eyes." Jack came to her aid. "I saw your soldiers execute many Chinese prisoners in cold blood. Just yesterday, I saw them use Chinese men for live target practice right here in the backyard of your police headquarters!"

"What are you implying?" The Colonel glared at Jack harshly. "Are you saying our soldiers are a bunch of murderers! Mr. Wells, let me remind you of something! China and Japan are at war!" The Colonel exploded. "We are samurai warriors. We fight and die in the name of our Emperor; we kill not because we enjoy killing; we kill because we must kill! These Chinese soldiers should fight like men and die like soldiers! I have nothing but contempt for these cowards! They all deserve to be cut down as like mokuzai, a piece of lumber!"

"Colonel, many of these Chinese soldiers are just mere boys!" Jack shouted back.

"Mr. Wells, aren't you being a little disingenuous? What we are doing in China is not that much different from what you Americans did to the native people in your land not so long ago."

"Colonel, I beg to differ. There is a big difference between what you Japanese are doing in China and what we did a long time ago—"

"No, no, no, Mr. Wells. There is no difference! Look at your history!"

"I know my history. What you are saying is untrue!" Jack protested.

"Mr. Wells, I don't mean just your American history, but the whole white men's history. For the past two hundred years, while you Americans were busy at conquering the American Indians, this little island nation called England had been busy colonizing other people's land around the world, building an empire stretching from Canada to Australia. In fact, your country was a part of that empire not long ago, and I don't see you criticizing the English for all the sufferings and killings they have inflicted on the indigenous people. And, it wasn't us who first started the Opium War on China to force the Chinese to smoke more opium!" The Colonel paused and then added thoughtfully. "Mr. Wells, let's face it: neither the West nor Japan had any legitimate reason to invade other people's land other than the fact that we could! We are stronger, superior, and we both have the imperative to acquire more land. Survival of the fittest! Might makes right!" The Colonel slammed down his fist.

"Colonel, I think your logic is warped. There is a big difference between our democratic West and your imperialistic Japan," Jack retorted.

"What is the difference? Just like other poor countries the West had colonized, China has only itself to blame for being so weak," the Colonel said as he took another glance at the black telephone. "Let me tell you something, Mr. Wells; the only difference is that times have changed. Japan has risen! Asia is no longer the white man's alone!"

"Colonel, Japan cannot justify what it is doing here in China. We Americans don't advocate colonialism."

"Really? Tell that to your General Douglas MacArthur," The colonel snickered. "Mr. Wells, I just wish you American would be less hypercritical and more understanding of the situations we Japanese are now facing."

"What do you mean?"

"Japan must take control of its destiny because you Americans can cut off our vital supplies of oil, iron, and coal from Southeast Asia at will. It is a matter of our national survival!"

"By invading China?" Jack scoffed.

"Do we have any choice? The West has already colonized the whole of Southeast Asia and not to mention India."

"China does not want to become a Japanese colony!" Lily protested.

"Young lady, I wish you could understand what we are doing in China is for the greater good for us Asians. If only China would cooperate, then we all can..." The Colonel paused and stared at the black telephone on his desk as it suddenly sprang alive, loud and ominous.

"*Moshi, Moshi.*" He abruptly jumped up, clicking his heels and bowing to the voice on the telephone. *"Hai, Yamashita desu!... Hai! Hai!"* Colonel Yamashita slowly put down the black receiver, stone-faced.

"Anything wrong, Colonel? What did they say?" Jack shot an alarming side-glance at Lily. Their eyes widened, and blood drained out of their faces.

After a long and excruciating minute, he said icily, "The Command Headquarters has issued their final order. According to our 'Three All's Policy,' all war prisoners are to be executed. No exception!"

"What! We are not war prisoners! I am American! You understand?" Jack protested at the top of his lungs.

Colonel Taro Yamashita—now a tightly wound military man—walked out of his office without another word. His eyes were blank, his face unfathomable, and that professor in him was long gone.

"This can't be happening! I am an American! Do you hear me?" Jack kept on yelling, but all the Japanese sentries seemed to be deaf as they roughly pushed him out of the door.

Soon, Jack found himself kneeling in front of a dark pit piled up with headless bodies as flocks of black crows cawed overhead. Already gathered nearby, Jack saw the same group of crisply dressed Japanese officers sitting on folding chairs, chatting and laughing as usual.

"This can't be real!" Jack cried hoarsely. "Lily, I think we are going to die!"

"Jack, I thought the Japanese were afraid of you Americans."

"That was what I thought…Lily, I don't want to die!"

"Jack, if we can't be together on this earth, maybe we can still be together in Heaven," Lily said softly.

Jack smiled at her and whimpered, "I wish it wouldn't end this way. Lily, I love you."

"Jack, I love you too. Let's pray." Lily tilted her head gently on his shoulder. "The Lord shall be our Shepherd. We shall not—"

But it was not Lily Jack felt on his shoulder, but the strong hand of the Colonel. "I know you two lovebirds would like to die together, but that would make it very difficult for me to cut off your head, my American friend!"

From the corner of his eye, Jack saw a pair of shiny boots. He dared not to look up, but he knew it was Colonel Taro Yamashita standing over him, staring down with that snickering, contemptuous smile. In his ramrod military posture, he slowly drew out his samurai sword from the scabbard. He picked up a dipper of clean water from a bucket next to his boots. Carefully, he dripped the water on both sides of the blade as drops splashed onto the blood-stained ground. Then he slid his sword through a white towel in a swift, continuous, fluid motion as if he wanted to make sure the blood of his last victim would be wiped clean. Tauntingly, he slowly wiped dry his cold steel blade and held it up in the air. Such a simple, magnificent killing machine!

In agonizing anticipation of his sharp blade, Jack submitted to his fate. His head bent forward, and shoulders drooped down. Bereft of terror, the waiting seemed to be an eternity.

Nonchalantly, the Colonel planted his feet firmly into the sodden dirt, legs spread apart. He held out his shiny sword with two hands, and in a swift motion, he swung it up in a perfect arc, and then he stopped. With a sadistic smile under his small mustache, he held up his sword in midair as if he wanted to prolong the agony of his victim.

"Yo!" He then let out a deep-throated animal grunt. His samurai blade came down swiftly in one clean fell swoop. No wasted effort, no splattering blood to soil his uniform; just two streams of warm blood squirted out into the air. The Colonel had beheaded many men with his sword before, but this was the first time he had sliced off a white man's head. Instead of bowing, the Colonel turned to his superior officers, raised his blood-stained sword, and shouted triumphantly, *"Banzai! Banzai!"*

And all the officers jumped up to their feet and shouted, *"Banzai! Banzai!"*

Jack fell over into the dark pit as many blank and soulless eyes stared up at him. "Oh, my God! Oh, my God!" he screamed.

"Jack, Jack, are you okay?" A hand reached out to him from the abyss.

"Lily, is that you?"

"Yes, it's me. You were having a nightmare."

"Oh, my God, I…I thought I was dead!" He shivered uncontrollably.

“No, you are not dead. Jack, I am here. Everything is okay.” Lily held him in her arms.

“It was so real! I even felt his sharp blade!” Jack sat up, touching the back of his neck.

“Jack, you must have had a really bad dream.” Lily rocked him gently in her bosom.

CHAPTER 32

It Is in Our Karma

In the wee hours of the morning, their boat quietly slipped into the Shanghai Harbor, passing the abandoned factory buildings and darkened billboards, where the Chesterfield Girl was no longer was smiling and the White Horse no longer jumping. There were no cruise ships on the empty water or people strolling along the deserted riverfront promenade. Jack only saw a couple of intrepid rickshaw pullers waiting patiently in front of the Cathay Hotel, hoping to pick up a fare.

"Thank God, Shanghai is still safe." The AP sighed with relief.

"Walter, make sure you get those pictures to all the newspapers, including the *North China Daily News*."

"Jack, these pictures will hit all the press first thing in the morning."

"It was nice meeting you, Mr. McDaniel. Can you send Jack a copy of your negatives? I want to send them to all the Chinese newspapers too."

"Of course, as soon as I get them developed."

"Walter, we should get together for a drink sometime."

"Of course. After all the things we have gone through?"

"You have a place to stay?"

"I think I am going to stay over there…I hope they still have a room," the AP reporter said jokingly as he looked up at the Cathay Hotel.

By the time they got back to Jack's apartment, it was almost four o'clock in the morning. Standing in the middle of his living room, Jack and Lily suddenly found themselves with nothing to say to each other.

"Lily, would you like to take a shower?" Jack finally broke the silence.

"Mm." She nodded nervously.

"Would you like a cup of tea?"

"Mm." She nodded again.

"It that a yes?"

"Yes, I would like to have a cup of tea," she whimpered.

"I am going to boil some water."

"I am going to wash up." Lily dodged into the bathroom. When she re-emerged, Jack was waiting outside the door with her tea.

"Here is your tea. Are you cold?"

"A little bit," she replied self-consciously, holding a lavender-striped towel around her wet body.

"I don't have any pajamas." Jack opened the hallway closet and pulled out his old cardigan sweater. "I used to wear this in my college days."

"It is kind of big."

"I know, but why don't you put it on?" Jack took away her teacup, slowly draped it over her wet shoulders, stepped back, and stared at her admiringly. "Yes, it is a little too big, but you look cute in it."

"You think so?" she replied coyly.

"I do." Jack slowly pulled her toward him, wrapping his hands around her nervous body. Her lavender towel fell on the floor.

"Jack, please." Lily feebly resisted with her hands on his chest. She began to tremble as his two big hands caressed her bare back.

"Oh, Lily, it is nice to hold you in my arms like this."

"Oh, Jack, please." She turned her face sideways.

Jack gently turned her face toward him, held up her chin, and whispered, "I love you."

"Oh, Jack!" She tilted up her face.

Hungrily, Jack lowered his moist lips to meet hers.

Lily began to purr as he gradually moved his lips down to her neck, her bare shoulders, and then her svelte body.

The need for giving of herself suddenly became urgent. Jack felt Lily's soft flesh pressed against his, slithering at his wanton groping and quivering as his wet lips traversed her porcelain white chest. He looked up occasionally, fearing she might be put off with his aggressive moves, but she was lost in her own ecstasy. "My God! Oh, oh… oh," she cooed like a little kitten, trusting and vulnerable. She arched up to meet his stiffened muscles. He grabbed hold of her more tightly as he rushed toward victory. And in his embrace, Lily blossomed.

The early morning mist blanketed the windows, the muted foghorn groaned in the harbor, and time stood still. They just lay there, motionless, savoring the precious moment as the rotating ceiling fan gently brushed the cool air across their naked bodies, now fused into one. After a long silence, he slowly eased up from her. "Do you mind if I smoke?"

"Do you want me to light it for you?" she asked sweetly.

"Sure." Jack handed her his Zippo lighter.

"I like the flower on your lighter." She ran her finger over it.

"I bought it at the Wing On Department Store, remember?"

"Yes," she replied reflectively.

"What are you thinking?"

"I remember the time when I saw you come up from the elevator. I was so nervous to see you. I thought you might…"

"I was a little nervous too."

"You were? I thought you might think badly of me after that night."

"No, not at all. After I had that talk with your friend, Jasmine, my feeling for you grew strong."

"Really?" Lily put her head on his chest. "Jack, I would have never imagined that when the first time I saw you in your father's garden, we would be lying here like this."

"Like this?" Jack slowly ran his finger over her naked chest.

"Jack!" she coyly pulled up the bedsheet.

"Lily, I remember that day very well too. You looked so pretty standing there in the garden with a flower basket in your arm."

"Really?"

"You didn't notice I was trying to get to first base with you?"

"What do you mean?"

"I wanted to know you better, but I didn't know where to start. You were so reserved."

"Of course, you are the Reverend's son."

"So what made you change your mind?"

"I don't know. We have gone through so much together ever since that day. After I got to know you better and things just happened." She slowly ran her fingers over his hairy chest as if she couldn't believe that she and this foreigner were lying together in bed.

"Yes, we have gone through a lot…."

"Jack, can I ask you a question?" Lily rested on her elbow. "Why did you go there that night? Out of all the places."

"You mean the Paramount Night Club?"

"Yes. Foreigners usually don't go there."

"My friend Bobby took me there because Jasmine works there."

"You knew her before?"

"No, I just happened to run into her at a Chinese New Year Party. She asked me to come."

"Jack, do you think our chance encounter at the Paramount was preordained?"

"I don't know, but it certainly had changed both of our lives."

"Jack, do you believe in karma?"

"I am not sure, but I have always been intrigued by it. What about you?" Jack blew out his smoke into the air.

"Jack, I've heard that lovers from their previous lives often find each other in this life and fall in love all over again. It is in their karmas that they will meet again, no matter where they are in the world."

"In the West, we call them soul mates."

"Jack, do you believe in souls?"

"Kind of." Ever since his college days, this Oriental concept of the afterlife had always fascinated him. Jack had often wondered what lies behind those curious liquid eyes of a baby, or that faithful look of a dog. There must be a certain self-consciousness staring back at him because their eyes are not vacant and their stares are not soulless.

"Your father said that after people die, they either go to Heaven or Hell; but in China, we believe that peoples' souls always come back. They just got recycled over and over again."

"Do you believe that?"

"I guess so. In China, people believe that if one had lived a virtuous life, he would come back as a man, blessed with lots of good fortune and many kids. If one had led an evil existence, he would come back to this life as a woman cursed with bad luck. If he had taken a life, he would become something less than a human, like a pig or a cockroach—a sort of retribution mandated by the Old Man Heaven. And for those who come back many times, we call them old souls."

"What do you think I am?"

"I think you are an old soul."

"What makes you think that?"

"I don't know, just a feeling."

"Lily, do you want to know a secret?" Jack gently stroked her hair. "Don't laugh if I tell you."

"Okay, I won't laugh."

"Remember when you were talking about China's olden days when Chinese scholars liked to sit in a teahouse, drinking wine, reciting poetry, and watching young ladies strolling by?"

"Yeah?"

"I could be one of those scholars sitting on the balcony, drinking wine, reciting poetry, and watching you walk by."

"Jack, you are an American."

"Yeah, in this life, but maybe in my last life, I might have been born Chinese."

"Really? What makes you say that?"

"I just have this visceral sense that I have been here in China before."

"What is visceral?"

"Just a feeling. Anyway, I seem to recall that I waved at you and you smiled back at me. You looked so pretty in that pink silk chi pao."

"Jack, you are so funny. Chinese girls didn't wear chi pao back then." Lily chuckled softly and paused. "Jack, you think we are soul mates?"

"Yes, I think we are," Jack replied firmly.

"You really believe that?"

"I do." Jack took another puff on his Camel.

"Jack, what about Joann? Is she your soul mate too?" Lily asked quietly.

"Eh...that was before I met you."

"I am sorry. I shouldn't have asked." Sensing the tension in his voice, Lily slowly moved away from him.

"C'mon, Lily, please. I need a little time to sort things out. I had another life before I met you, you know." Jack reached out to her.

"I know. I am sorry. I just thought…I am sorry."

"Lily, please don't keep saying you're sorry. I meant what I said. Lily, I love you."

"Jack, you don't need to say those words. I am not trying to make you say things you don't mean."

Oh, my God, she must think that I am just like all the other foreigners! "Lily, I hope you are not comparing me to Mary's father."

"No, I am not. It is just that…many of you American men take on Chinese girlfriends here in Shanghai, and then you leave them when you go back to your wives in America...I'm sorry, I don't mean to be so touchy."

"C'mon, Lily. I didn't know you even existed before I came to China. Things happen, but I can't change my past."

"Jack, you saved my life, and I am very grateful to you. According to the traditional Chinese belief, my life now belongs to you, but…I just thought you might have some feeling for me."

"What are you talking about? Your life doesn't belong to me. I do have a feeling for you, and I hope you have a feeling for me too!" Jack fumbled toward her.

"I do, but you are an American, and I am Chinese. I don't know how you really feel about me."

"Lily, I love you! Why can't you believe me?"

"Jack." She paused, and then said softly, "You are my first one. I am glad that you are. I'd rather die than let those Japanese devils rape me. If not for you, who knows what would become of me. I am very grateful to you."

"There you go again! Can we not talk about this grateful stuff? I thought you said you love me." Jack felt almost disappointed. *All that passion just because she was grateful to me?*

"Jack, I do. I believe that it is our karmas that have brought us together, but then again…"

"But then again what?"

"Perhaps in your last life, you loved more than one woman."

"That's a good one!" Jack chuckled. "Lily, even if that's true, it happened a long time ago. You know, back then, men could have more than one wife, or two, or even five wives."

"Jack, you're mocking me. I want to give you my heart, but I don't want to be your other woman. I don't want to come between you and Joann. I will leave as soon as there is daylight."

"Where are you going to go? You don't have any home to go back to anymore. Remember? The Japanese have burnt down the whole Chapei!"

"I-I think I am going to stay with Jasmine."

"Lily, I know you might think I am just like other foreigners, but I am not. Lily, please give me a chance to show you that I care for you. You can stay here as long as you want. I will sleep on the sofa."

"I don't want to impose on you."

"Lily, you are not imposing on me. From now, this is your home." Jack gently wrapped his arms around her.

"Thank you. Are you sure?"

"Yes. Very sure."

They stood together by the window as they watched the pink blushes peeking through the early morning skies and listened to the trams rumbling in the street below.

"What are you thinking?" Jack asked.

"I am just thinking…this is my country and I don't even have a home to go back to anymore."

"Lily, I understand how you feel. I am sorry." Jack held her tighter.

Silently, they stood together by the window as the early morning light cast a long shadow into the room. After a while, Lily sighed and said softly, "Jack, I wish we were born in another time."

CHAPTER 33

The Beginning of the End

"Good morning!" Mary jumped up from behind her secretarial desk when she saw Jack walking off the elevator. "Jack, where have you been? Everybody was looking for you." She followed him into his office.

"I just got back last night from Nanking."

"Nanking! What in the world were you doing over there? Everybody thought you were still in Shanghai!" Mary sounded surprised. "Your mother has been calling me for the past few days. Mr. Spencer even contacted the U.S. Consulate, but nobody knew where you were."

"Mary, I didn't go there because I wanted to. Man, you don't know the least of it." Jack plopped into his chair.

"Is Lily with you? Is she okay?" Mary asked quickly.

"She is okay; her friend has gone up north." Jack glanced around the room as if he was re-familiarizing himself with his office.

"Where north?"

"I don't know. I think he went to join the Communists. So, anything doing while I was gone?"

"Jack, I was just about to tell you."

"Tell me what?"

"Your father had a stroke, but he is okay now. I think."

"What?" Jack jumped up. "What happened?"

"That afternoon after you left, the Japanese soldiers went back to search the church again because their informant insisted that he saw a wounded man go inside. Your father tried to stop them, and in the struggle, he had a stroke."

"Oh God! I'm gonna go there right now!"

"Jack, it is only 8:30. I think he might still be sleeping. Your mother said he needs a lot of rest."

"Let me first go talk to Mr. Spencer, and then I'll go." Jack looked up and saw him already standing by the door. "Good morning, Mr. Spencer. I just got back last night from Nanking."

"What the devil were you doing in Nanking?"

"Mr. Spencer, I didn't go there voluntarily."

"You went there because…?"

"I was driving someone out of Shanghai, and on my way back, I ran into the Japanese China Expedition Forces on their way to Nanking. They decided to detain me."

"Did you tell them that you work for the Hongkong and Shanghai Bank?"

"I did, but it didn't make any difference to them."

"Jack, I'm glad you're back safely. How is your father?"

"I don't know yet. I am just about to go over there as soon as I finish up here."

"Certainly, by all means. Mary, would you please bring us a cup of tea?"

"Yes, Mr. Spencer."

Slowly, Spencer walked toward the window, holding a neatly folded *North-China Daily News* in his hand. "The paper has already labeled what the Japs did in Nanking as the 'Nanking Massacre.'"

"Did you see the pictures?"

"Yes, dreadful, absolutely dreadful. It was reported that over 200,000 Chinese were killed over a short span of just four weeks. Unfathomable what these Japs are capable of."

"I have seen some of the killings with my own eyes. I still can't believe that these young Japanese soldiers have it in them to do what they did to the Chinese. How can they live with themselves once they go back home to their wives, daughters, or sisters?"

"Jack, this much I do know. The Japanese are a bunch of profoundly insular island people. Their view of the world is often distorted by their opinion of themselves. Their sense of nationalism and devotion to their emperor are beyond fanatic. It is downright frightening! It seems that just about every Japanese man, woman, and child are willing to sacrifice themselves and die a glorious death in the name of their emperor. And that is why they don't feel anything for what they are doing to the Chinese. Actually, they all are very proud of what they did for their motherland."

"Yes, I have seen that fanaticism in their eyes. Those soldiers are trained to be like a bunch of killing machines with lust for blood. But I don't understand it. Why do the Japanese have so much hatred toward the Chinese? Aren't they of the same Oriental race?"

"Jack, Japanese don't consider themselves as Orientals. They detest us Westerners for lumping them together with other Asians."

"Why?"

"Therein lies the riddle." Spencer paused to take another puff on his pipe. "The Japanese want to be like us Westerners, but they can't. They are not white like us, and thus they internalize their anger into contempt toward their darker Asian brethren. Most Japs despise other Asians, especially the Chinese and Koreans."

"When I was in Nanking, I heard this colonel say something about their Japanese race was descended directly from some goddess, and thus they consider themselves superior to all other Orientals—just like the way the Germans think about their Aryan race."

"Yes, the Japs think they are better than all other Asians, and some of them even think they are superior to some of us. Imagine that!" Spencer smirked.

"Is that why they think it is in their destiny to be the leader of all their Asian neighbors?"

"Jack, I am afraid that they don't just want to lead their neighbors; they want to conquer them in the name of the 'Greater East Asia Co-Prosperity Sphere.'"

"I heard the colonel use that expression before."

"Jack, that is just an excuse the Japs are using to take over China and maybe the rest of Asia."

"Mr. Spencer, there must be something we in the West can do to stop their aggression."

"There is. If you Yanks can just cut off their oil supply, their war machine will come to an abrupt halt."

"It sounds like a good idea. Why hasn't anyone thought of that?"

"Many already have, but the cure would be worse than the disease."

"What do you mean?"

"Jack, an oil embargo would give the Japanese a legitimate reason to attack Burma, the Dutch East Indies, the Philippines—and

God forbid, even Australia—because they will claim that their national survival is at stake."

"You think they would be so brazen to take on the whole West?"

"I am afraid so. Jack, when it comes to their national pride, you don't know how fanatical these Japs can be. But unfortunately, at this moment, we Brits don't want to pick a fight with them, and I don't think your General Douglas MacArthur in the Philippines is anxious to take them on either. With Hitler rattling his saber in Europe, if we were to challenge the Japs here in Shanghai, I simply hate to see us Brits become the second white men to be defeated by these little yellow Gurkhas."

"Mr. Spencer, you sound pretty pessimistic."

"Jack, I am afraid that it is just a matter of time before the whole situation will come to an unpleasant end."

Puffing on his pipe, Spencer then said thoughtfully, "Jack, our British Empire has ruled supreme in this part of the world for one-hundred years. No one dared to challenge us until now. We were the *Da Lau Ban*—the Big Boss, as the Chinese like to call us; and the Japanese were the tail on the other end of the Bund. Now, the tail has risen, threatening to bite off its head. Jack, I am afraid that 1937 might well be the beginning of the end for our empire."

"I am sorry to hear that, Mr. Spencer."

"We had a good run at it for one-hundred years, but I am afraid that all good things must come to an end, and there is no point to cry about it, is there? Carry on!" Spencer said with a stiff upper lip as he strode out of his office.

"Jack, is everything okay? Mr. Spencer looked a little depressed," Mary walked in with the tea tray.

"He thinks that the Japanese might soon take over Shanghai."

"Bobby thinks so too. He said that soon it would not be safe for any of us to stay here anymore."

"Mary, what are you going to do if that happens?"

"I don't care. Bobby is going to take me to America; he is going to marry me!"

"Whoa, I am surprised. Congratulations! I thought Bobby wasn't the marrying kind. What made him change his mind?"

"Bobby thinks that the British will not be able to hold on to Shanghai much longer, and he worries that what happened in Nanking might happen here too."

"I hope not. So, when are you two planning to get married?"

"Next week."

"Why so soon? Aren't you gonna have a church wedding or anything?"

"Jack, to tell you the truth, we don't know enough people in Shanghai to fill even the first pew. Bobby and I are just going to the U.S. Consulate to get a marriage license. We want you and Lily to be our best man and bridesmaid."

"Sure, no problem. When?"

"We are thinking of next Saturday."

"You guys don't waste any time, do you?"

"Bobby said that he wants to get out of here before the shit hits the fan. Oh! I am sorry. I don't mean to be so vulgar."

"Mary, it is okay." Jack smiled. "I know what he meant."

CHAPTER 34

Bobby Gets Married

Inside the quiet U.S. Consulate, Mary, wearing a long white dress, and Bobby, in a double-breasted white flannel suit, quickly filled out their marriage certificate form and handed it back to the clerk behind the counter. After a glance, he looked up and asked suspiciously, "Who is this Hun Su Ling?"

"She is my mother," Mary replied anxiously.

"I thought you said you are British."

"I said my father is British."

"Then let me see your passport."

"I don't have one," Mary replied hesitantly.

"You don't have one? Why not?"

"Eh, I only have a Chinese passport."

"I am afraid that won't do."

"What do you mean, that won't do?" Bobby leaned over the counter.

"She needs a British passport to prove that she is a real British citizen."

"Like I said, I am an American, and she will be an American after we get married. So, what is your problem, sir?"

"I am sorry. I can't issue a marriage license to anyone other than to an American or a real British citizen."

"What the hell are you talking about? Her father is British!"

"But her mother is Chinese, and that would make her only half British. She has Chinese blood and a Chinese passport, and that would make her a Chinese. Our laws don't allow that."

"Don't allow what? What laws?" Bobby became agitated.

"Sir, you can't marry her because it is illegal."

"What the hell are you talking about? What's illegal?"

"Sir, have you ever heard of the anti-miscegenation laws that we have on the books in just about every state?"

"Don't use the big word on me. What does it mean?" Bobby asked brusquely.

"It means it is illegal for us white people—especially a white woman—to marry a nigger or any other colored people, Chinese included. I'm sorry. I didn't make the law."

"But she is not Chinese." Bobby leaned into his face.

"But fifty percent of her blood is Chinese. So that makes her a Chinese. I can't marry you two. I am sorry." The clerk was adamant.

"Does she look like a Chinese to you?" Bobby pointed to her blue eyes.

"Hey, Bobby, take it easy." Jack walked up from behind and asked calmly, "Sir, did you say that just about every state has this... whatever you call it...on the books? Which state does not have this law?"

"I am not sure...Eh, maybe Hawaii? But I am not sure."

"Good! Then just give her a visa. We will go to Hawaii to get married!" Bobby slammed down his fist on the counter.

"Sir, I cannot do that either," the clerk blustered.

"Are you bullshitting me! Why are you giving me such a hard time?" Bobby became angry.

"Sir, have you ever heard of the Chinese Exclusion Act of 1882?"

"No," Bobby said, "but that was a long time ago. What does that have to do with her?"

"It is still on our books, and it still prohibits Chinese—especially Chinese women—to emigrate into our country. Sir, I am very sorry," the clerk stammered.

"You are sorry?" Bobby shook his head in disbelief.

"Bobby, please do something!" Mary began to panic.

"Sir, can we speak to your superior?" Jack asked politely.

"I don't think it would do you any good."

"Why don't you give it a try? Please?" Jack persisted.

"Okay, if you insist." The clerk shrugged and quickly disappeared into the back office. A few minutes later, an elegantly dressed man appeared. "What seems to be the problem?"

"This jerk refused to issue us a marriage license. I reckon I am an American; this shouldn't be a problem!" Bobby shouted.

"I have already told this gentleman that we have a law on the books that forbids a white American from marrying a Chinaman."

"So, who is this Mary Lane?"

"I am."

"So, what is the problem?" The man took a close look at her tearful blue eyes.

"Sir." The clerk put the marriage paper in front of him and whispered something in his ear. The man-in-charge took another look at Mary, and then at Bobby, and just shrugged. "She doesn't look Chinese to me."

"Eh, what…what do you mean?"

"She looks more like a Hungarian."

"But…but she has a Chinese passport, and her mother is Chinese."

"Just put down that she is Hungarian. I think it is okay for a Hungarian to marry an American. No?"

"Are you sure, sir? But-but what about her passport?"

"I don't know. Just say that she lost it."

"Are you sure, sir?"

"Get them married first, and let me worry about the paper-work later." The man-in-charge turned to leave.

"Okay, I will do whatever you say," the clerk grumbled, shaking his head.

"Hey, buddy, thanks a lot," Bobby yelled out.

"You are mighty welcome!"

"I still think it ain't right to allow a Chinaman to marry an American." The clerk reluctantly stamped their marriage paper.

"Now, it is official. Congratulations, Mr. and Mrs. Robert Ferguson. Bobby, you now can kiss the bride," Jack declared.

"Mrs. Ferguson! I like the ring of it!" Mary beamed.

"Congratulations, Mary." Lily hugged her.

"For a while, I was really worried." Bobby wrapped his arms around his bride. "Let's get out of here!"

"Let's go dancing!" Mary hung on happily around his waist.

"Good afternoon, ladies and gentlemen, welcome to the Cathay Hotel." The hotel manager greeted them graciously.

"How are you, Freddy? Remember me?" Jack shook his hand.

"Yes, yes, of course, Mr. Wells, you are…with the Hongkong and Shanghai Bank, I believe."

"You have a good memory. Freddy, where is everybody?" Jack looked around the quiet lobby.

"Since Nanking fell, many foreigners don't want to come to Shanghai anymore. They are afraid that what happened in Nanking might also happen here in Shanghai. War is bad for business." He sighed and then took a discreet glance at Lily. "Would you two be needing a room tonight?"

"No, we are just going to your Jazz Bar for a drink. These are my friends, Mr. and Mrs. Robert Ferguson; they just got married."

"Congratulations are in order then, Mr. and Mrs. Robert Ferguson!"

"Freddie, later on, we would like to have dinner at your Tower Restaurant. Can you get us a table?"

"Certainly, we still have a few excellent tables with a harbor view. I will let them know."

"Thank you, Freddy."

"Mr. Wells, in case you change your mind, we still have a few choice rooms available." The hotel manager said quietly as he watched them walked down the hall.

The once-very-popular Tower Restaurant was now nearly empty, with many tables overlooking the harbor still unoccupied.

"Too bad we didn't come here last time. The view was so much better." Bobby waited for the waiter to pour their champagne.

"Bobby, the best view is right in front of you. Congratulations, Mr. and Mrs. Ferguson!" Jack raised his glass.

"I hope you two have a long, happy life together," Lily joined in.

"I'm so happy that I am married to such a wonderful guy, and have you two as our best friends." Mary held up her champagne glass. "Let us make a toast!"

"Here, here, to your marriage and our friendship!"

"We are going to miss you guys."

"Bobby, are you taking her back to Texas?"

"Hell no! Folks over there probably have never even heard the word 'Eurasian' before. We are goin' to Hawaii."

"Mary, I've heard Hawaii is a very beautiful place."

"That's what I've heard. It has lots of white beaches and palm trees. Lily, why don't you and Jack come with us?"

"Mary, you saw what just happened at the American Consulate. I don't think they would let me in."

"I wish you two could come with us. You and I could open up a dance studio together, and Bobby and Jack could run a bar on the beach," Mary said giddily.

"Yeah, Jack, why don't you think about it?"

"Bobby," Jack replied dourly, "I have already checked. I was told that U.S. immigration laws only allow a handful of Chinese college students and Christian missionary workers into the country."

"Hey, I got an idea. Maybe you can get your father to sponsor her for a missionary visa."

"Bobby, I don't think my father is ready to abandon his flock yet."

"Jack, I thought you told me that your mother wants to take him back to the States to get better medical treatment. This would be a perfect opportunity to do it. I think you should ask your mother and your dad will listen to her." Bobby urged him.

"Jack, Lily can get off with us in Hawaii, and you can meet us later after you settle in your father," Mary quickly added.

"Okay, I will ask my mother."

"Jack, do it soon. Only two ships are going back to the States in the next couple of months."

"Lily, would you like to go to America with me?"

"Yes…if they would let me in," she said softly.

CHAPTER 35

Praying at the Temple

With his father's recommendations, Lily got her missionary visa without much hassle, and with Bobby's connections, Jack booked the last two remaining cabins on the RMS *Empress of Japan* going back to the States. After resigning from the bank and helping his father tidy up the church's affairs, there was nothing much else left for Jack to do except idling away his days at his desk and staring out the window.

Meanwhile, heavy fighting between the Japanese Imperial Army and the Chinese Nationalist soldiers raged on outside of Shanghai, and food prices in the city, from a bag of rice to a pound of pork, seemed to double every week. Many nightclubs were closed and charity balls canceled. Anyone who could afford to leave was now desperately trying to secure a passage not just out of the Pearl of the Orient, but out of China. The once must-stop port of call now looked deserted.

Jack looked out the window with a melancholy stare. As he was about to light another Camel, Mary burst into his office.

"Jack, I'm so sorry to bother you."

"Mary, is something wrong?"

"Jack, I got some bad news for you." She closed the door behind her.

"What bad news. Is it about my dad?"

"No. Lily just called. She said that her friend, Jasmine, had drowned herself in the Whangpoo River!"

"What! Are you sure! When did this happen?"

"Last night. Lily told me that it might have something to do with her boyfriend."

"Where is she now?"

"She is at your place. I think you'd better go there fast. She sounded hysterical."

"If Mr. Spencer is looking for me, tell him I'll be right back." Jack grabbed his coat.

"Jack, I will go with you. I feel so bad for her. She has just lost her best friend."

"You think Mr. Spencer wouldn't mind?"

"I don't care."

Jack found Lily sprawled on the bed crying; her tears had already darkened the pillow.

"Hey, baby, I've heard." Jack gently stroked her tearful face. "What happened?"

"He secretly flew to Hong Kong yesterday without even good-bye to her." Lily picked up the Chinese *Shenbao* newspaper laying on her bed. The headline read: "Jilted Cabaret Girl Drowned Herself for Love!"

"I don't understand. What does it say?" Jack stared at Jasmine's lovely face on the front page.

"It says that she jumped into the Whangpoo River around midnight." Lily sat up, brushing aside her wet hair, and translated what she read: "According to the police report, the dead woman's name is Zheng Ting. She works at the Paramount Night Club under the stage name of Jasmine. It was rumored that the Number One Son of a certain rich textile factory owner had ditched her. He had secretly left Shanghai without taking her with him as he had promised."

"How could he do that to her?" Jack shook his head.

"Rich people in Shanghai can do whatever they want. Jasmine wanted to get married so badly; she was too blind to see that she meant nothing to him except being a rich boy's plaything."

"Man, and I thought he was a nice guy. She had so much bad luck in her life; I wished we could have done something to help her."

"The police said that she was pregnant at the time of her death. *Da Je!* My dear sister, why? Why didn't you say anything? I wish I were there when you needed me." Lily cried out as she gently ran her fingers over the picture of Jasmine's face. "Jack, she has no family here in Shanghai, and I don't even know any of her relatives from her village. Old Man Heaven, what had she done in her past life to deserve this cruel punishment?"

"I don't know, but I just wish she would have better luck in her next one," Jack mumbled.

"Jack!" Lily suddenly jumped up from her bed. "I must go to pray to the Old Man Heaven!"

"Where are you going?"

"I am going to Chenghuang Miao."

"Where?"

"She is going to the Temple of the City Gods," Mary explained. "I will call Bobby. I think he would like to come too."

The Chinese City, Nantao, was like a forbidden city to most foreigners; even though it was only a few blocks away from the International Settlement, few ever ventured into it. Following Lily, they negotiated their way along the narrow alleyways, sidestepping potholes and dodging hanging laundry. When they emerged from the narrow alleyways, Jack was surprised to see an airy open plaza buried deep inside. He hastened his steps, following Lily towards the faded red temple walls, passing old men playing Chinese checkers on stone benches and food vendors busy over the charcoal stoves. Inside the Temple of the City Gods, he trailed her along a large koi pond toward a tall pagoda-like building. Under the yellow-glazed roof overhangs, three golden statues of Chinese gods loomed over a group of monks praying at the altar. Jack could hear their hypnotic chanting echoing up the empty expanse of the prayer room and see worshippers kneeling on the slate floor with their hands clasped together, eyes closed, rocking back and forth as they pressed their heads to the floor, again and again.

"I'm going in." Lily quickly stepped over the brightly colored threshold. Standing outside, Jack saw her buy a few sticks of incense and a stack of paper money from a bald monk by the side door. He watched her kneel on a gold-colored cushion between two old ladies, and raise the incense over her head, and then rock back and forth, dropping her head onto the slate floor, again and again. Jack looked on, not knowing what to make of it as he thought back to the times she stood under the Cross singing "Amazing Grace."

"Jack, do you know that my father married my mother here in this temple?"

"Really? Your dad must be a romantic man."

"No, not really. He told my mother that his Holy Trinity Church would not perform their wedding service because she is Chinese, but the truth was that he was already married and my mother believed him. He lied!" Mary said in a broken voice.

"Are you okay, baby?" Bobby asked.

"For all these years, I have been busy coping with my own life and I have never thought of praying to the Old Man Heaven to grant her a better next life…Mother, wherever you are!" Suddenly, Mary stepped over the high threshold.

The bald monk by the door looked startled; he had never seen a foreigner inside the temple before.

Speechless, Jack and Bobby looked at each other and then turned to watch Mary and Lily walking up together to the altar, putting their paper money into an incense burner, and bowing to the three golden gods, over and over again.

"What is all that about?" Bobby whispered.

"I don't know."

"…maybe Mary is half Chinese after all," Bobby said quietly as he watched them walking away from the altar, holding hands and smiling at each other. "Baby, are you okay?"

"Yes, I feel much better now," Mary said.

"What did you pray for back there?"

"I prayed to the god of mercy to grant both of our mothers never to be poor again and to have a happy marriage in their next life."

Outside the temple gate, two rickshaw pullers, who seemed to have been waiting for them, quickly tossed away their unfinished cigarettes and cried out, *"Lau Ban,* rickshaw ride?"

"Bu yao, shei-shei, no, thank you." Lily waved her hand.

"Which way did we come from?" Jack glanced around the plaza.

"That way." Lily pointed.

"Okay, you lead the way."

"Lily, why don't you guys come to our place? I can make some lunch, and we can talk."

"Okay."

They followed Lily back into the same alleyway, and as she walked past a small noodle shop, she suddenly stopped.

"How many?" the proprietor asked ingratiatingly. "We serve the best Shanghai noodles. Your foreign friends like?"

"I thought I heard someone singing." She peeked inside, but she didn't see anyone singing except for a black vinyl record spinning on top of a square phonograph.

"Lily, we can go in if you are in the mood for some of their Shanghai noodles." Jack tried to comfort her.

"It is playing her song," Lily said numbly.

"What song?"

"The Jasmine Flower song. Can you hear it?"

What a beautiful Jasmine flower,
What a beautiful Jasmine flower,
Full of beautiful fragrant buds,
Everyone praised your whiteness and
Your sweetness. Allow me to pick one
And give it to another to share.
Oh, Jasmine flower, Jasmine flower....

"Jack, I used to sing that song with Jasmine when she taught me how to dance. We would dance and laugh. We had such a good time." Lily stood there staring down at the record player somberly.

"We were just like sisters. Now she is gone, and I have nothing to remember her by except for this song."

"I feel sad that she died this way. Jasmine was a beautiful person, just like the flower."

"Yes, she was just like the flower, beautiful but fragile."

CHAPTER 36

Hope Abandoned

The morning sun slowly rose from the East China Sea, casting long streaks of bright light into his bedroom. Jack twisted and turned in his bed. He hadn't slept well.

"Jack, are you awake?"

"Couldn't sleep."

"Me too."

"Today is the day."

"I know."

"How do you feel?" Jack rested his head on his elbows.

"I feel a little sad about leaving this place."

"I know how you feel. My dad is still reluctant to leave Shanghai. All he wants to talk about are his Sunday sermons and Chinese garden. I am afraid he is losing it." Jack sighed.

"How is your mother holding up?"

"She is a little stressed out. She feels the whole thing has been a failure; they didn't accomplish what they had set out to do here in China. She wants to come back as soon as my dad gets better."

"Jack, do you think it is a good idea that I go with you?" Lily asked unsurely.

"Of course. What do you mean?"

"I think your mother still wishes you would marry Joann. I am sorry. I didn't mean to hurt her."

"Lily, what is done is done. My mother is okay with it," Jack said quietly, but deep down, he felt a little guilty. He had always thought that he and Joann would eventually get married; he could not explain to her—or even to himself—how things could have turned out this way. He had written to her about his plan to take his father back to the States, and he tried to explain how he had fallen for this Chinese girl so far away from home. But after several tries, he decided it would be better for him to tell her in person.

"Jack, you don't have any regrets? I hope."

"No regrets." He pulled her closer.

"Hello there! Nice to see you again." The Sikh policeman greeted them as their taxi came to a stop at the foot of the Thibet Bridge.

"Hello, Patel."

"I say, why do you two keep on going back and forth while everybody else just wants to get in?"

"Any problem with that?" Jack snapped back.

"Sir, the problem is not with us; it is with them." He pointed toward a group of Japanese soldiers waving their rifles on the other side of the bridge.

"You don't need to worry about us anymore. We are leaving Shanghai for good. We are not coming back," Jack said loudly.

"Good for you! Maybe you can take me with you."

"No such luck, Patel."

"Have a good trip," the Sikh policeman said curtly as he stepped aside.

"Lily, aren't you glad that we don't have to go through this again?"

"Yes, my heart always skips a beat whenever I see these Japanese soldiers."

"I don't blame you." He squeezed her hand reassuringly.

As their taxis approached the New Hope Church, Jack saw his mother already waiting by the church door. "Mother, where is Dad?"

"He is still inside."

"Hi, Mrs. Wells, is the Reverend okay?" Lily hugged her.

"I hope so; he is the only one I've got. Let's go in to get him."

"Hi, Dad, are you okay?" Jack saw him standing on the empty stage with an unfocused stare.

"Son, where is Da Tu? I haven't seen him for days."

"Dad, Da Tu went north with that young Chinese man...I thought you knew."

"What young man?" His father looked puzzled. "Why isn't Lily up here to help me with my Sunday sermon?"

"Reverend, I am right here."

"Good, shall we?"

"Oh, dear." Mrs. Wells saw her husband searching for his Bible underneath the pulpit.

"Mother, what shall we do?"

"We might as well let him deliver his last sermon," she sighed.

The surprised parishioners and their families looked on, and slowly, they began to stand up from where they were sitting, squatting, and laying.

"My brethren and sisters, today I would like to talk…talk about God's eternal love. I…I want to…" he stuttered. His once-booming voice faltered.

"Wo dei tung boa jei mei men, Jin tian wo xiang yao he ni men tan tan Shangdi di ai…," Lily softly repeated his words, paused, and waited, but nothing was forthcoming.

"Mother, do you want me to go up there?"

"Thank you. I want to thank everybody," his mother quickly yelled out. "This will conclude Reverend Wells' last sermon, but we will be back!"

Just as Jack was about to run up the stage, he heard Lily start to sing. "Amazing Grace! How sweet the sound…"

Following her lead, all the parishioners too started to sing, and this little dimly lit prayer room again echoed with that yearning and hope, just like the first time when he heard it. As he listened, Jack began to feel a little sad that all his parents' aspirations in China were about to come to an end. They came with high hopes to Christianize the whole country but were forced to leave with only a handful of converts. He recalled what his boss had once said at the British Consulate last Christmas. "Reverend, converting one Chinaman is hard enough, but all of China?"

"Hallelujah! Praise the Lord!" Jack then heard his father thunder, waving his Bible.

"Dad, shall we go now?" He quickly ran up to the altar.

"Son, I have not finished my sermon yet."

"Dear, you need to say goodbye to everybody." His mother hurried over, gently patting on his father's trembling hand as she eased him down the stage, and then she turned to one of the parishioners. "Mrs. Lu, here is where we must say goodbye."

"Please take care of your health; we will never forget your kindness. We will be praying for you and the Reverend."

"You all must carry on God's work for a while without us, but we will be back."

"Mrs. Wells, don't worry; we will continue to study English very hard."

"Mrs. Lin, I hope they will send another pastor soon, but before that, you must all carry on with your Bible study without us."

"Nobody can replace our dear Reverend. We will miss him very much."

"He will miss you too. Goodbye."

"It is nice to meet you all. Goodbye." Jack waved.

"*Tsai-jian.*" Lily waved.

"Lee Li-wha, you make us Chinese proud. Study hard and come back to help China!"

"Lee Li-wha, you are such a lucky girl! Besides getting to go to America, you have caught such a handsome boyfriend!"

"Yes, Mrs. Lin, I am very lucky. I may even have a chance to go to college in America." Lily beamed. "I will study very hard, and I will come back to help China."

"What do you know? This girl who adored everything foreign may have a heart after all," another old woman walking behind them mumbled sarcastically in Chinese. "But I doubt that she will ever come back. Nobody comes back from the Golden Mountain. Why should they?"

"Lee Li-wha is a patriotic girl. She will be back."

"I doubt it," the old lady sneered under her breath.

"*Ai Ya,* Chow Tai-Tai, Lady Chow, you're such a sour vinegar. Let's all wish Lee Li-wha smooth sailing to the Golden Mountain and to have a happy life with Reverend Wells' son."

"I am not going to San Francisco. I'm going to Hawaii," Lily said softly.

"No difference, you are Chinese. They don't want you in their country," the old lady carried on.

"*Ai Ya,* Chow Tai-Tai, Lady Chow, you've got too much mouth. Why do you have to say such unlucky things to her? Her boyfriend is going to protect her."

"You don't think he will not get rid of her after he gets tired of playing with her? They all do; you know."

"The Reverend's son is a very nice boy. He is different."

"They are all the same," Mrs. Chow mumbled as if she was saying something she had already known.

"Lee Li-wha, don't listen to her. Have a good trip to America and a long and happy life with the Reverend's son!"

CHAPTER 37

On the Dock of Shanghai

The street leading to the Shanghai dock was even more chaotic than Jack remembered it. As their taxi inched closer toward the terminal, he saw a mob of anxious Chinese clamoring in front of the Chinese Customs House, and Sikh policemen, wielding their big wooden batons, tried to push them back. Jack and his mother held his father on each side as they worked their way toward the dock. Lily, clutching tightly onto her little suitcase, followed them closely behind. As they made their way through the trampling crowds, she suddenly heard a little boy crying out for his mother, and a young girl, no more than ten, was staring up at her with pleading eyes.

Lily stopped. "*Shao-mei mei, Yei men di mama baba le?* Little sis, where are your mother and father?"

"*Ta mendou sile! Riben Ren sahle tamen!* They are all dead! The Japanese devils killed them," the little girl cried out.

"What are you doing, Lily? We don't have much time." Jack looked back.

"Jack, I will be right there." She then turned back to the kids. "*Ni men zhu zai na?* Where do you live?"

"Chapei…they burned down our home," the little girl sobbed. "We couldn't find our aunt in the city."

"I am hungry." Her baby brother tugged on his sister's shirt.

"Lily, let's go! Our boat is leaving in an hour!" Jack rushed back.

"I know, I know. But they are hungry; let me get them some food." She hurriedly walked to a street vendor behind a steaming stove. "Please give me two dozen grilled dumplings."

"Anything else?" the man asked indifferently.

"And two bowls of your stir-fried noodles." She took out some coins from her pocketbook. She handed the little girl the dumplings and noodles, "*Shao-mei mei,* little sis, I only have one-hundred dollars left. Take it. I am sorry I don't have any more money. Take good care of your little brother. Buy him some candy, ha, sweet little girl."

"Lily, can we go now?" Jack rushed over, trying to ease her away.

"They are so young. They have just lost their parents, and they couldn't find their auntie in the city." Lily glanced back as she reluctantly moved away.

"Lily, I still have a bunch of Chinese money." Jack took out a stack of Shanghai dollars. "I have no use for them anymore. You want to give it to them?"

"That's a lot of money. Jack, are you sure?"

"Yes, I am sure. I just hope they can find their aunt soon."

"I hope so." Lily rushed back.

The little boy's eyes lit up when he saw her walking back. "*Jei-jei,* big sis, where are we going to sleep tonight?"

"I don't know…I am leaving Shanghai," Lily answered haltingly. "Here is some money the foreign uncle wants to give to you."

"Can we sleep with you?" The little boy looked up at her hopefully.

"Hsiao Chun, Little Chun, the big sister has her own family. We cannot sleep with them."

"Jei-jei, is that foreigner your family?"

"He is my dear friend. Ah, be a nice boy, *jei-jei* has to leave now." Lily gently patted his head; tears began to well in her eyes.

"Hsiao Chun, just take the money! The big sis is leaving China; she can't take us with her!"

The little boy stuck out his tiny dirty hand and took the money without a smile. "Can we be his dear friends too?" He looked up at her expectantly like a little lost puppy seeking some kindness from a stranger.

"We go now, Hsiao Chun, big sis has to go with her foreign boyfriend." The little girl pulled on her little brother's arm.

The glint of hope in the boy's eyes disappeared, and with a hesitant backward glance, he gave Lily a little wave and said in a tiny voice, *"Jei-jei, tsai-jian*. Big sis, bye-bye."

"Lily, shall we go now? You did your best." Jack gently pulled on her arm.

"The Japanese have killed their mother and father, they could not find their auntie in the city, and they don't have a place to sleep tonight! Just look at them! Just look at them!" She cried out in pain.

"Lily, we gotta go now! We don't have much time!"

"They have so few clothes on them. They might not make it through the night!"

The *Empress of Japan* suddenly let out a loud warning as its throaty horn reverberated throughout the harbor and something began to stir inside of her.

"I know, I know, Lily. Maybe there will be someone kind enough to take them in. There is not much else you can do for them. Let's go. Our ship is about to leave!" He again urgently pulled on her arm.

"Jack, the way the little girl looked at me reminded me of that girl I had left behind in Nanking. I saw the same fears in her eyes… and that little boy; he just breaks my heart; he reminds me of my little brother…"

"Lily, there are just too many homeless kids in Shanghai. You can't help them all," Jack pleaded.

"They are not homeless by choice! Jack, if I don't help them, who will?" She stared at the two little figures slowly walking away; her mind now seemed to be made up.

"Lily, you are not thinking…? Oh, man, you've got to be kidding! Do you know how many people would kill for a chance to go to America! Lily, you are throwing away an opportunity of a lifetime!" Jack could see what was on her mind.

"I know, Jack. I know, Jack…"

"Seriously, Lily, if you stay here, you'll have nobody left in Shanghai to fend for you!"

"They will be my family," she uttered in a disembodied voice.

"Lily, you got me!" he pled hoarsely. "I thought you want to go to Hawaii so you and Mary can open up a dance studio on the beach!"

"Yes, but..."

"But what? Lily, I love you. I thought you love me too!"

"I do, but I can't be your wife. Jack, maybe this is not our time."

"Lily, please don't say those things. Let's be real. You can't take care of them all by yourself. You don't even have your own place anymore. Remember? Please come with me. Our ship is about to sail!"

"Jack, I hope you understand if I don't help them, what will become of them?" She paused as her past flashed in front of her eyes. "Jack, I was all alone in these streets not long ago, I was frightened, and I wished someone would help me, but no one did. If it had not been for Reverend Henderson's kindness, I would not be the person that I am today. Perhaps it's time for me to return that kindness."

"Lily, what about us?" Jack cupped her face and kissed her salty lips, desperately trying to summon back that night's passions.

"Jack, I've left that poor little girl to fend for herself in Nanking, and I knew how much she needed someone to protect her. Now, how can I just walk away to seek a better life in America, knowing that these two kids might die in these cruel streets? They will forever weigh on my conscience."

"Lily, I will stay here then. There will always be another boat."

"Jack, your parents need you." She placed a tender kiss on his cheek. "I want to thank your father and mother for what they have done for me, but I need to catch up with the children before it is too late."

"Lily, you can tell them that yourself." Jack could feel her soft body slowly stiffen.

"Jack, I love you!" Lily suddenly pushed him away. "Children! Wait!"

"Lily!" Jack cried out imploringly.

As the evening breeze blew at her hair, she suddenly stopped. Slowly, she looked back with a sidelong glance and waved longingly as if she was saying to him, "Jack, I wish we'd been born in another time. *Tsai-jian,* until we meet again!"

"What happened? Where is Lily?" Bobby rushed back from the Customs House.

"I don't know; she is gone."

"What do you mean she is gone? What the hell are you talking about?"

"I don't know. The Japanese killed their parents…they were looking for their aunt in the city," Jack mumbled incoherently.

"Jack, what the hell are you talking about? Who are they?"

"She decided to stay with these two little homeless kids." Jack stared into the crowd.

"What made her do that? Are they her relatives or something?"

"No, she just said that this is something she must do."

"Does she know how many people would kill for a chance to go to America?"

"Yes, I told her that."

"Jack, I thought she loves you."

"I thought so too."

"Man, I hate to have to break this to Mary."

"How do you think I feel?!" Jack cried out.

The RMS *Empress of Japan* quietly slipped out of Shanghai Harbor. Jack and his parents remained on the deck watching the Pearl of the Orient slowly disappear into the darkening sky.

"My husband and I have just finished our dream house," Jack overheard an English lady standing nearby complain. "I hope my

Number One Boy will not let his dreadful relatives live in there. I must have a word with him when I come back!"

"Not this time, lady," Jack scoffed.

"Nonsense, I was born in Shanghai!"

"Lady, don't forget, this is not your country."

"I know that! Young man, I have been living in Shanghai longer than you have been alive," she replied indignantly. "I simply cannot understand what is happening to China."

"My dear, every country has its moment in the sun, and China had its moment," her companion said softly. "I am afraid that the Japs have finally slain the dragon."

"No, the dragon is not dead! It is just wounded!" Jack heard his father yell.

"Dear, it is getting cold. Shall we go inside?" Jack's mother gently nudged him away from the railing.

"I will be back!" he shouted.

"Yes, Dad. We all will be back." Jack patted on his shoulder.

"Son, what is happening to China?" Reverend Wells asked feebly.

"Dad, I wish I knew."

Like exploding bombs, faint thunders rolled across the East China Sea, furious waves pounded like a wounded dragon, and howling wind screamed like an angry sphinx. Jack stared at the empty cabin, still could not believe that Lily was not here by his side. He felt a void in him as if he had left a part of himself back on the dock of Shanghai. He wished she had not run into those two little kids and he had not offered them his left-over Shanghai dollars, but then again, how could he have known what was in her heart. *I thought she loved me, but she must love China more.* Jack sat down on the empty bunk bed and wrote.

My Dear Lily,

As our ship sailed out of Shanghai Harbor, I saw you crying. I was crying too. Darling, I felt your sadness as I watched you walk away from me. I tried to understand why you had to do what you did, but I cannot help but feel the aching pain that you are not here by my side. ...our karmas have brought us together, and I hope they will not keep us apart for long. Darling, I will be back.

Forever yours,
Jack"

EPILOGUE

... Many Years Later

In the summer of 1941, the United States government finally decided to shut off the oil spigot of Japan's war machine. With its national ambition at stake, Japan struck back. The sheer madness of this island nation to take on the most powerful country on earth seemed to have been lost on its people. Exactly four years after the Nanking Massacre, Japan brought the Total War to America. On December 7, 1941, the Japanese Imperial Navy attacked Pearl Harbor and seized the Shanghai International Settlement from the British and French. The Union Jack that had been flying over this once muddy riverbank of China for one-hundred years had stopped flying; and in its place, the Empire of the Sun unfurled over its skyline, proudly declaring to the world that Japan had finally driven the white colonialists out of China, and it was now its new master.

The glittering lights of Shanghai dimmed, the boisterous Cathay Hotel became subdued, the once-exclusive Shanghai Club became less exclusive; and the proud Shanghailanders were no longer so proud as they sat in the Japanese internment camps begging for scraps of food.

But after four years of brutal fighting in the Pacific, the seemingly invincible Imperial Japanese Army and Navy had finally met their match. In the crucible of war, Japan's claim to its divine racial superiority was laid bare; its Bushido spirit—the Way of the Warrior—was no match to the will of America's fighting men; and the Yamato damashii—the Japanese ways—shattered under Yankee might. On August 15, 1945, Japan unconditionally surrendered. As the Latter-day Commodore Matthew Perry—General Douglas MacArthur, the Supreme Commander of the Allied Powers in the Pacific Theater—triumphantly landed in Tokyo Bay. Japan's nightmare came true a century later.

Japan's burning aspirations to conquer its Asian brethren were crushed; its imperial reach exceeded its grasp; all sacrifices in the name of their Emperor came to naught; no territories were gained, but millions of lives were lost. While the souls of the dead Japanese soldiers were still being honored at Yasukuni Shrine by the Japanese citizens, countless innocent men, women, and children so painfully extinguished at these soldiers' hands were all but forgotten by the living, as if these poor souls had never been born.

The end of World War II did not bring peace to China. The Chinese soon turned on each other in the deadly struggle for power. The "Sick Man of Asia," the slumbering giant of the past, finally collapsed into convulsions; millions more died. In 1949, after years of fierce fighting with Mao Tse-tung's Eighth Route Army, Chiang Kai-shek's Kuomintang government finally lost its Mandate from Heaven—and his nightmare finally came true. But under the protection of the United States, he quickly re-established his Republic of China on the little island of Taiwan, clinging to the hope that he would triumphantly return to that China that once was his. But he never could.

Madame Chiang—along with her entourage of rich in-laws and cronies, and with millions of dollars siphoned off from the U.S.

Lend-Lease programs now safely deposited in the banks—settled into a comfortable but subdued life in the United States, hoping that one day they too would return to that China that once was theirs. But they never did.

The edifice of that famous Shanghai skyline sat along the Whangpoo River like an abandoned theater. The white colonists, the missionaries, and the privileged had all left the stage; only the poor, discarded, and true believers remained behind. The world-famous Bund—once the shining light of a new China, full of foreign ideas and motorcars—was now replete with forlorn gloom and incessant clicking of bicycle bells; the endless parties and careless gaieties at the crossroads of the world went silent, replaced by unsmiling faces and hardened stares. Young Chinese men and women in Mao's cotton jackets and the Eighth Route Army green caps rushed about with grim determination to erase China's century of humiliation and pain.

For the next quarter of a century, China turned inward once again. Like a mirage, the Pearl of the Orient by the East China Sea gradually faded in people's memories as if that Shanghai had never existed, and all the exciting charity ballroom dances and decadent cabaret shows never happened. But behind the bamboo curtain and beneath the somber gray skies, violent forces continued to churn.

China was reborn.

The intercom on the kitchen wall suddenly buzzed loudly. Jack Wells pressed the little button and hollered, "Who is it?"

"Mr. Wells, there is a Jap here to see you. He said his name is Anchora Tanata. He talks funny; I can't understand what he is saying," Max said over the intercom.

"My name is Akira Tanaka."

"Hey, mister, I'm talking here!" Max glowered.

"I said my name is Akira Tanaka!" Jack heard him shouting.

"Oh…yes, yes, please let him up!"

"Apartment 812, follow me," Max sneered.

Akira followed him across the checkered marble floor; the plastic flowers strung over the wrought-iron railings were still there, but the Venetian gondola scenes along the elevator lobby now looked a few shades grayer. Max slammed closed the elevator door and pushed on the well-worn brass lever. The machine groaned and hummed. In silence, they watched the floors receding below them. Both men looked very uncomfortable together in the small space as they gazed blankly into different directions. It seemed to be an eternity before the cab finally jerked to a stop.

"Thank you very much." Akira bowed and stepped out.

"You are not welcome!" Max violently pushed closed the door behind him, then mumbled, "Dirty Jap!"

Akira did not hear what he had said as he took a quick left-and-right glance at the dimly lit hallway.

"Hey, Akira!" Jack swung open the door, arms extended.

"Hello, Jack, long time no see!" He hastened his steps.

"That's right, long time no see." Jack grabbed Akira's hand. "How have you been? You haven't changed a bit since the last time I saw you."

"Not quite—you see these white hairs?" Akira tapped his forefinger at his temple.

"Me too. So, what brought you to New York?"

"I am on a medical tour with Todai, the Tokyo University Medical School. We have just visited Stanford, and we are going to have a meeting at Columbia this afternoon."

"Thanks for taking the time out to visit me."

"Jack, I wasn't sure you still lived here, but I thought it was worth a try."

"I am glad you still remembered where I live. Come in! Come in!" Jack pulled on his arm. "Let's talk in the living room. Can I get you something to drink? Sorry I don't have any sake."

"Coca-Cola would be fine, thank you very much," Akira replied politely. "We are on a pretty tight schedule. I have about an hour before I have to meet with my old professors."

"Sit down, sit down. It is a little messy." Jack put away a couple of books lying on the couch.

"I brought you and Mrs. Wells a little bonsai I got in Japan Town in San Francisco." Akira handed him a little ceramic planter with both hands.

"Thank you very much. It looks just like the one I saw in that Japanese restaurant back in Shanghai."

"Yes, Akashio. Ah, you still remember that." Akira smiled.

"Of course. I've never had a better Japanese meal since." Jack carefully laid down the bonsai on the fireplace mantel. "So, how many years has it been? Fifteen years?"

"Yes, fifteen years," Akira nodded as he slowly glanced around the spacious living room.

"Nineteen-thirty-seven seems so long ago. I thought we would never see each other again. So, Tanaka-san, how have you been? Married? Kids?"

"Yes, yes, married to the same girl, Yuki. I have a boy and a girl."

"I have a girl, twelve years old. She is my pride and joy." Jack moved away from the fireplace.

"So how is Joann? I hope she is well."

"Yes, she is doing fine. They are in the park and will be back soon." Jack took a seat on the other end of the couch.

"How are your parents doing?"

"Eh…they passed away last year."

"So sorry."

"I wish they'd had a chance to go back to China to see their New Hope Church one more time. With this Korean War, I don't know if even I could go back there anytime soon." Jack sighed.

"I too want to go back to China one day, but I don't think the Chinese would want to see another Japanese on their soil again."

"Akira, life is funny, isn't it? I thought World War I was supposed to be the war to end all wars, but then we had World War II. And now we are fighting with the Chinese in Korea. They were supposed to be our friends not long ago."

"At least we are on the same side this time," Akira said casually, walking toward the window. "You have such a wonderful water view. Everything is so wide open here. I wish I had more time to see America."

"Akira, are you sure you don't have time for lunch? Joann and my daughter will be back soon."

"So sorry, my schedule will not permit it, but we must have lunch next time."

"Okay, we must do lunch next time."

Suddenly, the front door swung open. A middle-aged woman and a pretty blond girl walked into the foyer.

"Hey, honey, we've got a visitor."

"Hello, Mrs. Wells. It is a pleasure to see you again." Akira quickly walked over and bowed.

"I'll be darned! Long time no see!" Joann hugged him. "Akira, this is our girl, Christina."

"How are you, Christina?"

"Hi! How do you do?" the young girl replied courteously.

"Christina, this is your dad's old friend from Japan, Mr. Akira Tanaka." Joann pulled her closer.

"Christiana, I've known your mother and father for a long time."

"I know; my dad already told me."

"Why are we all standing here in the hallway? Let's go sit in the living room, and I will go fix you guys some lunch."

"Honey, Akira can only stay for a few more minutes."

"It won't take long. You two must have a lot to talk about."

"So sorry, Mrs. Wells. I am scheduled to meet my colleagues for a medical conference at Columbia in half an hour."

"Are you sure? How about a cup of coffee?"

"Thank you, Mrs. Wells. Perhaps we can all have tea in Tokyo someday. We are rebuilding the whole city."

"Jack and I want to take Christina to see your country, and China, too. I hope this Korean War will be over soon before she goes to college."

"Yes, yes, of course. I will be honored if you all can come to visit me. Japan has changed a lot since the war. We are now a democratic country."

"Yes, we'll plan on it, Akira."

"Mrs. Wells, I am very happy to see you two again. Now, I must go to meet my colleagues at Columbia University." He bowed.

"Akira, it is nice to see you again." Joann gave him a light kiss on his cheek.

"Akira, let me walk you out." Jack held open the door.

The afternoon sun shone brightly on the sidewalk, and the cool breeze from the Hudson River brushed gently across their faces. As they walked toward Broadway, the two men suddenly found themselves with nothing to say to each other; the distance of the years seemed to have come between them. After a few awkward minutes, Jack finally said, pointing to the brownstone where Wong's Chinese Hand Laundry used to be, "I used to do all my laundry in that store. I wonder where they all went?"

"Maybe they went back to China…Did you know them well?"

Jack stared at the dark empty window behind a row of garbage cans and replied softly, "No, I didn't know them that well. In fact, I don't think I knew any of them well."

"Me neither. I had encountered many Chinese during the China Incident, but I don't know any of them personally except for that Chinese girl. Jack, whatever happened to her? May I ask?"

"You mean Lily?" Jack suddenly stopped walking. "She and I were supposed to go to Hawaii together, but at the last minute, she changed her mind."

"Why? I don't understand. I thought she would be very happy to leave China with you."

"I thought that too. But she decided to stay behind to help out two little homeless kids."

"But why?"

"She…she said she felt sorry for them because the Japanese soldiers had killed their parents."

"Oh…I'm sorry to hear that," Akira mumbled awkwardly, and then quickly asked, "Do you know where she is now?"

"No. I wrote her several times, but she never wrote me back. No one seemed to know where she went. She might have gone up north," Jack said pensively.

"Did you ever go back to try to find her?"

"I tried, but I didn't know where she went to, and no one knew what village she came from. By the time I was able to go after I settled in my father, China was already mired in wars on several fronts. Then, World War II broke out, and after that, the Communists came. The last letter I sent her never even got into China."

"Did she ever write to you?"

"No. I've forgotten to give her my address in New York…I should have."

"I knew you must have cared for her a lot. Otherwise, you wouldn't have risked your life for her in Nanking."

"Yes, I did care for her a lot…I still love her, but I think she loved China more," Jack said with a touch of bitterness.

"Jack, I am so sorry. War can do terrible things to people. It not only destroys lives, but it also interrupts dreams. If not for the China Incident, I could have finished my doctoral at Columbia and stayed here teaching."

"China Incident? I have heard you use that expression before."

"In Japan, we refer to the unfortunate arms conflicts between us and China as 'the China Incident.'"

"I see…" Jack shook his head. "What a euphemism!"

"Jack, we Japanese have paid a terrible price for this war. Millions of our brave soldiers have died and with nothing to show for it," Akira said defensively.

But you started the war! Jack held back his thought. "Akira, we Americans have paid a terrible price too."

"Yes, we all have."

"And for what? After all of these killings and suffering, China is now our common nemesis." Jack replied grimly recalling what he had seen in Nanking. "Ironic, isn't it, Akira? Now, we Americans are trying to kill the Chinese too."

"It seems that human conflicts never end." Akira nodded in agreement.

"Hey, by the way, whatever happened to that colonel?"

"Which colonel?"

"Colonel...Taro Yamashita, I think that's his name. Did he ever give you any more trouble after that day?"

"No, but he did reprimand me for interfering with his order. But at the time, there was too much going on for him to dwell on just one Chinese girl."

"Was he ever tried as a war criminal?"

"No. Why? I don't think he had killed anyone. He was just like me, a commissioned non-combatant officer; we all had to follow our orders. Anyway, soon after that day, I was transferred out of the military hospital to Unit 731 in Manchuria to do some medical research, and I never saw him again."

"What kind of medical research did you do over there?"

"Eh…bacterial stuff," Akira answered evasively. "Jack, one of the reasons I am here is to collaborate with your American scientists on the bacterial research."

"But I thought our government had banned that kind of research."

"Maybe…I don't know. Jack, I cannot discuss this kind of thing. I hope you understand," Akira paused and said nostalgically as he watched the Columbia students in suits and ties streaming in and out of the campus gates across the street. "I miss my college days; those innocent times."

"Well, Professor, I won't keep you from your appointed rounds."

"Goodbye, my good friend," Akira said affectionately.

"Sayonara, my friend." Jack watched him walk across Broadway and disappear behind the campus gate. Slowly, he let out a deep sigh as if he couldn't believe that it was not so long ago, he too had attended that college.

"Honey, I am in the kitchen fixing you lunch."

"Okay, I will be right there," Jack replied absentmindedly as he slowly sat down on the windowsill. He tapped out another Camel from his silver case and clicked on his old Zippo lighter several times before it gave out an orange glow. The white lilies etched on his lighter had long faded, leaving just a faint mark. He gazed at it for a moment and then looked out the window. In the distance, he could see the George Washington Bridge hovering over the glistening Hudson River and the Gothic church tower gleaming under the bright morning sun.

Much remained the same, and much had changed. The sounds and furies of those tumultuous years in that faraway place gradually receded from his memory like the unmarked miles on a lonely country road where love was found, then lost. Jack had long acquiesced to how things had turned out for him, but his heart still yearned for what could have been. Jack had long ago given up on ever hearing from Lily again, but in 1972, after President Nixon first paid a visit to Mao Tse-tung in Peking, the icy relationship between the US and China slowly began to thaw. A year later, Jack unexpectedly got an airmail postmarked "Hong Kong." *Could it be from her?* With trembling hands, Jack tore it open.

Dear Mr. Wells:

You do not remember me. I was that little girl you saw on the dock of Shanghai thirty-five years ago. I am writing to you because it was our mother's last wish.

After we saw you go inside the Customs House, we stayed outside watching your boat leave the dock of Shanghai, and then our mother took us back to her village to live. Mr. Wells, I was too young then to understand how much sacrifice she had made for my brother and me. Only years later, I realized that she had given up such a golden opportunity to go to America with you, to attend college, and to have a lifetime of happiness with you. Our mother had given up all that just for us. My brother and I owe our lives to her.

Times were tough during those war-torn years; we had little to eat, but we managed to survive. Our mother worked very hard as an English teacher and dance instructor to put food on the table. After China was liberated in 1949, she had a hard time adjusting to the new China. During the many political meetings, she was often denounced and attacked by her colleagues her past. They accused her of being a decadent bourgeois because she loved Western dances, and an American Imperialist's running dog because of her past association with your father's church. And during the Cultural Revolution in 1965, the Red Guards even forced her to dance in the street with a dunce on her head as they paraded her in mass demonstrations. They demanded that she confess her past mistakes, but she told them that there is nothing wrong to love singing and dancing.

Our mother often talked about you. She told us how nice you were, how funny you were, and how brave you were. And I told her that someday I would write to you and tell you how much she had missed you, but all contact with America was forbidden then. During those turbulent times, our mother got thinner and weaker. She passed away in the spring of 1969, and I buried her next to her parents. Our mother had suffered much. I just wish that she will have a better next life and her karma would bring her back to you again.

I couldn't tell you all this until after your president visited our country, and only after much searching, I was able to get your address from someone who once knew your father.

My brother and I have our own families now. He is working as a supervisor at the Shanghai Port, and I am teaching English at Fudan University. I knew how lucky we were—if you had not decided to give us your left-over Shanghai dollars on that day, I don't think we would have become what we are today. Mr. Wells, my brother and I will always be grateful for what you had done for us. And someday, I hope we can pay back your kindness.

Respectfully yours,
Jasmine Lee

With an aching heart, Jack slowly put down the letter as he tried to remember what these two kids even looked like, but the only image that stayed with him was Lily's sad smile as she cast her last glance back at him on the dock of Shanghai long ago. Sometimes, he still wished he hadn't trifled with fate, but then again, who could have known such a simple gesture of kindness would have changed his life this way. Jack smiled wryly as he thought back to what his father had once told him: "*Son, life has many twists and turns. Do the right things; by helping others, you will be helping yourself, for compassion has its own reward.*"